PAST & PRESENT

A MARKETVILLE MYSTERY

JUDY PENZ SHELUK

Superior Shores Press

PRAISE FOR PAST & PRESENT

"Psychological realizations and self-inspection are an exquisite touch to this story that keeps readers not only engaged, but completely cognizant of the forces that motivate families, murderers, and investigators alike… The result is a tense, emotionally gripping, multifaceted mystery that serves both as a perfect continuation of Callie's life story and as a fine stand-alone read for newcomers." — *Diane Donovan, Senior Book Reviewer, MIDWEST BOOK REVIEW*

"A well-crafted story that keeps readers engaged as history blends into the present." — *Debra H. Goldstein, award-winning author of the SARAH BLAIR mystery series*

"Sheluk nails it with this intriguing mystery that stitches together an investigation into the past with people's lives in the present—including that of protagonist Callie Barnstable. Treat yourself to a new present-day read—you won't be disappointed." — *Edith Maxwell, author of the Agatha-nominated QUAKER MIDWIFE MYSTERIES*

"An intriguing small-town mystery populated by engaging characters you want to spend time getting to know. Ocean liners, immigration, and family ties; the past is always present—an idea Ms. Sheluk explores to great effect." — *Micki Browning, Agatha-nominated author of THE MER CAVALLO mystery series*

"An engaging journey into the past that ripples into the present. Sheluk's well-written narrative and clever banter follows protagonist Callie Barnstable as she seeks answers for a client; each photo, memorabilia, and news article reveals an intriguing picture of love, family secrets…and murder. A top-notch mystery that keeps you guessing to the end."— *KINGS RIVER LIFE MAGAZINE*

PRAISE FOR SKELETONS IN THE ATTIC

"A smartly constructed mystery in the good old-fashioned and highly readable sense." — *Jack Batten, The Toronto Star*

"Callie's plight grabs the reader from the get-go and, as the plot twists and twists again, you follow her with heart in mouth. Is there any way for this to end well? Yes, there is, and you won't see it coming!"— *Catriona McPherson, bestselling author of The Reek of Red Herrings*

"A thought-provoking, haunting tale of decades old deception." — *Annette Dashofy, USA Today bestselling author of the Zoe Chambers mystery series*

"A complex plot, an extremely likeable protagonist, and a bombshell ending you never saw coming." — *Diane Vallere, National bestselling mystery author*

"A fine, winding investigative piece that redefines the concept of 'dirty laundry' and whether or not it should be aired in public or secreted forever" — *Diane Donovan, Senior Book Reviewer, Midwest Book Review*

"Her father's sudden death. Her mother's disappearance from long ago. Inheriting the house where her childhood began. These items all connect to the journey that Callie must face and what a can of worms this roller-coaster ride opened in this debut series." — *Dru Ann Love, Dru's Book Musings*

"A beautifully crafted page-turner." — *Ellen Byron, bestselling author of the Cajun County Mysteries*

PRAISE FOR THE GLASS DOLPHIN MYSTERIES

THE HANGED MAN'S NOOSE

"A thoroughly engaging debut mystery… well-plotted, well-paced and just plain well done!" — *Elizabeth J. Duncan, award-winning author, the PENNY BRANNIGAN and SHAKESPEARE IN THE CATSKILLS mystery series*

"A small town with a dark past, its inhabitants full of secrets, a ruthless developer, and an intrepid reporter with secrets of her own come together to create a can't-put-down-read." — *Vicki Delany, bestselling author of the SHERLOCK HOLMES BOOKSHOP MYSTERIES*

"Compelling characters with hidden connections and a good, old-fashioned amateur sleuth getting in over her head." — *James M. Jackson, author of the SEAMUS MCCREE mystery series*

A HOLE IN ONE

"What fun! A twisty tale chock full of clues and red herrings, antiques and secrets, and relationships that aren't what they seem." — *Jane K. Cleland, award-winning author, JOSIE PRESCOTT ANTIQUES MYSTERIES and MASTERING PLOT TWISTS*

"A bang-up mystery! Two friends, two murders, secret pasts, and a touch of romance. Who could ask for more?" — *Lea Wait, USA Today bestselling author, SHADOWS ANTIQUE PRINT and MAINELY NEEDLEPOINT mysteries*

"A captivating page-turner…you don't have to love golf to love *A HOLE IN ONE*." — *Kristina Stanley, bestselling author of the STONE MOUNTAIN MYSTERIES*

ALSO BY JUDY PENZ SHELUK

NOVELS

Glass Dolphin Mysteries

The Hanged Man's Noose

A Hole in One

Marketville Mysteries

Skeletons in the Attic

Past & Present

A Fool's Journey

SHORT STORY COLLECTIONS

The Best Laid Plans: 21 Stories of Mystery & Suspense (Editor)

Live Free or Tri

Unhappy Endings

SHORT STORIES

Plan D (The Whole She-Bang 2)

Live Free or Die (World Enough and Crime)

Beautiful Killer (Flash and Bang)

Saturdays with Bronwyn (The Whole She-Bang 3)

Goulaigans (The Whole She-Bang 3)

This is a work of fiction. Names, places, and events described herein are products of the author's imagination, or used fictitiously. Any resemblance to actual events, locations, organizations, or persons, living or dead, is entirely coincidental.

Past & Present: A Marketville Mystery (Book 2)

Copyright @2018 Judy Penz Sheluk (www.judypenzsheluk.com)

Edited by Ti Locke

Proofreading by Rosemary Graham

Cover design by Hunter Martin

Published by Superior Shores Press

ISBN Trade Paperback: 978-0-9950007-3-5

ISBN e-Book: 978-0-9950007-4-2

First Edition September 2018

Second Edition April 2019

Third Edition August 2019

In memory of my mother, Anneliese Penz

FOREWORD

If you're the sort of person who reads the dedication at the front of a book, you'll have noticed that *Past & Present* has been dedicated to my mother, Anneliese Penz, who lost a lengthy battle with COPD and related health issues in September 2016. Until the very end, she was handing out bookmarks for SKELETONS IN THE ATTIC and THE HANGED MAN'S NOOSE to any doctor or nurse who would take one (and I suspect she may have slipped a couple into their lab coats when they weren't looking).

I take comfort in the fact that the last book my mother read was SKELETONS IN THE ATTIC, the first book in this series. She was so pleased that I'd dedicated the book to my father, Anton "Toni" Penz, who succumbed to stomach cancer at the age of forty-two.

From the beginning, I planned to include two characters named Anton and Anneliese in the sequel to SKELETONS, but I didn't have a plot, let alone a plan. Quite honestly, I was stuck.

Then I discovered a small blue leather train case with cream trim, an ivory plastic handle, and brass locks at the back of my mother's clothes closet. Inside, she'd carefully preserved documents from the past, among them her German passport issued in England in 1952, her landed immigration papers from England to Canada documenting her journey on the T.S.S. *Canberra*, old photographs and postcards, and some costume jewelry. The idea for *PAST & PRESENT* was born: the past reaching out to the present.

Although much of the historical data in these pages is based on fact, and Callie's research often mirrored my own, this story is very much a work of fiction. I like to think my mother and father are together again, handing out bookmarks in heaven.

Judy Penz Sheluk

1

It's been thirteen months since I received the phone call, a detached voice on the other end telling me that my father had died in an unfortunate occupational accident. Thirteen months since I sat in Leith Hampton's Toronto law office for the reading of my father's will. Thirteen months since I found out that I, Calamity Barnstable, answers to Callie, had inherited a house in Marketville.

It was a house I didn't know existed. In a commuter town better suited to families with two kids, a cat, and a collie than a thirty-six-year-old single female who thrived on the anonymity of city life and condo living.

If that wasn't overwhelming enough, there was a catch. According to the terms of my father's will, I was required to move into the house for one year and find out who had murdered my mother thirty years earlier. A mother who disappeared when I was six years old, and one I barely remembered—a state of mind encouraged by my aforementioned father. There had been no photos of her around our house, no fireside chats about how they'd met. In the Barnstable household, it was like Abigail Doris Barnstable had never existed.

To say that my comfortable, condo-living existence as a bank call center clerk was flipped upside down would be an understatement. One month I was fielding queries about lost credit cards and debit card fraud, and the next month I was acting like some sort of unofficial private investigator. In Marketville, no less.

The house my father had bequeathed to me was nestled within a cul-de-sac chock-full of mostly well maintained 1970s bungalows, split-levels, and semis, the streets named after provincial wildflowers. Trillium Way. Coneflower Crescent. Day Lily Drive. Lady's Slipper Lane. You get the idea.

I say mostly well maintained because my inheritance, 16 Snapdragon Circle, was the singular notable exception. The front lawn had long ago succumbed to dandelions and twitch grass. The roof had been patched without any attention to matching the existing shingles. The windows were spattered with bird droppings, dirt, and bits of egg from Halloweens past. Some houses needed a little bit of TLC. What this house needed was a good coat of fire.

I might have hopped into my aging Honda Civic and driven back to Toronto that very moment except for four things. First, I no longer had a place to live, having sublet my condo to a co-worker. We'd always gotten on well enough, but we weren't about to become roommates.

Second, I'd quit my job at the bank and was in no hurry to return. Working in a fraud unit at a bank might sound fascinating, but the reality was that all the interesting cases were immediately bumped up to my supervisor.

Third, I'd promised Leith I'd take on the "assignment"—a term I use for lack of a better word—not because I wanted to, but because if I didn't do it, there was a scheming psychic named Misty Rivers who was more than willing to take on the task. After all, free lodging and a thousand dollars a week—the compensation for taking on the job—were powerful motivators, for me, as well as for Misty. But even with all of that on the table, I still might have taken a runner. And then reason number four sauntered over from the house next door to join me.

Royce Ashford was about forty, good looking in a rugged handyman sort of way, the kind of guy you'd see on one of those

TV home improvement shows. Well-defined biceps, sandy brown hair cropped close to his scalp, warm brown eyes. I imagined six-pack abs under his shirt and hoped my loser radar had taken a leave of absence. When it comes to men, my judgment is sorely lacking. Whatever you do, don't ask me about Valentine's Day. My memories have nothing to do with the velvety petals of long-stemmed red roses, and everything to do with the thorns.

But back to Royce. It wasn't so much that I was looking for a relationship. I wasn't. But it had been glaringly apparent that my inheritance was in desperate need of renovations, and judging from the logo on his golf shirt, he owned Royce Contracting & Property Maintenance. According to Leith, a man I semi-trusted, my father had planned to hire Royce, and until this crazy house business, I'd trusted my father's judgment better than my own. Besides, if you can't trust your next-door neighbor, who can you trust?

So that's how I ended up moving into 16 Snapdragon Circle and living in Marketville. As for finding out what happened to my mother thirty years ago, that's a long story, one that I'm not quite ready to revisit or retell. Suffice it to say that some things are better left in the past. Maybe one day I'll bring everything into the present, but today isn't that day.

After everything that I've uncovered in the last few months, from too many buried family secrets to an actual skeleton in the attic, you'd think I'd want to hightail it back to Toronto. But I find myself enjoying the slightly slower pace of living in Marketville, not to mention a phenomenal trail system that spans three towns. It's a terrific resource for runners—or should I say plodders—like me. I've even managed to find a running group that includes every age and pace imaginable, young to old, slow to warp-speed fast. We like to joke that we're crazy enough to run in plus thirty and minus thirty. That's Celsius, for you Fahrenheit folks. On the Fahrenheit scale it's eighty-six degrees to minus twenty-two. Doesn't have the same catchy ring to it, does it, but you get the drift.

Then there's Royce. We're still treading lightly, friends first and all of that, but the attraction between us continues to bubble under the surface like a lava lamp. I'm not quite ready to burst that bubble just yet, but I'm also not willing to walk away from it.

There's also Chantelle Marchand, my across-the-street neighbor. As an only child of two only children, I am intrigued and amused by Chantelle's stories of growing up as the fifth kid in a six-kid family. She's also become a really good friend. The best friend I've ever had, if I'm being honest, not that I've had a lot of friends. I've always been more of a group friend sort of girl. You know the type. Lots of people to hang out with, always up for a movie, or to go out for dinner, but no one close enough to get into the whole true confession thing. When it comes to true confessions, I'm more about getting them than giving them.

My only other true friend is Arabella Carpenter, and she's busy running the Glass Dolphin antiques shop in Lount's Landing, a small town about thirty minutes north of Marketville. We still get together, but it requires planning, not one of my strong suits. With Chantelle it's as easy as walking across the street and saying, "Hey there."

Not that Chantelle and I hit it off on first meeting, although I'll admit that was as much on me as on her. Chantelle is one of those women who rocks every look, from blue jeans to bustiers to evening gowns, and she does it as effortlessly as kicking off a pair of sneakers for five-inch stilettos. My eyes are probably my best feature—black-rimmed hazel, in case you're curious—but Chantelle's are a smoldering shade of charcoal that scream "come hither." She's also got the sort of highlighted blonde hair that looks natural, despite the hundred dollar plus price tag to get it there, and, unlike my own curly brown mop, it manages to stay sleek and stylish in all manner of wind and weather. She attributes her killer body to genetics, but she's also a Pilates, yoga, and spin instructor at the local gym. Chantelle might be closer to thirty-nine than twenty-nine, but you'd never know it from looking at her. It's hard not to hate someone like that, you know?

But here's what most people don't know. In spite of it all, Chantelle is wildly insecure. Getting dumped and divorced for an adolescent—her words, not mine, but quite accurate nonetheless—

will do that to you. Trust me, I know. Not about the divorce part, I've never been married, but the getting dumped part, that I'm all too familiar with.

Anyway, I've decided to stay in Marketville for the time being, although not in this house, which is filled with far too many memories. Besides, it's time to start over. I've spent enough of the last year digging through the past.

With Royce's help, and some money from my father's estate, I've done enough renovations to get the house ready for resale without going into debt. My realtor, Poppy Spencer, a referral from Arabella, assures me that I'll get top dollar, if not into a bidding war. In the meantime, it's time to figure out where I'm going to live and what I'm going to do to earn a living.

2

Poppy Spencer slid her tablet toward me. "This Victorian detached on Edward Street ticks all the boxes."

Poppy is a successful-looking businesswoman in her late forties, with steel-gray eyes partially hidden behind dark designer frames. Her short brown hair had been artfully highlighted with glints of copper and gold and I suspected she paid more for one haircut and color than I paid my hairstylist in an entire year. Probably more on manicures, too, judging by her perfectly polished French-tipped fingernails. I leaned across the granite-topped island in my newly renovated kitchen to review the listing. Edward Street was in the heart of Marketville, the town's original main street which had, over the years, morphed into a trendy destination spot filled with independently-owned ethnic restaurants, trendy cafés and bistros, and upscale clothiers. Despite its mostly Victorian architecture, Edward Street had long since abandoned the historic vibe that Main Street in Lount's Landing embraced. This was where the smart suburban shopper went to get wined, dined, and decked out. In other words, a good location for a residence-based business.

FROM THE MULTIMEDIA slideshow on Realtor.ca, 300 Edward Street looked charming, but it was getting close to the outer fringe of the street, a less desirable section of Edward. It was also currently home to a physiotherapist's residence and practice, and I wondered how much it would need in renovations. I wasn't sure that I wanted to go through the dust and debris again, not to mention the expense. It always cost more than you thought, as Royce had warned me before we got started on the Snapdragon house. I should have listened to him, but you know what they say: experience is the best teacher.

Then there was the part of me that yearned for one of the many new builds popping up on every farmer's field from Marketville to Lount's Landing to Lakeside. Of course, those homes wouldn't be ready for a year or longer, which was hardly helpful given my decision to move out sooner rather than later.

"I was thinking of something more contemporary."

"We can certainly look for something more modern, but the reality is you won't find anything like that on Edward. Are you willing to consider houses in a subdivision?"

A resale in one of the newer subdivisions might be a good compromise. "Possibly."

"That's not a problem if you just plan to live in the home. However, you mentioned starting your own business. There are almost always restrictions regarding the operation of a business in a residential subdivision. A home office wouldn't be an issue, but there are bound to be complaints from neighbors if you plan to entertain clients. We'd have to check the town's zoning bylaw to see what's allowed before putting in an offer. The nice thing about Edward Street is that it's zoned residential-commercial."

I hadn't thought about entertaining clients, which probably didn't bode well for my business planning acumen. Then again, I hadn't quite come up with a concept. "I suppose I could go and look at it during the open house on the weekend." I could ask Royce and Chantelle to come with me.

Poppy was already on the phone to the listing broker. "Perfect," she was saying, "my client and I will see you in an hour."

"An hour? What happened to going during the open house?"

"It's a seller's market," Poppy said. "Which will be good for you, when we sell your property. But it works both ways. We've got to get in there *before* the open house this weekend." She tapped her French-manicured fingernails on the granite. "Do you want to bring anyone with you?"

It would take ten minutes to drive there, which didn't leave a lot of advance notice. But I knew that if I didn't bring someone along, Poppy would have me signing on the dotted line before I'd properly thought things through.

"Let me try Chantelle and Royce."

CHANTELLE WAS at home and thrilled to be asked along. The news wasn't as positive when it came to Royce, who was out on a job, but he did promise to do a home inspection should I decide to put in an offer. That made me feel better, and a small part of me secretly hoped he was stalling because he didn't want me to move away.

Three Hundred Edward Street was a red brick Victorian with gingerbread trim painted a pale shade of buttercream yellow, and a wraparound front porch that welcomed visitors. The front door opened to a narrow reception room on the left side, a kitchen at the rear, visible from a pass-through window, and a polished wooden stairway to the right, leading to a second floor.

"There can't be more than six hundred square feet of living space on the main level," I said, fishing around in my purse for my cocoa butter lip balm. I'd been weaning myself of the habit, but every now and again I found myself reaching for it like a baby with a pacifier.

"Six-hundred and fifty, to be exact," Poppy said, consulting the listing, "but plenty of space for an office and reception room."

"Did you notice the baseboards?" Chantelle asked. "They have to be eight inches high and all original oak. So are the staircase and the floors. Gorgeous. Someone took good care of this home."

We made our way into the kitchen. It was what my father would have called a one-bum kitchen; there was barely space for a refrigerator and stove, and a dishwasher had been bypassed to increase the modest cupboard space. But the white cupboards were cheery, the countertops gold-veined black quartz, and a window looked out over a small backyard filled with perennials in various stages of bloom. There was even a door leading out to a stone patio. I could imagine having tea out there in the morning, a glass of wine at dusk. I glanced at Chantelle and knew she was thinking the same thing.

There were two bedrooms upstairs, about equal size, one facing the street, and the other the backyard. Both were being used as current owner's treatment rooms. "The closets are really tiny," I said. "I'm not looking for a walk-in, but these are miniscule."

"Any closets at all are a find," Poppy said. "A lot of older homes don't have closets. People used wardrobes to hang their clothes. Of course, they owned fewer clothes."

"You can get one of those space saver systems," Chantelle said. "I'm sure Royce would install it for you."

I wasn't convinced. "Let's check out the bathroom."

It had been updated, with cedar walls and a large walk-in shower in place of a bathtub. The idea of clients using it didn't thrill me.

"I don't know. It's not really what I had in mind. I was thinking of something with a bit more privacy. At least another bathroom."

"There's another bathroom in the lower level," Poppy said. "That's the one your clients would use. This upper level would be your private living space and the main level would be your office and kitchen area. Come on, let's go check out the basement."

⚲

THE BASEMENT, or should I say the finished lower level, had seven-foot ceilings, which should have made the space feel claustrophobic, but the walls had been painted off-white and, though small and narrow, there were plenty of windows. Along with a generous powder room, there was a laundry room and furnace area. A separate, windowless, room had been blocked off for storage. I don't love basements, but as basements went, this one wasn't too bad.

"The shelving and file cabinets stay," Poppy said, consulting the listing again.

That would save me some money and add storage, but I still wasn't convinced. "I've got to think about it."

"It won't last," Poppy said. "Not in this market. Of course, you have to be comfortable with your decision. There are other properties."

"Not like this," Chantelle said. "You can't let this house go. It ticks all the boxes."

"I admire your enthusiasm," I said, "but you're not the one buying it."

"Then I'll go in with you."

"You want to buy a house with me?"

Chantelle shook her head. "Not the house. The business. You can do your investigative thing, and I can supplement it with my knowledge of genealogy. It will be perfect."

And that's how we started Past & Present Investigations.

3

———

I've never purchased a house, but Arabella Carpenter had steered me right. When it came to real estate, Poppy left no stone unturned. After reviewing comparable properties on the market—a challenge given the uniqueness of every property on Edward Street —and after Royce determined the amount and cost of work required to suit my needs, Poppy wrote up an aggressive offer.

The dollar amount of the offer terrified me, but Poppy assured me that after the sale of Snapdragon Circle, I'd pretty much break even. I hoped she was right. I had some savings from the sale of my late father's heavily mortgaged townhouse in Toronto, but I figured I'd need that to live on while I got my business going.

A saner person might have gone back to working nine-to-five, but having had a taste of freedom this past year, the thought made me shudder. Surely I could earn enough to pay for food, taxes, and the occasional night out.

Besides, I wanted to resolve the issue of my father's untimely death. I'd never bought into the verdict of occupational accident, but I'd been too busy trying to solve the mystery of my mother to do much about it. Now I'd have the time to look into it properly. Maybe I wouldn't be successful, but I owed it to my father to try.

SELLING Snapdragon Circle turned out to be a snap, pun fully intended. Poppy and Chantelle helped me stage the house, and I had to admit it looked amazing. All my hard work had paid off, from painting every single wall and ceiling to stripping the carpets to expose the original hardwood. Getting a new roof and hiring Royce's company to renovate the kitchen had also proved worthwhile; Poppy predicted almost a doubling of my investment. In the meantime, the house was listed with "offers accepted in five days," and Ella Cole, my nosey sixty-something next-door neighbor, kept me from wandering the streets by providing endless cups of tea, coffee, cookies, and gossip while the showings continued unabated. The hours leading up to offer day were stressful to the max. What if no one bid on the property? What if the offers were insultingly low? I didn't have to worry. At the end of an exhausting day, I'd turned down a half dozen offers and accepted one for more money than I'd dreamed possible. Poppy Spencer virtually preened at the results, but I didn't fault her for it. She'd earned her commission and then some.

Then reality came crashing down on me. I was planning to start a business investigating missing persons from the past, cases that either A) no one else was interested in or B) everyone had given up on. I wasn't a private eye. I didn't even have any qualifications beyond what I'd learned searching for my own mother.

What the hell had I been thinking?

CHANTELLE CALMED me down with generous pours of Australian Chardonnay and take-out rapini and artichoke pizza from Benvenuto, a local Italian restaurant. To assuage her guilt—you don't stay a size two by chowing down pizza on a regular basis, no matter what your genetics are or how hard you work out—she'd brought a large tossed salad to go with it, balsamic vinaigrette on the side.

"The first thing we have to do is to get business cards and a website," she said, nibbling on a slice and somehow managing to keep rapini from stringing her teeth.

I'd been planning to order business cards and had been working on a website. I wasn't an internet guru, but the template I'd selected from my web host seemed easy enough to navigate, and I considered it a work in progress.

"If you approve the logo I designed, and we decide on our titles, I can order the business cards. I'm just not sure whether to go with Calamity or Callie."

"Hmm… I know you don't like to be called Calamity but it does have a ring to it. How about Calamity with Callie in parentheses?"

It was a good compromise. I showed Chantelle what I'd come up with, an intertwined pair of Ps for Past & Present, tucked inside a magnifying glass. I thought it had a sort of Sherlock Holmes feel to it. At least that's what I was going for.

"It's fantastic," Chantelle said. "As for titles, how does 'Partner' sound?"

"Partner." It felt right on my lips. "I like it. As for the website, it's in the works. There's nothing yet in the way of content, but we can go live at any time. I thought we might start by writing up bios. Yours should be relatively easy because of your genealogy credentials. I'm struggling a bit with mine. There's embellishing the truth, and then there's being an outright liar."

"I can help you with your bio. I'm good at that sort of thing. I've also got a friend who's a decent photographer. I'm sure she'll give us a break on the cost."

I hadn't thought about photos, but Chantelle was right. We needed to show our faces. "Okay. That should do it then, as a start."

Chantelle shook her head. "I don't think so. What about the rest of our team?"

"The rest of our team?" I picked off an artichoke, wishing Chantelle had gone with something less exotic. When it came to pizza, I preferred double cheese with hot peppers, maybe some extra sauce if I was feeling adventurous. I didn't mind artichokes, but I preferred to eat them mashed up in a hot spinach dip, with some nacho chips on the side. The thin black corn ones that made you believe you were eating something healthy.

"Our team," Chantelle said again, taking my mind off the nachos.

"Go on."

"Here's what I'm thinking. I'll be the point person for the genealogical side."

"That goes without saying."

"Glad you agree. Now, as for our resident psychic—"

"Resident psychic?"

"An absolute must, to my mind, and I'm thinking Misty Rivers is just the ticket. She could pull a tarot card each week, post a message on the website." Chantelle waved her hands as if to say, "Details, details."

"What sort of post?"

"It needs to allude to looking into the past. *Misty's Messages* or *Reflections*, something along those lines. "

I'd grown to accept Misty over time, but despite her claims to mystical ability, I suspected she was about as psychic as I was.

"I don't know. It seems a bit gimmicky."

"Every business has some sort of gimmick."

Did they? I was mulling that over when Chantelle spoke again.

"I've already run the idea by Misty."

I felt my spine stiffen. "You've already discussed this with her?"

"Yes, and before you get all bent out of shape, she's excited to be part of it."

I'm sure she is. "And just how will we pay Misty for her psychic prowess?" I knew I sounded bitchy and attempted to soften my words with a smile. It must have worked, because Chantelle smiled back.

"Easy peasy. If one of her posts brings in a client, we'll pay her a finder's fee."

"A finder's fee. I suppose that could work."

"Of course it will work. If we decide to make Misty an administrator on the website, she can even enter the posts herself."

I wasn't sure I wanted Misty having admin privileges, but this was no time to squabble, and I certainly didn't want the website to become my full-time job.

"Anyone else for this 'team' of ours?"

"Shirley Harrington."

Despite my reservations on the team approach, I had to admit Shirley would make a good addition. As head librarian in charge of archives at the Cedar County Reference Library, she'd been invaluable in my search for information about my mother's disappearance. "I like the idea of bringing Shirley on board, but the last time I spoke to her, she had retired from the library and was doing the snowbird thing in Tampa. I don't think she's planning to come home until mid-April. She promised to call me when she comes back. I do know she's planning to join a couple of golf leagues. I don't know how much free time she'll have."

"I'm sure she'll appreciate being considered, regardless. Spending the winter in Florida is one thing, but when she gets back to Marketville, retirement may not look as rosy, even with lots of golf thrown into the mix."

"I hate to admit it, but you have a point. Anything, or should I say, anyone else?"

Chantelle beamed. "I thought you'd never ask. Arabella would make a terrific resource. I was in Lount's Landing yesterday on another matter, so I popped into the Glass Dolphin and chatted with her about it."

I couldn't imagine why Chantelle was in Lount's Landing, and while I took her at her word, I couldn't help but feel slighted. This was supposed to be *my* business and Chantelle was already running the show. "What did she say?" I tried to keep the edge out of my voice and didn't quite succeed.

Chantelle's charcoal eyes narrowed. "You don't have to sound so snippy about it. I know you and Arabella have been friends since high school, but it's not like we don't know each other. Besides, I really was in Lount's Landing on another matter. A potential client, if you must know."

"Sorry, I'm being ridiculous. Asking Arabella was a great idea. I should have thought of it. What did she say?"

"She agreed to take part on an as-needed basis. We'll also list the Glass Dolphin antiques shop on our website, and she'll reciprocate. If someone brings us something old and possibly antique, we can email her photos and ask for her opinion. If she thinks it warrants a visual appraisal, we'll take the object to her shop in Lount's Landing."

"That sounds good for us, but how does it benefit Arabella?"

"She does quick email appraisals now, but she covers herself by saying she can't guarantee her appraisal without seeing the object in person. Arabella said ninety percent of the stuff emailed to her doesn't have any significant monetary value, and is often not antique or vintage. If she thinks there's a possibility of value or historical interest, she'll set up an appointment for an appraisal. Her rates vary based on how much research she needs to do. Occasionally, when someone brings an item in for appraisal, they'll want to sell it to her, or leave it with her on consignment."

"How would we pay her?"

"We would bill her fee back to our client. With their permission, of course."

"It sounds as if you two have everything covered." I heard the edge creeping back into my voice. So did Chantelle.

"I was trying to be proactive, and you're welcome. Besides, it's not like you haven't consulted Arabella in the past. Or have you forgotten about the locket and poster already?"

I hadn't forgotten. Both had played a significant role in last year's search, and as much as it pained me to admit it, Chantelle was right about all of it.

And that's how Past & Present Investigations ended up with a team. Now all we needed was a client.

4

____

With plenty of paint, cleaning supplies, and Royce's vision and muscle, Chantelle and I were able to transform 300 Edward Street into a multifunctional space. The main floor was an office space, the upper level was mine alone, complete with tiny master bedroom and minuscule guest bedroom, not that I was expecting any guests. The basement was reserved for storage, filing, a client bathroom, and laundry.

Our first team meeting started out very sis boom bah minus the plaid skirts and pompoms. Chantelle was clearly pumped, and Misty seemed to share her enthusiasm. I was a little more apprehensive, likely because I was the one paying the bills. I'd never owned a business before, and I didn't want to fail. I also didn't know where to start, where to advertise, or how to generate traffic to the website.

"Social media," Chantelle said. "That's our first step. A Facebook business page is a must. We can consider rolling out Twitter, Pinterest, and other platforms later. For now, let's focus our attention on Facebook and try to build a following."

"How do we build a following?" I asked.

"I think it's important that we grow it organically," Misty said, fluttering silver-sparkled blue fingernails. "It's better to have ten bona fide followers who might be interested than one hundred who could care less."

I nodded. It made sense. "No argument from me. What about Chantelle's *Misty's Messages* idea, where you pull a tarot card once a week or so?"

"I love the idea," Misty said. "I can also set up a page that explains tarot. It's important to have content people can get behind to draw them to the site. Any other ideas?"

I suppose I could mention looking into my father's death, but posting that quest online seemed far too personal.

Chantelle came to the rescue. "Maybe if we pull a card today it will inspire us, Misty. Did you bring your tarot cards with you?"

Misty had. She pulled the deck out of her purse, shuffled the cards, and asked me to split the pile in three. "Select one card from any pile."

I flipped over the top card in the middle pile. It was the King of Pentacles in reverse. "What does it mean?"

Misty reached over and patted my arm lightly. "It means you're worried about money. That what you have isn't enough."

Maybe Misty was psychic after all.

⚲

Chantelle and Misty had just left when my phone rang. I checked the call display. Arabella Carpenter.

"What's up?"

"I just referred a potential customer to Past & Present Investigations. Her name is Louisa Frankow. She lives in Lakeside. She brought some paperwork into the shop, hoping to get some information."

A potential customer. "What sort of paperwork?"

"Her grandmother's immigration card to Canada in nineteen fifty-two, her passport, postcards, photographs, and letters. Nothing of monetary or historic value."

Nothing of monetary or historic value. My earlier optimism was waning. "What brought her to the Glass Dolphin?"

"Louisa's grandmother came to Canada from England by ocean liner. That's how everyone emigrated in those days. The ship's name is included on her immigration card."

"How does that translate to antiques?"

"We have a fair bit of ocean liner memorabilia at the shop, along with several vintage posters promoting travel by air, rail, and sea. Emily started posting photos of the posters and related items on our website and Facebook page, along with some trivia to add interest. The campaign has been so successful that I've created a special travel corner inside the store. Maps, posters, vintage jewelry and memorabilia, an old train case from the 1950s."

Emily was Emily Garland, Arabella's partner at the Glass Dolphin. Arabella's heart was in the past and she had a gift for bringing the past into the present. Emily was a true millennial and social media was in her blood. As a former journalist, she was also adept at research. They seemed as unalike as two people could be, but they were terrific partners.

"So Louisa found the ocean liner posts on Facebook and thought you might have something from her grandmother's ship."

"Actually, the Facebook posts brought her to the Glass Dolphin, but it was the train case that really seemed to resonate with her." Arabella chuckled. "It's funny. I added that as an afterthought, something that would make the travel corner seem more authentic, but it's the item customers want to talk about. It seems everyone's mom or granny had a case like it and I could've sold a dozen train cases if I'd had them. Anyway, Louisa looked at the train case for a bit, left without saying anything, and came back two days later with the documents."

"Did you have anything that tied into her mom's ship?"

"Unfortunately, no. That's when I thought of you and Chantelle."

"Hmmm. I suppose we could do some research on the ship, but I'm not sure how we could help her do something she should be able to do herself."

Arabella laughed. "There's a winning attitude."

I felt myself blush. "Point taken. How can we help?"

"Here's what I know. Louisa's grandmother died long before she was born. Her mother was raised in foster care from the age of three. Unfortunately, she died of cancer a couple of weeks ago, one month shy of her sixty-fifth birthday. Louisa found a train case in her mother's closet, similar to the one we have in the store. Inside were her grandmother's documents, letters, and photographs."

"And now she wants to find out everything she can about her grandmother."

"Exactly. Louisa also intimated there was some mystery surrounding the grandmother's death, although she didn't provide any specifics. I have no idea if there is or was a grandfather in the picture."

It was starting to sound intriguing. Whether it paid a bill or two remained to be seen, but I wasn't about to turn down a client.

"Thanks, Arabella. I appreciate it."

"I know what it's like to start a business, and I want to support you, but I'll be honest. I debated contacting you about this."

"Why?"

"Because you're still not ready to face what you've learned about your parents. Sooner or later you'll have to come to terms with… everything. This digging into the past, it might be painful for you."

Well, well. It appeared that Past & Present wasn't the only thing Chantelle and Arabella had discussed. "I'm perfectly capable of separating business from my personal life. As for my mother, I much prefer later to sooner, but thanks for your concern."

"That's good news, because I've already given her your coordinates," Arabella said, ignoring the sarcasm in my tone. "Just keep me posted, okay?"

The promise extracted, I hung up, too excited at the thought of an actual job to stay annoyed. Besides, the rational side of me knew that Chantelle and Arabella only had my best interests at heart.

I went upstairs and pulled a file folder labeled "Dad" from under the bed.

That's when the doorbell rang.

5

Louisa Frankow was a slender woman, about five foot two, with brown eyes the color of milk chocolate, and golden hair that fell in soft waves to her shoulders. I wondered if her hair color was natural and decided it had to be. I've never seen a shade of honey gold like that come out of a bottle. Why was it everyone's hair was always nicer than mine?

She was dressed conservatively in black slacks and a blazer, a white silk blouse open at the neck. Diamond studs in tiny earlobes. No rings. I pegged her to be in her mid-thirties, about my age, give or take a year on either side.

She was carrying a small blue leather suitcase with cream trim, an ivory plastic handle, and brass locks. It was the right size to be a train case, used for toiletries and intimate essentials back in the day. I've learned quite a lot about luggage over the past year. It's the sort of thing people like to keep their secrets hidden in.

"I probably should have called and made an appointment," Louisa said, staring at the file folder in my hand. "I can leave if you're busy and make an appointment to come back another day."

I shook my head. "This can wait. Arabella told me you were coming." Not entirely true, since Arabella hadn't mentioned a specific date or time, but Louisa looked as if she was ready to jump out of her skin. "Come on in and have a seat. Wherever you're most comfortable."

I'd set up the office space to include a six-foot long mission table and eight wooden chairs that could best be described as an eclectic mix. The table weighed a ton, and it had cost more than I'd wanted to spend, but it had plenty of drawers, allowing it to work as conference table, dining table, and desk. Arabella had given me a healthy discount on the lot. I'd also created a small, but intimate, seating area underneath the kitchen pass-through, with two reproduction mission oak recliners upholstered in an abstract fabric of hunter green, gold, and burgundy. Those I'd found on Craigslist for a song, and the extra-wide wooden arms meant I didn't need end tables, which was just as well, given the lack of space.

Louisa stared at the table. "It's probably best to sit at the table so I can show you what's in the suitcase."

"Can I get you something to drink? Tea? Coffee? Sparkling water?"

"Sparkling water would be great. Lemon if you have it."

I did. I went into the kitchen, took out a serving tray, then poured two glasses of water, sliced some lemon, opened a box of assorted chocolates, and put a few on a glass plate, along with some fresh strawberries, and cocktail napkins. Pleased with my presentation, I took everything into the office and placed it on the table. Louisa had taken a seat, the suitcase in her lap, as if she wasn't quite ready to share the contents with me. I needed to make her feel comfortable.

"Here you go. Help yourself, and tell me what brings you to Past & Present Investigations."

Louisa took a sip of water. "May I rest the suitcase on the table?"

"Of course."

"Thank you." She popped open the brass locks. Inside the case were several plastic storage bags, the kind you used at the airport to store your liquids. "I didn't even know my mom owned this. It belonged to my maternal grandmother, not that I ever met her. My mom was raised in foster care. She aged out at sixteen, shoved out of the system without any support. The experience soured her."

"What about your father?"

"Not in the picture. My mom got pregnant at eighteen. I don't know whether it was a one-night stand or she fell for the wrong guy. She never elaborated. I do know that whoever he was, he didn't contribute a dime of support. I've certainly never met him. Nor do I care to."

"Did your mom ever marry?"

"Never even dated anyone again, or if she did, she certainly never brought him home. We weren't rich, but I didn't want for anything." Louisa grimaced. "Well, that may not be entirely accurate. I longed for affection. My mom had a hard time displaying any emotion. Every feeling she ever had was neatly compartmentalized. Not surprising considering her upbringing and my deadbeat dad. But she did her best. We did our best."

I wondered if Louisa had ever been married, or if she'd followed in her mother's footsteps.

"You're probably wondering if I ever married," she said, reading my mind. "The answer is, yes, three times. Husband number one when I was barely legal age to tie the knot. He turned out to be a gambler. He lost our toy poodle in a poker game, if you can imagine that. Husband number two was a drinker who couldn't hold down a job when he went to the trouble of finding one. Husband number three was a serial cheater who didn't even try to hide his infidelity. I left him two years ago and swore off men. I earn a decent living as a credit manager. It helps that I'm bilingual, especially if I'm traveling in Quebec." She named a national automotive glass company. I knew they owned a couple hundred windshield replacement retail stores across Canada.

"What's in the train case that makes you want to dig into the past?"

Louisa removed one of the plastic bags, pulled out a photograph and handed it to me. "This is my grandmother. Her name was Anneliese Prei."

The resemblance to Louisa was uncanny. Despite the sepia tones of the old photo, it was obvious that her hair had the same honey-gold soft waves, and that her eyes were the color of milk chocolate. Even the mouth, full lipped and pouty, was identical. But it was the tilt of her nose, the slightly haughty way she held herself, which took her from look-alike to doppelgänger.

"She was beautiful. You look like her. You're older, of course, and she has an edge about her that you don't seem to possess, but overall, the resemblance is uncanny."

"I always assumed that I took after my father. I certainly don't look anything like my mom. When I saw this picture, it was as if my grandmother was calling out to me from the grave."

Maybe she was and maybe she wasn't. Either way, I understood. I'd felt the same way the first time I saw a photograph of my mother.

"And now you want to find out everything you can about her."

Louisa nodded, her brown eyes serious. "My mom always believed that my grandmother had come to a bad end."

"What sort of bad end?"

"I honestly don't know. My mom was only three when her mother died, and I'm guessing there wasn't any other family, including a responsible father figure. If there were, she wouldn't have wound up in foster care, would she? But my mom used to experience terrible nightmares. She'd wake up screaming 'bad man, bad man.' Might have stemmed from a repressed memory."

The repressed memories of a three-year-old child and nightmares of a bad man weren't much to go on, especially since the holder of the memories was dead. Once again, Louisa seemed to read my mind.

"My mom had a manila envelope with some photographs from when she was in foster care. There aren't many, but they might help. I'll drop it off later this week." Louisa managed a rueful smile. "One manila envelope, for a child who lived in foster care for thirteen years. It's beyond sad, when you think about it. Anyway, I don't know why I didn't bring the envelope with me. I'm afraid I'm not thinking clearly these days."

"Not thinking clearly goes with the territory after you lose someone you love, especially your mother, no matter how complicated or strained the relationship was. But yes, anything you might have of your mom's could prove helpful. Are there any other photos?"

"A few photographs, along with some birthday cards she gave me over the years, all stored in an old Laura Secord chocolate box. I can't imagine anything in the box will be much help. The cards, what could they tell you beyond the fact that she was a proud mother? As for pictures, she didn't take many. She worked as a receptionist for an office furniture company, not exactly a lucrative career choice, but there weren't a lot of opportunities for someone with a grade ten education, even back then. Money was always tight. Food, rent, and bus fare came first, though she would always spring for my annual school photo." Louisa attempted another smile. "I don't think she wanted me to feel left out."

"Could you take a look at the photos? I'm interested in any that include other people."

Louisa nodded. "I can do that."

"Can you think of anything else?"

"There's a jewelry box, but I don't think there's anything in there of any real value."

I thought about the Art Deco locket I'd discovered in the house, and how important it had become in finding out more about her past. "You could be right, but I'd still like to see it, if you don't mind."

"Consider it done."

"Perfect." I pulled the train case toward me. "What can you tell me about the contents?"

"What you see is what you get. Some old postcards from the ship my grandmother came over on, a handful of black and white photographs. I've stared at them for hours. I even tried to do some research on my own, but I've never been good at solving puzzles, and my job is quite demanding. Time is the one thing I don't have to spare. I do, however, have some money, thanks to my mom's estate. It turns out she was quite a miser." Louisa laughed, a harsh, humorless sound. "All those years of scrimping and saving, for what? To die alone at sixty-four?"

There was no adequate response. Louisa picked up on my silence, no flies on this potential client.

"Arabella seemed to think your team could offer a solution."

A solution? With enough money, time, and luck, we could probably offer some answers to the past. Whether it was a past she would welcome remained to be seen. As much as I wanted this first job, Louisa had to know what, and who, she was getting into. Arabella had a motto that authenticity matters. If we were to succeed at Past & Present Investigations, and be proud of what we were doing, transparency was a must.

"We aren't private investigators. Each of us brings something different to the table, but if you're looking for a PI—"

"I've had quite enough experience with private eyes after my serial cheater, thank you very much. Arabella told me about your team. What I know about genealogy would fit in a thimble. I don't have the time or the interest to dig through old papers. The stuff in this suitcase might tell you a story, so too my mom's jewelry and whatever's inside the chocolate box, but I'm not much of a visionary. Most of all, I was swayed by Misty's tarot message on your website. It was as if she was writing it especially for me."

"Hmmm, yes," I said, as if I had a clue. Had Arabella given Misty a heads up? She must have. I made a mental note to ask. "In that case, I think our team can help you, although it could take some time."

"I'm not expecting miracles, and I realize it may take several weeks. As long as I get regular updates, I'll be satisfied that you're making progress, or at least trying to." A savvy business owner might have left it at that, but I felt compelled to caution Louisa. "Sometimes secrets are best left buried in the past. We may find out things you'd rather not know."

"I'm aware that there are risks involved. I wish I could explain what force brought me to you. I can't. Anneliese Prei has a story to tell, and I need to find out what it is."

I thought I had been ready, too, when I'd embarked on my quest to find out what happened to my mother. As it turned out, I wasn't ready at all.

But this wasn't about me, or my mother. This was about a woman named Anneliese Prei. A woman who had immigrated to Canada for a better life, only to wind up dead three years after her arrival, cause of death as yet unknown. I looked at the photo. To me, Anneliese had a look of slightly arrogant self-confidence, a sort of feisty inner spirit that life tends to chip away at until it's all but gone.

Maybe that's what had killed her, maybe it was something else. All I knew was, like Louisa, I had to find out.

6

Louisa and I settled on an hourly rate, deposit, and a baseline for the overall budget. I drew up the paperwork, including a voucher for the train case and its contents, and felt a tug of excitement when she signed the contract and wrote a check payable to Past & Present Investigations.

The legalities taken care of, I recorded the few details Louisa could provide. Her mother's name was Sophie Marta Frankow, born March 23, 1953 in Toronto to Anneliese Prei, father unknown. Was it possible his last name was Frankow?

"It's possible," Louisa said, "but Frankow could have been the last name of one of the foster families. Unfortunately, my mom refused to talk about it."

Unfortunate didn't begin to describe it. The chance of getting past privacy laws to uncover any information were remote. Hopefully Chantelle would have an angle.

℘

I FIRED up my computer as soon as Louisa left and went to our website. It was time to read what Misty had written.

Despite my earlier reservations, I was impressed at the page Misty had created. A carousel of tarot cards rotated beneath the words "Misty's Messages," with a small photograph of Misty on the left side of the website banner. Misty was a plump fifty-something woman with fluffy bleached blonde hair and jet-black eyes. The picture had been subtly photoshopped to smooth out the most obvious wrinkles without going overboard, and her into-the-camera gaze made her look approachable.

The main page for *Misty's Messages* had several clickable tabs, which I knew from my website tutorials were called child pages. I clicked the tabs: *History of Tarot, Major Arcana, Minor Arcana,* and *Court Cards.* No content yet, but text that said COMING SOON. I was impressed; Misty had accomplished a lot in a very short time, and it demonstrated her desire to be part of the Past & Present team.

On her *Messages* page Misty explained that she used a Rider-Waite deck for her tarot readings.

Originally published in 1910 by William Rider & Son of London, the illustrations for the Rider-Waite cards were drawn in 1909 by Pamela Colman Smith under the direction of Arthur Edward Waite. Smith's richly detailed and symbolic drawings transformed the standard tarot deck. Today, Rider-Waite is one of the most popular tarot decks in the English-speaking world. See History of Tarot for more information.

The *History of Tarot* was linked to the "COMING SOON" child page.

Today's *Message* had captivated Louisa. It featured the Eight of Wands: eight thin logs pointing toward the ground, with leaves falling against a clear blue sky and a rolling, treed landscape.

THE EIGHT OF WANDS (ELEMENT: FIRE)

This is the only card in the minor arcana that does not include people, animals, or mythological creatures. Notice how the eight wands work in tandem, each pointing in the same downward direction, as if in harmony with each other, the leaves and the earth. The overall impression of the card is one of peacefulness, movement, teamwork, and determination.

MISTY'S MESSAGE: This is the perfect time to take action. Working with a team will help you to produce the results you desire.

I had to grin. I knew from past research that reading of the tarot was at the interpretation of the reader, although there was a general consensus on what each card represented. Misty had taken the Eight of Wands and made it all about purpose and teamwork. Not only was it clever, Misty had earned her first finder's fee, split fifty-fifty with Arabella. Not a bad start.

It was time to tackle the train case and sort the contents. I felt the muscles in my neck relax. I could do this. We could do this. I called Chantelle, provided a brief update, and paced the room until she arrived.

AFTER JUMPING UP AND DOWN, hugging each other, and making a large pot of Earl Grey tea, Chantelle and I were ready to start.

The first plastic pouch I removed contained a green cardboard passport. It was stamped *BUNDESREPUBLIK DEUTSCHLAND* and *REISEPASS.*

"A passport for the Federal Republic of Germany," Chantelle said, stating the obvious.

I opened up the passport. The black-and-white photo inside showed a serious Anneliese Ruth Prei. It was issued in London, England, on February 12, 1952, with an expiry date of February 12, 1954. Anneliese was described as having an oval face, brown eyes, no identifying marks, height one hundred and sixty-five centimeters.

Canada may have gone metric in the 1970s, but everyone I knew still weighed themselves in pounds and measured themselves in feet and inches, including me. "How tall is one hundred and sixty-five centimeters?"

Chantelle tapped on her keyboard. "About five foot four," she said. "What else does it say?"

"It lists her current location as Nottingham, and her birthplace as Stettin, Pommern."

"Stettin, Pommern." Chantelle tapped away at her keyboard. "Got it. Pommern was a province in Prussia. Stettin is now Szczecin, not sure if I pronounced that right. It's spelled s-z-c-z-e-c-i-n. It's a port city, on the Oder River, which flows from the Baltic Sea. It says that Stettin became part of Poland after World War II. Here's a Wikipedia entry. 'In April 1945, Nazi authorities of the city issued an evacuation order, and most of the city's German population fled.' My guess is that Anneliese fled to another part of Germany, and at some point, made the necessary arrangements to immigrate to England. Something or someone made her want to leave England and come to Canada."

"It's someone," I said, pointing to a handwritten entry in the passport. "This is her Canadian visa application, approved on June 12, 1952, in Liverpool. The word FIANCEE is written in block letters and underlined."

"So there was a man waiting for her in Canada. What else does the passport tell us?"

"She was immunized on June 17 and arrived in Quebec City, Quebec, on July 7." I flipped through the pages. There were no more entries until the back page, where a paper record had been pasted in. "Look at this. Foreign exchange for traveling expenses, a special allotment for emigration. Looks like Anneliese received fifteen pounds."

Chantelle started typing. "About forty Canadian dollars, according to my historical currency converter. It would be worth about three hundred and fifty dollars in today's money. Which is interesting, but not something that warrants more than a footnote in our investigation. What can the immigration identification card tell us?"

"Anneliese R. Prei became a landed immigrant in Quebec City on July 7, 1952. That ties with the passport, which is no surprise.

The ship was the T.S.S. *Canberra*, Greek Line. It departed from Southampton, England."

"According to Wikipedia, the *Canberra* sailed for the Greek Line from 1949 to 1954," Chantelle said. "Unfortunately, the Greek Line stopped operating in 1975."

"So it's a dead end."

"Not necessarily. Hang on while I go to the Canadian Museum of Immigration." Chantelle's fingers flew across the keyboard. "Here it is. The T.S.S. *Canberra* had seven hundred and thirty-three passengers on that journey. It would be nice to get a copy of the passenger list, although I'm not optimistic. A lot of those records were destroyed, and there are privacy laws, which can be quite restrictive. However, I do have a contact at the Museum. I'll send her an email. Ancestry.ca might also have a record." She pulled a pen and a spiral-bound notebook from her purse and made a note.

The cover of the notebook had an autumn scene of a rocky-edged lake, a red canoe docked at shore. It was the sort of picture you'd expect from Tom Thomson or the Group of Seven. "Pen and a notebook. I thought I was the last of a dying breed."

"There have to be more of us out there," Chantelle said, grinning. "Maybe we can start a notebook club. Of course, only pretty notebooks will be allowed, none of those five-subject kind you used in school."

"That goes without saying."

"What else do we have? In case I want to write more notes."

"The only other thing in here is an envelope with three postcards from the ship." I took the postcards out and laid them one by one on the desk. The pictures on the postcards were black and white, the paper yellowed with age. All three had captions in German. "There must have been a lot of Germans on that ship, even though it left from England."

Chantelle nodded. "That makes sense. Many of the immigrants from England at that time were originally from Germany."

I picked up the first card. It depicted a wood-paneled room with a beamed ceiling and patterned carpet. A large piano was clearly the main attraction, with end tables and frilly, floral upholstered chairs and love seats positioned throughout the room. The caption read T.D. *Canberra - Erste Klasse Musik Salon.*

"I wonder why it's the T.D. *Canberra* instead of the T.S.S. *Canberra?*"

"I've come across that before with my genealogy research," Chantelle said. "T.S.S. stands for twin-screw steamer or steamship. T.D. stands for *Turbine Dampfschiff,* which translates to turbine steamboat."

"You are a veritable wealth of information. Can I assume that *Erste Klasse Musik Salon* translates to First Class Music Salon?"

"You can."

I turned the card over. "There's nothing written on the back. I wonder if Anneliese ever saw the inside of that salon. It looks very stiff and formal, doesn't it? Not the sort of place where you'd be doing a singalong with the pianist."

I studied the next postcard. This room had wood plank floors, a small piano, ceiling fans, and a few upholstered chairs. It was still nice, but it didn't have the opulence of the music room. "T.D. *Canberra - Touristenklasse Aufenthaltsraum,*" I said, stumbling over the pronunciation. "The first word means tourist class, but the other is beyond my cyphering abilities."

Chantelle was already on it. "It means lounge. This must be where the tourist class hung out."

I turned the card over. Blank again. The final postcard, captioned T.D. *Canberra – Touristenklasse Speisesalon,* was clearly a dining room, showing three long tables, seven chairs to a side, although the impression was of a much larger room with several more tables. A white tablecloth and napkins were in stark contrast to the dark furniture and bare wooden floors.

"Okay, we have blank postcards from the ship Anneliese came to Canada on," Chantelle said. "Obviously she kept them as mementoes of her journey, but they don't really tell us much."

"Except this one of the dining room does have this on the back." I pointed to a hand drawn heart with the number seven written inside it. "What do you think it means?"

"The tables and chairs on the ship would have been numbered, and the passengers would have sat at the same table, with the same people, every night. My guess is that Anneliese fancied someone at the table."

"That's my thinking, as well. But how do we find out which passenger?"

"We're just getting started. Maybe one of the three other storage bags in this suitcase will help us connect the dots. Or at least get us to the map that has the dots on it."

Connecting the dots. I remembered Louisa's words, how she felt when she saw Anneliese's photograph for the first time, as if her grandmother was reaching out to her from beyond the grave. I hoped Anneliese would trust us and keep on reaching.

7

I unzipped the first plastic pouch and carefully removed five black-and-white photographs of Anneliese. Once again I was struck by Louisa's uncanny resemblance to her grandmother.

I recognized the *Canberra's* tourist class lounge in two of the photos. Unlike the postcards, which featured empty rooms, these pictures included people sitting, chatting, and milling about. I turned them over to find a penciled alphanumeric notation of 406-C and 412-C, almost certainly jotted by the ship's photographer. Unfortunately, the demise of the Greek Line and the absence of a photographer's name made further identification impossible.

There was, however, a date of June 30, 1952 written in blue fountain pen ink on the back of both. Anneliese? A quick comparison of the spiky, Germanic handwriting against the signature on her passport confirmed it.

I studied the first shipboard photo. Anneliese stood next to the small piano, a half smile playing on her full lips. The other shot showed Anneliese laughing, surrounded by a group of people.

She wore a barber pole striped shirt with a large winged collar and softly puffed three-quarter length sleeves, paired with a slim-fitted A-line skirt, a row of decorative buttons down the right side.

Sling-back, peep-toed pumps completed the look. It was obvious that Anneliese liked fashion, and with her tiny waist and slender ankles, she wore it well, but it was more than that. Everything about Anneliese Prei exuded quiet confidence.

The third picture had been snapped in front of the chateau-styled Royal York Hotel in Toronto. Now dwarfed by mega-high-rise office towers and condominiums, in 1952 the twenty-eight story Royal York was the most prestigious address in town. Anneliese wore low-heeled pumps and a wide-strap sundress with a square neckline and white scalloped trim. It was difficult to determine the color, but I imagined it to be a deep shade of lavender. The dress was fitted at the waist and flared out to just below her knees, accentuating her trim figure. I flipped it over and noted the same handwriting, "July 9, 1952."

"There's something different about her in this photo, but I can't put my finger on it."

Chantelle glanced at the photograph. "Her hair has lost a bit of its bounce, but otherwise, she's as crisp as a newly minted bill, not so much as a crease in that cotton dress of hers. Maybe coming from the temperate climate of England to the heat and humidity of Toronto in July sapped her energy. She landed in Quebec City, there would have been a train trip to Toronto, a lengthy journey back then."

The long journey was a plausible explanation. But my gut told me there was more to Anneliese's lack of bounce than hot weather and the trials and tribulations of travel. I placed the pictures side by side, studying Anneliese's expression. There was something about her smile, her eyes…

"That's it." I pointed to the pictures taken on the ship. "In these two, Anneliese has a mysterious half smile, as if she's hiding a secret, but she also looks positively radiant. In the one taken in front of the Royal York, there's tension there. She's smiling, but the smile doesn't quite reach her eyes. It's the kind of expression you see on people's faces when they're forced to pose for a picture."

Chantelle nodded. "You're right. Damn, you're good at this reading between the lines stuff."

"I'm going to have to be if we want to succeed." I slid the next photo out of its plastic storage bag and felt a stir of excitement. "This one might actually provide our first solid clue."

Anneliese was wearing the same dress as in the previous photo. She looked more relaxed, the smile more genuine. She was standing on the front porch of a narrow, nondescript two-story duplex.

"I'm not seeing a house number, which is disappointing, but it's the kind of house you might find in the old part of Toronto," Chantelle said. "Somewhere like Danforth Village, where a twenty-five-foot lot would be considered a wide."

I knew Danforth Village, a neighborhood in the east end of the original part of Toronto. Most of the existing houses had been built in the 1920s and '30s, although you'd be hard pressed to find one that hadn't been renovated from top to bottom. Now considered centrally located, in 1952 it would have been on the outskirts of the city. "At least now we know where Anneliese settled. She must have moved in here with her fiancé."

Chantelle shook her head. "I don't think people cohabited before marriage in those days, or if they did, it certainly wasn't mainstream. It's more likely she rented a room there, along with other new immigrants. It's not like there were a bunch of apartment buildings back then."

"There's still one more photo. Maybe that will tell us more."

In the last photograph, Anneliese was standing on the front porch of an attractive two-story brick house. She wore a below the knee pencil skirt in a light color, probably off-white or cream, paired with a softly flared short-sleeved jacket that skimmed her slender hips. Matching elbow-length gloves, a cap with a dark ribbon, and a three-strand pearl necklace completed the ensemble. Her blonde hair had been pinned back from her face in a loose bun, revealing pearl drop earrings that matched the necklace. A light-eyed man in a black suit, black tie, and white shirt stood next to her, his arm wrapped possessively around her waist. His hair appeared to be even blonder than Anneliese's and as straight as a poker.

I flipped it over. It was dated October 11, 1952. "Do you think this might be her wedding day?"

Chantelle nodded. "Without question. It would make sense, as well. Those days, when you immigrated to get married, you were expected to tie the knot within six months, or you were sent back to where you came from. Sooner was definitely considered better. The pearls may have been a wedding gift from her husband."

"There's an old superstition that pearls bring tears. I wonder if Anneliese cried on her wedding day."

"Actually, ancient Greek culture believed that pearls would promote marital bliss and guard against tears on the wedding day," Chantelle grinned. "Or night, as the case might be. Anyway, that's where the tradition of giving pearls to a bride comes from, although you're correct. A lot of people associate pearls with tears and would never want to wear pearls on their wedding day, let alone accept them as a gift from the groom."

Chantelle always amazed me with the trivia she came up with. Her knowledge of pearls was no exception. "What about the house? Based on the narrow lot and overall style, it could be in the same part of city, which would also make sense. Anneliese's fiancé would have rented her accommodations close to him."

"The double gabled roofline is definitely distinctive. You don't see that often. The trim is quite unique as well. If I were renovating I might restore it, but I can't imagine replacing it. A trip to Toronto might be in order for a walkabout."

"I'm always up for a trek to Toronto and a good walk, but I'm not seeing the purpose. It's unlikely any of the original owners still live in the area. Nursing homes would be more like it, if they're still alive. Besides, we're only guessing on the area."

"True," Chantelle said, drumming her fingers on the table. "I've got it. Old telephone books."

"Old telephone books?"

"If Anneliese Prei had a phone, she would be listed, along with her address."

"I hate to rain on your parade, but it's unlikely that Anneliese would have had her own phone in a rental property. It's more likely there would have been one phone for all the residents. Lots of people didn't even have telephones back then, and those that did often shared a party line."

"Anything else to add?" Chantelle asked, a note of exasperation in her voice.

"Actually, yes. There's the little problem of not knowing her married name."

"We can make an educated guess that it was Frankow."

"We can try that," I conceded. "But where are we going to find a Toronto telephone book from 1952?"

"The Toronto Public Library." Chantelle turned to her attention back to her laptop and started typing. "Damn. They've digitized almost all of the nineteenth and early twentieth century Toronto city directories up to 1922, but they can't add a directory online until the ninety-year copyright protection expires. Here's the kicker. They have some print copies available, but none for 1952. The first telephone book after 1951 is 1957."

I had to admit it was frustrating, but one thing I'd learned during the past thirteen months was that there was always another place to look. I was pondering the possibilities when Chantelle spoke up.

"What if we posted the photograph on Facebook with a link to our website? It's possible someone might recognize the house."

"I don't love the idea. It opens up our investigation to any nutcase out there, and I'm not sure how Louisa would feel about posting her grandmother's picture for the world to see. I'd rather try your walkabout idea first, if we determine knowing the address is necessary. Which I don't think it is, at least not at this point."

"Fair enough. But if we do decide to post the photo of the house, we can always hire a photographer and have them remove Anneliese from the image. They can work miracles these days with all the digital advancements."

The issue shelved for the moment, I replaced all five photographs back inside the storage bag. "Which one do you want to open next? The thin one or the thick one?"

"Let's leave the thick one for last."

Great minds think alike. "The thin one it is."

8

___

The thin one contained a Certificate of Marriage between Horst Frankow and Anneliese Prei, dated October 11, 1952, at the City of Toronto in the Province of Ontario. The Marriage License had been issued on September 25, 1952.

"We were right about the last photo of Anneliese being taken on her wedding day," Chantelle said. "And about the Frankow part. What I don't understand is why Sophie would have ended up in foster care if there was a father in the picture."

"Another mystery. Unfortunately, this marriage certificate won't help us much."

When I'd researched my mother's disappearance, her marriage certificate had been a huge help, even listing the current addresses of the bride and groom. Not so with this one, which offered nothing more than the basic facts: names, date, place, along with the signatures of the witnesses and City Hall magistrate. Even the witnesses' names were a dead end. John J. Johnson and David P. Smith. There had to be a lot of Johnsons and Smiths out there. The magistrate would be long retired, and likely to have performed thousands of civil ceremonies. I guessed the witnesses had probably been supplied by City Hall for a nominal fee.

Chantelle was more optimistic. "You never know. Ancestry.ca has a pretty good selection of marriage certificates on record. At the very least, it might lead us to find out more about Horst Frankow. It's another thing I can check when I'm on there." She recorded the details of the certificate on a new page of her notebook.

"You do know that we can make copies with our printer," I said, teasing her.

"Waste of paper. We're on a budget. Besides, I like to have all my notes in the same place." Chantelle started tapping her fingers on the table again, her brow furrowed in concentration. "Can I see the photograph from Anneliese's wedding day again?"

"Sure." I slid it out of the pouch and handed it to her. "What's bothering you?"

"Her outfit. In the snapshots from the boat, she wore things that emphasized her tiny waist. So why was she wearing a loose jacket on her wedding day?"

I went back through the notes I took with Louisa. Sophie was born on March 23, 1953. I did some mental math. "Anneliese was almost four months pregnant on her wedding day."

"Give me a minute to check my files," Chantelle said, back at her keyboard.

Patience has never been one of my virtues. "What are you looking for?"

"I thought I recognized the outfit, and I was right. It's part of another project I've been working on, the grandmother was a seamstress in the 1950s." Chantelle pointed to a picture on her computer screen. "It's almost identical to what Louisa is wearing in the photo."

The outfit was a Butterick pattern, number 6194, and it had been listed under the category of 1952 maternity clothes. The material of the jacket and skirt was lightly patterned versus plain, but it was definitely the same style. Even the cap was the same, ribbon and all.

"I suppose there weren't many patterns for maternity ensembles," I said. "I wonder...do you think the pregnancy was planned?"

"It's possible, but doubtful," Chantelle said, typing. "Here's an online pregnancy calculator. A March 23 birth date would have meant conceiving around June 30."

"You think Anneliese got pregnant on the ship?"

"I think it's a possibility we have to consider."

"What if Anneliese and Horst slept together right away? Sophie might have been premature."

"Maybe the thick pouch will hold the answer," Chantelle said, ending the debate.

I unzipped the top and pulled out a tissue-wrapped photo album with a pink cover and yellowed pages that may have been white or cream at one time. A cautious flip through the pages, about two dozen in all, revealed that each snapshot had been painstakingly positioned inside black cardboard corners, two photos to a page, with several blank pages at the end. All the photos were black and white. I went back to the first page, careful not to damage the aging paper.

The first picture was of a chubby-cheeked baby, the words "Sophie Marta Frankow, March 23, 1953," written beneath it in Anneliese's now-familiar handwriting.

"She was a cute baby," Chantelle said, "but her coloring definitely isn't the same as Anneliese or Horst. We know Anneliese's eyes are soft brown, and based on Horst's fair complexion and blond hair, we can safely assume his are blue. Sophie's eyes look almost black. So does her hair. Love the little curl on top of her head, though."

The curl *was* cute, but Chantelle had a point. Both Anneliese and Horst had blonde hair. That wasn't conclusive proof of anything, a newborn's hair color and texture could change over time, and we had no idea about Anneliese or Horst's genetics. Even so, the baby in the picture didn't look premature to me, not that I was an expert.

I went through the album, page by page. Anneliese was with Sophie in every one, playing on the front yard of the double gabled house, sitting on the porch with her daughter in her lap. Horst was in the odd picture, always with his hand resting firmly on

Anneliese's arm, or wrapped tightly around her waist. There were no pictures of him holding the baby, let alone playing with her.

"Anneliese looks radiant when she's alone with Sophie," I said. "Is it just my imagination, or does her expression look strained whenever Horst is in the shot?"

Chantelle shook her head. "I don't think it's your imagination. I had the same impression. She's always smiling and happy, except when he's standing or sitting next to her. Look at the way he's posing in every single one. It's as if he's trying to control Anneliese. And there are no pictures of him interacting with Sophie."

"Maybe we're reading too much into it," I said, but I had to wonder. Did Horst know or suspect that he wasn't Sophie's birth father? Did anyone else? Today, it might not be such a big deal, but in 1952, raising another man's child might have been considered scandalous.

"One thing is certain," Chantelle said, interrupting my thoughts. "Anneliese never lost her sense of style. She had to be one of the hippest moms on the block."

Was that another reason for Horst's apparent possessiveness? Was he the jealous type, and if so, how much did that jealousy impact their lives? I studied the photos again, page by page, noting the special occasions recorded by Anneliese, month after month. First birthday. Christmas. Valentine's Day. Easter. Halloween. Repeat. The photos ended with one taken at Sophie's third birthday party on March 23, 1956. Her hair hadn't gotten any blonder, either. If anything, it had gotten darker and curlier. She was blowing out three candles on a lopsided chocolate-frosted cake, clearly homemade. Anneliese stood behind her, clapping her hands and laughing.

"Sophie went into foster care at age three," I said. "Anneliese must have died shortly after this picture was taken."

Chantelle wasn't listening. Instead, she was sliding her hand across the bottom of the suitcase's satin lining. "I'm not sure about this seam in the left hand corner."

"The seam?" Sometimes I had to wonder about the stuff Chantelle worried about.

"Just trace your fingers along it and tell me if you feel anything funny."

I humored her and did what she asked. Nothing. "No, can't say as I do."

"Do you have a magnifying glass?"

"Of course I have a magni…wait, you want to examine the seam with a magnifying glass?"

That netted me an exasperated sigh. I took a magnifying glass from what I'd come to think of as my "Detective Callie" drawer and slid it in her direction.

Chantelle explored the seam, viewing it from every possible angle. I was starting to lose patience when she handed me the magnifying glass and pushed the train case toward me. "What do you think? Has it been carefully re-stitched? Or is my imagination in overdrive?"

I mimicked her actions. Still nothing. I shook my head.

"Never mind. Can you get your sewing basket?"

"My sewing basket?"

"Yes, your sewing basket. The one with your sewing tools. Like needles and thread and one of those stitch remover gizmos."

"Sorry to disappoint but my father never encouraged sewing. I don't own a sewing basket, and I have no idea what a stitch remover gizmo looks like. I might have one of those lame hotel sewing kits from a hundred years ago when they gave them out with the shower caps and the shoe shine thingamajig." I paused for effect. "No, wait. I don't."

"Spoken like the spoiled only child that you were, no hand-me-downs to alter, hems up, hems down, no knees or elbows to patch."

It was a running gag between the two of us. My being a spoiled only child while Chantelle wore rags as the fifth kid of six. Except today, it didn't seem all that funny.

"It's not as if my father dressed me in the latest runway fashions," I said, hating the pissed-off tone in my voice. "He just didn't think to teach me about stuff like sewing."

"Yeah, yeah, chill out. It was an observation, not an indictment." Chantelle grabbed her handbag from the back of her chair and rummaged through it. "Here you go. It's not an official stitch remover, but these nail scissors should work. Just be careful not to damage anything."

"Why don't you do it, if you're such an expert?"

Chantelle rolled her eyes, but I could tell she was relieved. I watched as she carefully snipped each stitch until the secret compartment was revealed.

Unlike the previous contents in the upper part of the train case, there were no plastic storage bags under the lining. In their place was a single envelope. Part of me wanted to dive in, head first. Another part felt as if I was crossing some sort of invisible line. "What do you make of it?" I asked Chantelle.

Chantelle bit her lower lip, appraising the contents before her. "I would say that Sophie was the one responsible for the storage bags, everything neatly compartmentalized."

I nodded. It fit with Louisa's description of her mother. "What else?"

"My guess, and it is just a guess, is that this train case with the photo album, marriage certificate, and collection of postcards, pictures, and travel documents, was the one thing Sophie had to bring from foster home to foster home. At some point, she decided to protect each and every item in plastic for posterity."

"Do you think Sophie knew about the envelope under the lining?"

"I don't believe so. Even after my prompting, you didn't find anything wrong with the seam, and truthfully, if I hadn't been forced to learn needlework skills, I don't think I would have either. I think it's safe to say that that hidden compartment was a secret Anneliese took to her grave."

"We need to look at what's inside, but I don't know, it feels wrong somehow. Do you feel the same way I do? Like it's an invasion of privacy?"

Chantelle shook her head. "Not at all. We were hired to find out what happened to Anneliese Prei. Unless we decide to walk away, it's going to get personal. You of all people should know that, especially after everything you've been through these past few months."

Put like that, the decision was an easy one. It was time to find out what Anneliese had been hiding all these years.

IT WAS a Certificate of Baptism and Birth for Sophie Marta Frankow dated March 25, 1956, two days after Sophie's third birthday. I stared at the names on the certificate, trying to push back the sick feeling in the pit of my stomach.

"Are you okay?" Chantelle asked, concern etched on her lovely face. "I get that you recognize the last name, but surely it's a coincidence."

"You're probably right," I said, knowing that she wasn't. I turned my attention to the document at hand.

"Certificate of Baptism and Birth," I read out loud, as if doing so would change what was written there. "This certifies that Sophie Marta Frankow, daughter of Anton Osgoode and his wife Anneliese Ruth née Prei, was born on the twenty-third day of March, 1953 at Toronto, Ontario, and received Christian Baptism on the twenty-fifth day of March, 1956."

"His wife" had been crossed out, raising the question of who would have done that. The pastor? Anton? Anneliese, after the fact? I knew the question was rhetorical, that there would be no way of ever finding out, but I couldn't help but wonder.

The certificate was signed by G. Walther, Pastor, and witnessed by Adam Bradford and Helena Bradford. The purple stamp signifying the name and address of the church had been faded to the point where the only legible text was "St.," "Chur," and "Toronto," the last t and o in Toronto almost invisible. Unless Chantelle could find out something about a G. Walther, a pastor in 1953, the church would remain unknown, not that the name of the church really mattered.

It didn't even matter that Sophie's father wasn't Horst Frankow. We'd suspected as much, even if we hadn't expected to find written proof in the form of a Certificate of Baptism. It was the surname of the father that Chantelle and I recognized.

Osgoode. As in Corbin and Yvette Osgoode. My mother's parents. My grandparents. And we were far from close, given that they'd disowned my mother when she came home pregnant at seventeen. That disassociation had remained, even after I was born.

I'd recently started working on a family tree on Ancestry.ca. Call it closure, or validation, or just plain curiosity after everything Chantelle had told me about genealogy. As a result, I'd learned that Anton Osgoode was my great-grandfather, and that he'd died in 1987 at age sixty-six. There had been no record of anyone named Anneliese, at least not in what I'd discovered so far. I also knew that my great-grandmother Olivia was still alive at the age of ninety-one, at least the last time I checked, and that she had never remarried.

It also meant that I was related to our client, Louisa Frankow, though my boggled state of mind was currently unable to figure out what that relation might be. Possibly half first cousin once removed?

My thoughts slid off course to an added twist. I suspected that in some way, Corbin Osgoode had been responsible for my father's occupational accident. I just hadn't been able to prove it. Yet.

Past & Present Investigations had just taken on a whole new meaning.

9

———

Chantelle got ready to leave. She promised to search for a passenger list from the *Canberra*, as well as start the genealogical research on Anneliese Prei and Horst Frankow. She could have pushed me on the Anton Osgoode stuff, but she didn't, and that's one of her greatest strengths, the ability to read people's emotions and respond to them. I appreciated her all the more for her innate sensitivity.

"I'll add checking the *Toronto Star's* newspaper archives to our to-do list," I said. I might have been feeling shell-shocked, but we still had a job to do.

"Good idea. I'd recommend starting in 1950 and working through the years." Chantelle shot me a pitying glance. "It's not going to be an easy job."

"Nor one I'm looking forward to." I thought about the hours spent at the library looking at microfiche for news items about my mother. It was slow, tedious work, though Shirley, a former librarian, seemed to thrive on it. But it could pay dividends, as I'd discovered for myself. I made a list of names. "Anneliese Prei, Anneliese Frankow, Horst Frankow, Sophie Frankow, Louisa Frankow, and Anton Osgoode. Am I missing anyone?"

"The pastor, G. Walther," Chantelle said. "And Adam and Helena Bradford. They were witnesses at the Baptism, and could be Sophie's godparents."

"Which brings us to another mystery. I'll admit that I'm not well-versed in religion, but aren't godparents supposed to look after the child if something happens to the parents? Why would Sophie have gone into foster care if she had godparents?"

"Unless Anneliese had a will specifically naming the godparents as custodians, they wouldn't have a legal obligation to look after Sophie."

"Hmmm. I think it's unlikely that Anneliese had a will."

"Agreed. Of course, it's also possible that the godparents were the ones to put Sophie in foster care. Whatever their story is, they have to go on the list."

"Done. I'm also going to give Louisa a call. I'd like her to bring over Sophie's jewelry box and the rest of the photos sooner rather than later."

"As long as I'm here when you go through them." Chantelle gave me a quick hug. "I'll leave it up to you on how much you want to tell Louisa."

Meaning, would I tell her that we were related. I knew I'd have to, at some point, but not yet. Not until I figured out how everything tied together. I called Louisa at her office and got her voicemail saying she'd be out of the office for the next week. I left a message saying we'd already made some progress, but could really use Sophie's photos and jewelry box when she returned. I started a written report as soon as I hung up, including billable hours. For a moment I felt a bit like the late Sue Grafton's fictional private detective, Kinsey Millhone, albeit without the index cards and black all-purpose dress. The thought made me smile.

What didn't make me smile was the thought of contacting Olivia Osgoode. I hadn't made an effort yet, given my strained relationship with my grandparents, most notably her son, Corbin. He had shunned his teenaged, pregnant daughter, my father, and, in turn, me. I also knew arranging a meeting was necessary and soon, in light of her age. I hoped all her faculties were still intact.

But how would I find her? I searched for her name only and came up empty. No surprise there. How many ninety-one-year-olds had Facebook pages or residential landlines in their own names? Plan B would be to call every retirement residence in Cedar County, but the thought of doing that exhausted me, especially since my queries would almost certainly be blocked for privacy reasons. That left Plan C: call the Osgoodes and ask. I slid a tube of cocoa butter lip balm out of a drawer and smoothed it on, pondering the ramifications of contacting my grandparents. Part of me wanted to keep them at arm's length while I attempted to investigate Corbin from the sidelines. The other part considered the old adage, "keep your friends close, and your enemies closer."

I picked up my cell, flipped through my contacts, and dialed. If I got lucky, Yvette would answer the phone, and I wouldn't have to deal with Corbin.

I got lucky.

If Yvette Osgoode was surprised to hear from me, she gave no indication, though a hint of sarcasm rang out strong and true.

"Callie. To what do I owe the pleasure?"

I wanted to call her grandmother, but the name stuck in my throat. Calling her Yvette seemed disrespectful, although I wasn't quite sure why. I decided not to call her anything, and plunged ahead with my prepared story.

"I'm working on my family tree."

"Are you? I hear a lot of people do that these days."

No offer of help, not that I expected any. "I'm hoping to get in contact with Olivia Osgoode. My great-grandmother."

"I'm well aware of who Olivia Osgoode is." Yvette's tone was positively acerbic. "What I don't understand is why you feel the need to contact her. She's old, cantankerous, and she has a tendency to live in the past. She's never expressed the slightest interest in meeting you."

Sucker punch to the gut delivered. "Perhaps she followed her son's lead. Regardless, I'm willing to take my chances at rejection. I've had plenty of experience in that department." Sucker punch right back at you, *Grandma*. As for Olivia living in the past, couldn't that work to my advantage? I wanted her to revisit the past, not get all caught up in the present. I wasn't looking for a family reunion.

There was a lengthy silence on the other end of the line. I forced myself not to speak. This was a battle of wills, one that I was determined to win.

After what seemed like an eternity, Yvette spoke. "She's at the Cedar County Retirement Residence. It's in Marketville, at the corner of Mavis and Lester. Room eighteen on the third floor. It's up to her if she wants to see you. I won't interfere either way, not that it would matter if I did. She's always found me insufferable, a feeling that I assure you is mutual."

I resisted telling a mother-in-law joke, thanked her for her time, and hung up before we could get into anything remotely personal. Whatever road Yvette was ready to go down with me, I wasn't willing to join her. At least not while Corbin was alive.

I checked my phone for the time and was surprised to find it approaching four o'clock. It would be too late to pay Olivia a visit. I'd volunteered at a retirement home during high school as part of my community service hours. The one thing I'd learned was that dinner hour started early, as did bedtime.

Temporarily frustrated, I closed my eyes and considered other avenues to explore. There's something about closing my eyes that helps me shut out the world and allow my subconscious to take over. It didn't take long for an idea to take hold. I could study the photographs from the *Canberra*.

I selected the two photographs of Anneliese in the ship's tourist class lounge and placed them side by side on the table. Except this time, I wasn't looking for Anneliese.

It took me a few minutes to zero in on every other person in the photos, and compare them, disregarding anyone who appeared in only one. That left me with three people, in addition to Anneliese: two women, and one man. I wasn't particularly interested in the women, especially since neither were standing anywhere near Anneliese. I was, however, interested in the man. In the photo of Anneliese by the piano, he was standing across the room, but he was definitely looking in her direction. Even better, in the picture where she was mixing and mingling, he was standing next to her. He wore a tweed suit, striped tie, white shirt, and a wide smile.

I pegged him to be about thirty years old. Height five foot eleven give or take an inch on either side, which I deduced from Anneliese's recorded height on her passport of five foot four, along with an estimation of the two-inch heels on her peep-toed pumps. His hair was almost black, the waves slicked back in the style of the day, his eyes deep set and equally dark, his nose straight and narrow. Broad shoulders on an otherwise trim build, despite the fashionable, if baggy, pleated trousers. A handsome man who carried himself with the self-confident assurance of the good-looking.

I pulled a magnifying glass from a drawer in the table and hovered it over his features, taking them in one by one until no doubt remained. Age, hairstyle, and fashion differences aside, this man was a dead ringer for my grandfather. True, Corbin Osgoode's hair was now on the snowy side of white, but I'd seen pictures of him in his youth. He'd had the same wavy black hair, the same trim, broad-shouldered physique, the same self-assurance. I'd always assumed it was because he had nosebleed money. One look at Anton made me realize it was more than that.

It all added up to one thing: the tall, dark, and handsome stranger in the photo was my great-grandfather, Anton Osgoode. The plot had indeed thickened.

⊕

I forced myself to make some dinner, if you consider heating up canned French Canadian pea soup making dinner. I'm not usually a tinned soup kind of person, preferring to make my soup from scratch, but there was something about this brand of pea soup that I found comforting, perhaps because it had been one of my father's favorites. Add a crusty roll, and you were golden. Not that I had a crusty roll. I did, however, have a loaf of rye bread in the freezer. It would have to do.

I considered my next move while sopping up soup with slices of lightly buttered rye toast. I'd have to tell Chantelle what I'd discovered, that much was a given. But first I'd pay a visit to Olivia Osgoode. A surprise visit, if Yvette had kept my phone call to herself. I remembered her reaction to the mention of Olivia's name, and thought that the odds were in my favor.

I pushed the remaining bread and soup aside and started planning my strategy. Everyone needed a strategy. Didn't they?

MORNING DIDN'T ARRIVE SOON ENOUGH for me. I'd had a sleepless night, unaided by a generous glass of Australian Chardonnay before bed. If anything, the wine had served to keep me awake. Live and learn.

I stopped at the supermarket and bought a bunch of red and white carnations, the freshest-looking flowers in an otherwise sorry-looking selection. Not sure whether to go with chocolates or cookies, I settled for a box of chocolate-coated cookies. It was now or never.

CEDAR COUNTY RETIREMENT RESIDENCE was brand new and seriously swanky, a five-story red brick building with generous green space surrounding it, and plenty of free parking for visitors. A quick online search revealed it cost upwards of five thousand dollars a month, without extras like meals delivered to your room, or day trips to the mall or doctor. Olivia's government pension wouldn't cover the rent, but when it came to money, the Osgoodes weren't exactly hurting.

The lobby featured oversized porcelain tiles in a rich, creamy shade, a tray ceiling sprinkled with pot lights around a large, oval skylight, and pale gold walls. Two curved sofas, upholstered in muted burgundy striped satin, framed a round mahogany table. An enormous bouquet of mixed flowers stood in the center.

I made my way to the glass-and-granite reception area, where an attractive platinum blonde in her early thirties greeted me with a condescending smile and an inquisitive stare. Clearly most visitors were regular. Or regular enough. A first-time visitor with carnations and chocolate-covered cookies was viewed with suspicion.

I had my spiel memorized. "I'm here to see Olivia Osgoode. She's in room eighteen on the third floor."

"East wing or west wing?"

Damn Yvette for leaving out that little detail, no doubt intentionally. "I'm not sure, to be honest." I put on my brightest smile. "I'm her great-granddaughter, Callie."

Platinum Blonde raised a thinly plucked black eyebrow. "Olivia didn't mention that she was expecting any visitors."

"I'm trying to surprise her."

At this, Platinum Blonde's mouth puckered in disapproval. "We don't encourage surprise visits with our older residents."

Weren't all of their residents older? I bit back a snarky response. "I did clear it with my grandmother, Yvette Osgoode. She had no objection."

The name drop worked. It would appear that Yvette Osgoode was a force to be reckoned with, even if her feelings for Olivia were less than loving. I followed Platinum Blonde's directions down to the west wing elevator, pressed the button for up, and waited for the ding. I could do this.

I could.

10

———

Olivia Osgoode's room was compact, but well appointed, with a living room and a separate kitchenette equipped with bar-sized refrigerator, microwave, kettle, and coffeemaker. Two white colonial doors, both closed, undoubtedly led to the bathroom and bedroom. The décor and furnishings were surprisingly modern: hardwood floors the color of cognac, glass and chrome coffee and end tables, a wall-mounted flat screen television, and a black leather sofa with matching chair. There were a couple of rose pink throw pillows on the sofa, the walls painted to match, the only hint of a feminine touch. The overall impression was one of a downtown Toronto condo rather than a retirement residence.

Olivia sat upright and rigid in the chair. She was a fine-boned woman with translucent skin that had been lined by age in the gentlest of ways, as if an artist had painted in the wrinkles, and then smudged the paint to soften them. She assessed me with clear blue eyes and I got the distinct impression she didn't suffer fools gladly. Unfortunately, a fool is just what I felt like, standing before her, carnations and chocolate-coated biscuits in hand.

"You have your father's eyes," she said. "Jimmy Barnstable

wasn't nearly good enough for my granddaughter, but he did have nice eyes. Black-rimmed hazel. You don't see that often."

I wasn't sure how to respond to that, so I opted for silence and stood before her like a chastised schoolgirl. She must have taken pity on me, because when she spoke again, it was to direct me to a crystal vase in the cupboard above the refrigerator for the flowers, and to another cupboard for napkins and a plate for the cookies. I managed to take care of both tasks and set everything on the coffee table without dropping them, a miracle given the unexpected weight of the vase and my shaking hands.

"Tea would be nice with the cookies you brought." Olivia said. "You'll find a tin of Earl Grey in the pantry, along with a teapot. I can't abide the idea of tossing a teabag in a mug and pouring some hot water over it. Pure laziness. The key to a perfect cup of tea is to ensure the water reaches a proper rolling boil. Then rinse the teapot with some of the boiling water before putting in the tea and filling the pot with water. Let it steep for exactly four minutes, not three and not five. In the meantime, you'll find bone china mugs in the cupboard above the cutlery drawer, along with the sugar pot. There are creamers, milkettes, and fresh lemon in the refrigerator. I try to keep them on hand for visitors, though those are often sadly lacking, present company excluded. I take my tea black."

I took my tea black as well, which at least eliminated one of Olivia's instructions. I plugged in the kettle, found the teapot and bone china mugs, and waited for the kettle to come to a boil. When it finally did, I rinsed the teapot before adding the water and tea, and set the chronometer on my watch. At exactly four minutes, I poured the tea, brought the mugs to the table, and took a seat on the sofa, grateful for the reprieve. I'd been here less than ten minutes and was already exhausted. It was easier to run a marathon.

Olivia took a cookie and dipped the tip into her tea with arthritic hands. It was a small gesture, but it made her seem more human somehow, less imperious. I followed suit, and for a brief moment we enjoyed our tea and cookies in companionable silence.

"How did you find me?" Olivia asked, setting down her mug.

"Yve—My grandmother told me where you lived."

"Anywhere but with her and my son," Olivia said, drily, "although Corbin insists on managing my financial affairs. He believes that I'm no longer capable of doing it myself, as if growing old is synonymous with becoming stupid. I could almost understand that, but he doesn't trust me to hire a professional, either. He'd rather tell me how much he's doing for me." She summoned up a sad smile. "I'm not complaining. I have my meals and snacks delivered to my room, or I can eat in the dining room with the droolers, deaf, and dim-witted. There's a well-stocked library on the main floor, and nursing care when I need it. There are worse places to live. But enough about me. What brings you here after all these years?"

She made it sound like I was the one who'd stayed away when the reverse was true. The Osgoodes had been the ones to abandon me, the child of their teenaged daughter, Abigail, and the unworthy Jimmy Barnstable. I bit back a bitter response, knowing it would end our conversation.

"I'm working on my family tree."

An arched eyebrow. "Why?"

"I have a friend, Chantelle, who's into genealogy. She made it sound interesting."

"And is it?"

I shrugged. "It's too early to tell."

"I can assure you we're not nearly as dull as our family tree might suggest."

I leaned forward. "Is that so?"

"Not so fast. I need time to think about it. Do I want to share the story, or carry it with me to my grave? I'm not sure. Besides, I'm an old woman, ready for her afternoon nap."

"I'm sorry. I should have prepared you for my visit. Instead, I've barged in here unannounced and overstayed my welcome."

"Not at all. I appreciate the courage it took for you to come here. It couldn't have been easy." She paused, her bright blue eyes taking the whole of me in, top to bottom and back again. After a few moments she nodded, as if arriving at a decision.

"Come back tomorrow at noon. Bring me a homemade tuna

sandwich on whole wheat. Albacore, not the stuff that looks and smells like cat food. Packed in water, not oil, oil makes it too greasy. No salt, light on the pepper. Real mayonnaise, not that sugary salad dressing concoction they force us to eat here. Use enough that the sandwich is moist, but not so much that it makes the bread soggy. The tiniest bit of butter, not margarine. If you don't have butter, leave the bread dry. Lettuce and thinly sliced cucumber and tomato. In turn, I'll save some of the cookies you brought for dessert. They're quite lovely. A nice combination of arrowroot biscuit and chocolate."

I wrote down her order the minute I was outside of her room, making sure I had every detail right. Olivia was testing me, and I intended to pass.

11
———

Olivia Osgoode took a dainty bite of her tuna sandwich, which I'd made to her exacting specifications.

"He was a philanderer, you know," Olivia said, setting her plate down on the table. "My husband, Anton. Your great-grandfather."

"A philanderer," I said. "Are you saying that Anton cheated on you?"

Olivia nodded. "His first dalliance was shortly after our wedding, although I was blissfully unaware of it for some time. Not that finding out would have made a difference. I got pregnant at eighteen in a time when we called it 'the family way' and marriage was the only option. Even if we weren't tear-our-clothes-off passionate about one another, we got on well enough. Things were different back then, at least they were for unwed mothers. I didn't want to be an unwed mother. I certainly didn't want to wear the stigma of a divorce."

I couldn't begin to imagine a time when social mores were so rigid they could compromise someone's right to happiness. "Did you love Anton?"

"I loved my son, Corbin, more than life itself," Olivia said, ignoring my question. "Did you know that I suffered through three late-term miscarriages after he was born? That was another thing no one spoke openly about, along with menstruation and God forbid—the ultimate taboo subject—sex. For a while, people would ask Anton and I if we were planning to have more children. After a time, the questions stopped. With every miscarriage, Corbin increasingly became my world."

I could imagine my grandfather being doted on from cradle to college. It went a long way to explaining the man he'd become. "What about Anton's world?"

"I thought he felt the same way. Or at least I did until I found out about Sophie."

I creased my brow and tilted my head to the right, my attempt at looking confused. "Sophie?"

"That's the part of the family tree that isn't quite so dull," Olivia said, "although I need you to promise that you won't share what I'm about to tell you with Corbin or Yvette. They don't know, and there's no reason for them to find out. Especially after all these years."

"You have my word."

Olivia stared at me with shrewd blue eyes. I held her gaze without flinching, easier said than done. After what seemed like an eternity, she continued.

"Her name was Sophie Frankow, that's spelled s-o-p-h-i-e, not s-o-f-i-e, last name f-r-a-n-k-o-w. She was Anton's illegitimate daughter and Corbin's half-sister."

I feigned a look of surprise bordering on shock, and pulled a pen and notebook from my purse. "Sophie Frankow," I said, writing it down. "Do you know when she was born?"

"March 23, 1953." Olivia closed her eyes, as if trying to block out the memory. "It was ironic, really. March 23 also happened to be our wedding anniversary. Of course, I didn't know about Sophie, at least not then. It would be another three years before her mother darkened my door. And I do mean darkened. The day Anneliese Frankow came knocking was the worst day of my life."

The admission seemed to cost Olivia because she slumped back in her chair, looking every moment of her ninety-one years and then some. I worried that she'd send me away again, but instead she asked if I'd make her another cup of tea while I cleaned up the dishes and got out the cookies.

"There's brandy in the bottom cupboard," Olivia said as I took care of things. "I don't imbibe often, but I could use a generous dollop in my tea. Feel free to join me."

I found the brandy and poured a shot into one of the bone china mugs. I planned to abstain, nothing against brandy, which I quite enjoy, especially straight up in a snifter, but I was driving. Besides, I needed to keep my wits about me. This might well be the last time Olivia allowed me to visit, and I didn't intend to miss a thing.

Two cups of fortified tea and three chocolate-coated cookies appeared to revive Olivia. By the time she pushed her mug and plate aside, the color was back in her cheeks, no doubt heightened by the brandy.

"Where was I? Before we stopped for tea?"

"You were telling me about the day Anneliese came to your house."

Olivia nodded, her lips pressed together in a tight line. "It was the Tuesday before our wedding anniversary, about ten o'clock in the morning. I was just getting ready to go to the market. I've always believed in shopping fresh every day, or at the very least, every other day, none of this stockpiling of groceries for me. Anton was out of town, something of a regular occurrence, especially in the 1950s and early '60s. He was a buyer for Eaton's, fine china and glassware."

Family owned and operated since being founded in the nineteenth century, Eaton's Department Store had once been a household name across Canada, employing thousands. Unfortunately, alleged mismanagement by the last two generations of the Eaton family had resulted in the chain's bankruptcy in 1999, sending shock waves throughout Canada. But working as a buyer for Eaton's in the 1950s would have been a coveted position.

It also explained why Anton had been traveling on the T.S.S. *Canberra*. While there were importers of china and glass at the time, a company the size of Eaton's would have a buyer meet directly with manufacturers like Royal Doulton, Royal Albert, and Waterford Crystal, and that buyer would almost certainly be wined and dined. I couldn't wait to tell Chantelle. "It sounds like a great job."

"It was both well paid and prestigious," Olivia said, a note of pride in her voice. "In 1956 the average wage ranged from seventy to a hundred dollars a week. Anton made considerably more, and he invested it wisely. Corbin likes to pretend that his wealth is all about his business acumen, but the reality is he had a considerable financial cushion with which to start Osgoode Construction. But I digress."

Digress? As interesting as Anton's backstory was, at this rate I'd be staying for supper. I gave Olivia what I hoped was an encouraging smile. It seemed to do the trick, because she got back on track.

"As soon as I saw the woman at my front door, I knew she'd been involved with Anton. She was his type. Blonde, brown doe eyes, pouty mouth, nice legs, trim figure, tiny waist. She reminded me of Vera-Ellen. Anton was infatuated with Vera-Ellen."

I must have looked a bit lost, because Olivia smiled ever so slightly.

"You have no idea who Vera-Ellen was, do you? She was a dancer and a movie star. She co-starred in a few musicals in the late forties and fifties. Her best-known role was in *White Christmas*. The movie also starred Bing Crosby, Danny Kaye, and Rosemary Clooney, who, by the way, is George Clooney's aunt."

I tended to avoid Christmas movies, with the exception of the Alastair Sim version of *Scrooge*, finding them maudlin at best, and mind-numbingly dull at worst, especially the ones that reminded me of a cheesy romance novel. But I vaguely remembered *White Christmas*. I'd seen it years ago as a kid. There had been a lot of singing and dancing. Had I watched it with my mother? I knew now that she loved old musicals, had in fact named me Calamity Doris after Doris Day's musical portrayal of Wild West frontierswoman, Calamity Jane.

"I sort of remember *White Christmas*," I said, knowing that I'd be googling Vera-Ellen the minute I got home. "It was a long time ago."

"It's been a long time for me as well," Olivia said. "As you can imagine, the thought of watching Vera-Ellen in anything was quite unappealing after Anneliese came to visit. Which brings me to the day that changed my life forever."

12

The day that changed her life forever. I held my breath, worried that the slightest sound would discourage Olivia from continuing. I exhaled softly when she began.

"She came to the door with a young girl dressed in a pink and white snowsuit," Olivia said, a slight tremor in her voice. "She introduced herself as Mrs. Anneliese Frankow, a friend of Anton's, and the girl as her daughter, Sophie. She emphasized *Mrs.*, not that it mattered. The girl didn't have Anneliese's coloring, though I could have overlooked that. I could even have overlooked her black hair with eyes to match. What I couldn't overlook was the girl's obvious resemblance to Anton. She wasn't much more than three, if that, but Anton Osgoode was stamped all over her face."

I tried to imagine what it would have been like. I've dated a two-timing triathlete, as well as a guy who'd dumped me for someone else on Valentine's Day, but to the best of my knowledge neither of them had fathered a child while we were seeing one another. "It must have been a shock."

"Not as much as you might think. By then, I'd figured out that Anton's business trips frequently included a fling or two. He tried to be discreet, but there were always signs. A faint trace of perfume lingering on his shirt, lipstick on his handkerchief, a matchbook in his coat pocket with a cabin number scrawled inside the cover. I chose to turn a blind eye. In return, Anton rewarded me with expensive souvenirs, silk scarves, and jewelry. It was easier for both of us that way. At least it was until I met Anneliese and saw Sophie. That, as they say, was a game changer."

"What did you do?"

"I invited them in."

"You invited them in?"

Olivia smiled. "You seem surprised."

"I'm not sure I would have been so accommodating."

"It had nothing to do with being accommodating. I had to find out why she'd come to our house three years after Sophie's birth, and the last thing I needed was one of the neighbors listening in. There was enough gossip among the bored housewives on our street." Olivia laughed. "As you can imagine, the thrill of cleaning, cooking, and laundry only went so far as a means of entertainment."

I found myself laughing with her. And liking her. I hoped she felt the same way about me. "What happened next?"

Olivia stopped laughing. "Corbin had been playing in his room. He was eleven by then, and very much into building model airplanes. He came wandering out to see who was at the door. Anneliese's face lost all color, and for a moment I thought she might faint. It was clear from her expression, or lack thereof, that she'd been unaware of Corbin's existence."

I nodded and tried to think of something appropriate to say, but Olivia kept talking.

"I was confident that Anton kept his infidelities confined to shipboard romances, another reason I was able to tolerate them. Anneliese's reaction seemed to confirm that belief, but it was more than that. Despite his philandering ways, Anton was an honorable man. He wouldn't have walked away from the responsibility of a child. Not if he knew about her."

"What happened next?"

"Anneliese apologized for the intrusion, saying she'd made a mistake, and left, Sophie in tow."

I felt the crush of disappointment. I had naively believed that Olivia would have the answer to all my questions. Instead she'd led me to Anneliese and left me hanging. "Did you tell Anton about her visit? About your suspicions about Sophie?"

"Yes, and I've been haunted by that decision every day since."

"Why haunted?"

"Because two weeks after Anneliese came to my house, little Sophie knocked on her neighbor's door. She was crying and babbling something about a bad man and her mommy. The neighbor tried the front door and found it unlocked. Anneliese was inside, lying face down on the kitchen floor. The medical examiner determined that she'd been struck on the back of the head with a blunt object. Death was instantaneous. Anneliese's husband, Horst Frankow, was the prime suspect. It's always the spouse or the lover, isn't it?"

"I can't claim to be an expert. It certainly seems that way in books and on TV."

Olivia acknowledged the truth of that.

"What happened to Horst Frankow?"

"According to the newspaper, neighbors and friends claimed that Horst often flew into a jealous rage without provocation. There was also evidence of abuse, bruises and whatnot."

It went a long way to explain why Sophie ended up in foster care. It also reminded me that I needed to make searching newspaper archives more of a priority. "Sophie said something about a bad man. Surely she wouldn't refer to her father that way."

"You wouldn't think so, but I doubt the word of a three-year-old was given much weight, especially back then. Regardless, there must have been enough evidence against Horst for the police to make an arrest. He was charged with murder and convicted of manslaughter. The sentence was life imprisonment to be served at Kingston Penitentiary. He died three weeks after being incarcerated, stabbed in the shower by another inmate. Never even had a chance to file a formal appeal." Olivia gave a grim smile. "Apparently wife killers don't last long in prison."

Horst Frankow's trial and death was also one more thing for Past & Present to delve into. "There is one thing I still don't understand."

"What's that?"

"You said you were haunted by the decision to tell Anton about Anneliese's visit. You didn't say why."

Olivia's eyes flickered toward the intricately etched crystal vase, filled with the red and white carnations I'd brought yesterday. It was a furtive glance, so quick that I wasn't entirely sure I'd seen it. And then Olivia said the words that had haunted her for five decades.

"The police never found the blunt object that killed Anneliese."

13

———————

We were sitting on the back patio, sipping white wine, and nibbling on hummus, pita, and assorted raw veggies. I'd just finished getting Chantelle up to speed on my visits with Olivia.

"How are we supposed to tell Louisa that Anneliese was murdered by her husband?" Chantelle asked. "I know she suspected her grandmother had come to a bad end, but not like this."

I hadn't told Chantelle everything. While I'd shared Olivia's confidences, including Anton Osgoode's position as a buyer for Eaton's, his involvement with Anneliese, and his ongoing infidelity, I'd stopped short of telling her about the crystal vase. It wasn't as if Olivia had come right out and said she suspected her husband of bashing in Anneliese's head. It could be that her glance at the vase had been nothing more than a glance, and I was reading more into it than there was.

But my gut told me that Olivia believed Anton was the bad man little Sophie had seen kill her mother. That she'd carried the guilt of her belief throughout the rest of her life.

I had wanted to ask Olivia about the vase. The etching on it was so intricate, a cornflower, along with two birds holding a ribbon in their beaks, an envelope beneath one of the birds. Was it a gift for

Anneliese, something Anton would have brought back from England as a buyer for Eaton's? If so, how did the vase come into Olivia's possession?

It had been the wrong time to ask. If I pushed Olivia too soon, she may have stopped talking, or worse, never invited me back. And I very much wanted to be invited back.

I had taken my cue from her subtle yawn, offering to take her out for lunch on my next visit. The haste in which she accepted made me realize just how much she craved company, and an outing. I'd promised to call her in a couple of days to set a date, time, and place.

"Earth calling Callie, come in Callie," Chantelle said, laughing.

I forced myself back to the present. "I'm sorry, I was thinking about Olivia. I like her. Incredible, isn't it, that I might actually like a member of the Osgoode family? Anyway, in answer to your question, we don't tell Louisa. Not until we have all the facts we can find. Three-year-old Sophie babbled something about a bad man when she ran to the neighbor's house. She suffered from nightmares about it her entire life. I don't believe she would have referred to Horst, the man she knew as her father, as a bad man. She would have said something like, 'My daddy hit my mommy,' or something along those lines."

"What are you saying?"

"I'm saying we need to find out as much as we can about the murder. Perhaps we even end up clearing Horst Frankow's name."

Chantelle took a sip of her wine. "It complicates things, but I'd like to try."

We clinked glasses, toasting the decision. I hoped clearing Horst Frankow's name didn't come at the cost of discovering Anton Osgoode was guilty.

"One other thing," Chantelle said. "I don't know exactly how to say this but…doesn't it seem more than coincidence that our first case involves your family?"

"The thought crossed my mind," I admitted, and recalled trying to find my mother, the planted clues, the information withheld. "Then again, maybe Louisa was onto something. Maybe Anneliese is reaching out from beyond. All I know is that I need to see where this goes."

"Fair enough, but where do we start? How does someone go about investigating an old murder?"

"The murder of a young mother of a three-year-old girl, husband accused and convicted, that must have made headlines, especially back then. I'm planning to go to the Toronto Reference Library next week."

"Good plan, but what about other resources? Do you think Leith Hampton could steer us in the right direction?"

The thought of calling Leith Hampton didn't sit well with me, but then again, neither had the idea of calling on Olivia, and look at where that had led. If I wanted to do Louisa Frankow's case justice, I had to set aside my personal feelings. "I'll call him tomorrow. Now enough business for today.

We ordered pizza and opened a bottle of Chardonnay; another was chilling in a terracotta clay cooler, a housewarming gift from Royce Ashford. I felt my face flush at the thought of Royce. We hadn't seen each other since he'd completed the minor renovations on the house. Our friendship hadn't really gotten to the relationship stage, but I missed him, missed knowing he was next door. I made a mental note to call him and invite him for dinner. He loved my lasagna. The old adage, "the way to a man's heart is through his stomach," seemed impossibly old-fashioned, but I found myself planning the meal.

LEITH WASN'T in the office when I called him in the morning, but his receptionist assured me that he would be available in the early afternoon, after he returned from court. I hopped onto the Past & Present Facebook page and was pleased to see that Misty's first tarot message had already produced dozens of Likes and Comments. Misty was prompt at responding, and her answers were both articulate and entertaining.

Inspired by Misty's success, I decided to create a website page I titled *Research.* I included a clickable sidebar widget on our main page, and called it RESEARCH HELP WANTED. My plan was to prepare a new Facebook post, and duplicate it on the website.

I've learned Facebook posts have to include animals or video to produce results. I googled "1952 trains, Canada" and found a few possible photographs. I selected a copyright-free image of an old train, along with a photo of the Gare du Palais train station in Quebec City, and included a message asking for any information on train travel from Quebec City to Toronto in 1952.

I wondered if Chantelle had heard back from the Canadian Museum of Immigration. We'd been so busy talking about Olivia and Anton that we hadn't discussed anything else. I was just about to give her a quick call when my phone rang. I checked the call display. Leith Hampton.

"Leith, thanks for returning my call."

"How have you been, Callie? I know you sold the house on Snapdragon Circle."

I filled him in on buying the Edward Street property and starting Past & Present Investigations. His silence while I prattled on spoke volumes. Leith wasn't a huge fan of my sleuthing adventures.

"I assume this call has something to do with this new business venture?"

"You assume correctly. I'd like to find out more about a murder that took place in 1956. I thought you might be able to assist."

"Nineteen fifty-six. You aren't kidding about the past part. Unfortunately, it's not my area of expertise, and I've got a big case going to court next week. I can, however, recommend someone who might be able to help. Fellow by the name of Howard Portland. He's been retired for years, but at one time he was one of the best criminal prosecutors in Toronto. Beat me more than once, not that I hold that against him. I had dinner with him a few weeks ago. He's writing a legal thriller set in the 1950s, and if anyone can help you, it's Howard. Tell him I referred you." Leith rattled off the phone number and wished me luck.

I called the number. A baritone voice answered after three rings. "Portland."

"Mister Portland. Howard. My name is Callie Barnstable. I'm the co-owner of Past & Present Investigations. Leith Hampton gave me your phone number."

"Did he? In that case you can call me Mister Portland." He chuckled. "Just kidding. Howard is fine. What can I do for you?"

"We're working on a case that involves a murder which took place in 1956. Leith seemed to think you might be able to help."

"Help you with what?"

"Research, resources, whatever tidbit of information or insight you might be willing share. The information we have right now is sketchy and superficial. I was hoping to fill in some of the blanks."

"I'm willing to try, however, I prefer to do so in person. If you don't mind."

"Not at all, in fact I'd prefer it. Where would you like to meet?"

"Where's your office located?"

"Marketville."

Portland laughed. "Well, I'll be damned. That's where I live."

We set up a meeting for ten o'clock the following morning, me promising to offer unlimited refills of black coffee, Howard insisting that no food was required. I knew I should call Chantelle and invite her, but I wasn't ready to talk about Anton Osgoode's possible involvement and I didn't know if his name would come up. I justified my decision by telling myself she had plenty to do already, what with her job at the gym, and her genealogy research.

Denial can be a wonderful thing.

14

Howard Portland was a clean-shaven, athletic-looking man in his late sixties, with close-cropped steel gray hair, bushy white eyebrows, and piercing gray-blue eyes magnified by no-nonsense wire-framed glasses. He was wearing a blue and gold Boston Marathon T-shirt, and I recognized him as one of the warp-speed runners from my Sunday running group, not that we'd ever exchanged more than a few words in greeting. He smiled in recognition, set his brown leather briefcase down on the floor, and shook my hand in a firm, but friendly grip. We chatted briefly about the run club, the insanity of getting up at the crack of dawn every Sunday regardless of weather, and our future race plans. It turned out we were both planning to run in the 30K Around the Bay road race in Hamilton come March, his fifth time, my first. I figured Howard would be halfway home by the time I finished.

The running pleasantries out of the way, and coffee made and poured, we got down to business.

"First, tell me everything you know about the case," Howard said. "Don't leave anything out. The smallest detail could be significant."

"I only know what my great-grandmother, Olivia Osgoode, told me, and she's ninety-one years old with an axe to grind when it comes to the woman who was murdered."

Howard grinned. "How sharp an axe?"

"The woman who died had an affair with her husband."

"That's one sharp axe. Tell me what you know about the victim."

"Her name was Anneliese Ruth Frankow, née Prei. She was originally from Germany, immigrated to Nottingham, England, after the war, and subsequently immigrated to Toronto in July 1952 to marry a man named Horst Frankow. I don't know much about Horst yet, but my guess is that they were German expats that met in Nottingham. The marriage took place in October." I paused, knowing that I was treading into the point of no return.

Howard picked up on the hesitation. "What aren't you telling me?"

"My great-grandfather, Anton Osgoode, Olivia's husband. There's reason to believe he's the one who had the affair with Anneliese."

"Maybe you should start at the beginning."

I updated Howard on Louisa's quest to find out more about her grandmother, the train case, and how the Certificate of Baptism for Sophie Frankow listed her parents as Anneliese Frankow and Anton Osgoode.

"I'm not close to my grandparents on either side, a long story with no bearing to the case at hand. Until I met Olivia, I'd never met any of my great-grandparents, but I've been dabbling at creating a family tree. I knew that Anton Osgoode was my great-grandfather. Finding his name on Sophie's Certificate of Baptism, that was…unexpected."

"I can imagine. Is Anton still alive?"

"He died in 1987 at the age of sixty-six. I visited Olivia at the Cedar County Retirement Residence, hoping for the best and expecting the worst." I smiled. "I actually found myself enjoying her company. She told me Anton was a serial cheater, and she chose to ignore it."

"That's not as uncommon as you might think, especially for that generation. Divorce was a dirty word, and divorcees viewed with great suspicion. Did Olivia know about the child?"

"Not at first." I told him about Anneliese's visit with young Sophie in tow. "Anneliese left when Corbin came out of his room to see who was at the door."

"So Anneliese had been unaware of Corbin's existence."

"That's the general consensus."

"Where does the murder come in?"

"Anneliese was killed in her own home two weeks after she visited Olivia. Three-year-old Sophie was in the house, though whether the killer saw her is unknown. What is known is that she ran to a neighbor's house, crying and talking about a bad man hurting her mommy. The medical examiner determined the cause of death was blunt force trauma to the back of the head. The murder weapon was never found." I left out my thoughts about the vase. I needed Howard to help me find out the facts, not get embroiled in speculation.

"Did the police make an arrest?"

"They arrested Anneliese's husband, Horst Frankow. Neighborhood gossips called him jealous, with a temper, and Anneliese often had unexplained bruises. He was charged with murder, convicted of manslaughter, and sentenced to life imprisonment in Kingston Penitentiary. He died in prison less than a month later. Stabbed in the shower, according to Olivia."

"Kingston Pen was a maximum security prison. Horst Frankow may have been a jealous husband, but he wasn't a hardened criminal. He would have been ill prepared for life there. Whoever stabbed him might have done him a favor. What's interesting is the conviction of manslaughter."

"How so?"

"Manslaughter would indicate that the defense claimed Frankow committed the murder in the heat of passion as a result of sudden provocation." Howard opened his briefcase and pulled out a yellowed document titled *Statutes of Canada 1953-54*. He flipped through the pages, opened it to Section 203, and handed it to me.

There was a lot of legal jargon, but the bottom line was that sudden provocation meant the accused had lost self-control and acted upon it before there was time for his passion to cool. I stifled a grin. No politically correct pronouns used back in the 1950s.

"My read on it is that the defense used Horst's hot temper to their advantage," Howard said as I handed the document back to him. "Premeditated murder would have almost certainly resulted in the death penalty."

It was a plausible explanation. "Where can I go to find out more about the murder?"

Howard paused to consider. "Old newspapers would be the easiest. In Toronto, that would mean the *Toronto Star*, *Toronto Telegram*, and, because we're talking about a murder, I'd also check the *Globe and Mail*, even though it's a national paper. A young mother being killed in her own home, especially in 1956, would have garnered country-wide attention."

I'd been planning to check out the *Toronto Star* archives, but I hadn't considered the *Globe*, and I'd never heard of the *Toronto Telegram*.

"I'm not familiar with the *Telegram*," I said.

"No surprise, given your age," Howard said. "The *Tely* ceased publication at the end of October 1971. Everyone talks about the dire state of print publishing today, but even then, it wasn't a license to make money. The *Telegram* closed after ongoing financial difficulties. That didn't stop the *Toronto Sun* from publishing its first newspaper that November with many of the same writers and staff. The *Sun* continued to support a Progressive Conservative Party political agenda in the manner of its predecessor, whereas the *Star* has always been staunchly Liberal."

I remembered Royce telling me the best way to get the true story was to read the various versions of it in different newspapers, a reason he subscribed to the *Sun*, *Star*, and *Globe*. "Where would I find archives for the *Telegram*?"

"I don't believe there are newspaper archives available to the public for the *Telegram*," said Howard, "but the *Toronto Telegram Photograph Collection* is held by York University Archives and Special Collections. The collection is quite extensive. Even without having access to all of the university's collection, there are well over ten thousand photographs online."

I felt a stir of excitement. Surely there would be at least one photograph, if not more, in the *Telegram* collection. It would take a lot of time, but at least I could do it from the convenience of 300 Edward Street. I was writing down the information when Howard made my day.

"I'm sure you're aware that the Toronto Public Library now has a comprehensive online reference library which includes the *Star* and the *Globe and Mail.*"

Online records? Meaning no microfiche? "I wasn't until just now, but thank you. Is there anything else you can recommend?"

Howard nodded. "The Archives of Ontario holds a continuum of criminal justice records created from the time the police undertake an investigation into a criminal act, to the court trial and sentencing, to the resulting incarceration, probation, or parole." He gestured to my computer. "How about I find the link for you?"

I turned the screen and slid the keyboard toward him.

Howard's typing speed was as impressive as his running. "Here you go," he said, after barely a minute had passed.

The PDF was titled *Criminal Justice Records at the Archives of Ontario.* A Table of Contents offered an Introduction, along with six search categories: Investigation Records, Prosecution and Indictment Records, Court Records, Judges' Benchbooks and Judgments, Correctional Records, and Probation and Parole Records.

I wanted to jump up and hug Howard, but something told me he wasn't the demonstrative type, unless you counted a high five after a run.

"This is a great resource. I had no idea it existed."

"You would have found it eventually. I just saved you a bit of time." Howard rose and made his way to the front door. "Call me if you need any help navigating the system, or better yet, call the Archives of Ontario. The reference archivists are extremely helpful."

"I'll do that. Thank you for everything."

"Anything for a fellow runner, but I will caution you not to get your hopes up. A lot of early files didn't make the transfer from wherever they were stored originally to the Archives of Ontario. But you might get lucky."

Get lucky? For the first time since learning about the murder of Anneliese Frankow and Horst's incarceration I felt back in control, and luck had absolutely nothing to do with it. I was doing this investigation thing, step by step, past to present, and I was doing it with a little help from my friends, old and new.

15

———

The Introduction in *Criminal Justice Records at the Archives of Ontario* made it clear that permission would be required to access any of the documents. A quick review of each category defined the criteria, narrowing my potential search. First, however, I'd have to find out which documents I wanted to access. There was a link to an online database to be used in conjunction with the PDF. Fair enough. I'd start at the beginning and see where it led me.

The first category, Investigation Records, was a dead end:

> The Archives of Ontario holds records of investigations and inquests conducted by the Ontario Provincial Police (OPP), local coroners, the Centre for Forensic Sciences, and the Fire Marshall's Office. Please note that the Archives does not hold the records of any municipal, regional, or national police (i.e., RCMP) services.

Since the murder took place in Toronto, the Toronto Police Department would have investigated it. Or would they? Maybe, in 1956, the OPP would have been in charge. I opened a new window, searched for Toronto Police, and found a Wikipedia entry:

The Toronto Police Service is the police force servicing Toronto, Ontario, Canada. Established in 1834, it was the first municipal police service created in North America and one of the oldest police services in the English-speaking world.

I checked the Toronto Police Service's website next, disheartened to find that copies of police reports were available only to those parties involved in the incident or their representatives, with consent.

The next section under Investigation Records was the Coroner's Records. Listed by area and date range, there was nothing for Toronto, per se, but there was a listing for York County. I knew that Toronto had seceded from York County to become Metropolitan Toronto. A quick Wiki search revealed the year to be 1953, not that it mattered. The available coroner's records ended in 1955, one year before the murder of Anneliese Frankow.

The Centre for Forensic Sciences case files came next, and the details were encouraging:

> Provides forensic services to police forces across Ontario. The files usually contain a police report describing the crime scene and the evidence found, the notes taken by Laboratory staff while examining the submitted samples, and the Laboratory's report to the police.

I clicked on the link and was taken to the archives page for Forensic Sciences. I felt a faint flutter of hope when I saw the date range available: 1932-1961.

The flutter quickly faded.

> Case files between 1931 to 1951 are arranged in alphabetical order. Case files between 1951 and 1961 are arranged by case file number. No list or finding aid is available for this series.

I might have had a chance of requesting the correct file using an alphabetical search, but I had no hope of knowing the case file number. Would it be possible to request files by date, and weed through them looking for the Frankow murder? I pulled a yellow legal pad out of a drawer and made a notation. There might be more questions than answers. Making a list would make those questions manageable.

The Investigation Records category exhausted, I went to the next category on the PDF, Prosecution and Indictment Records, and reviewed the available options. The Crown Attorney Prosecution Case Files 1865-1984 seemed to be a fit. I reread the description.

These files were compiled by the Crown Attorney while prosecuting a criminal case before the General Sessions of the Peace, the County Court Judge's Criminal Court, High Court of Ontario, or Supreme Court of Ontario. Each case file lists name of the accused, charge and plea, dates of court appearances, trial notes, names of witnesses, verdict and sentence. The file also contains a copy of the initial crime report and a summary of the police investigation. For more information, search the Archives Descriptive Database using the phrase Crown Attorney and the name of the county or district of interest.

I clicked the link for the descriptive database and entered "Crown Attorney, York County, Toronto," and after a moment's thought, added "1956" to refine the search. This still netted me a list of fifty-one entries, with the keywords highlighted. Only one entry ticked all three boxes: the York County Summary Conviction Criminal Appeal Files. The York County part wasn't a problem since Toronto had been part of York County before it seceded. The appeal files part, however, was a problem. As the prosecutor, the Crown had won the case. There would have been no need for the prosecution to appeal. And Horst had been killed in prison before he had the opportunity to appeal.

I stood up and stretched, trying to release the tension that had built up in my neck and shoulders. Court Records, the next major category on the PDF, could wait for a half hour. It was time to burn off some stress. It was time for a three-mile run.

ONE OF MY favorite things about Marketville was the twelve-mile paved trail system that ran through the center of town and followed the Dutch River through parks and green space, past wetlands and historic cultural sites. In short, a runner's paradise. Even better, the trail system was just steps away from my new digs on Edward Street.

There were other runners, couples holding hands, and moms with babies in strollers also enjoying the trail. I smiled as I ran by them, getting nods, waves, and the occasional high five. With the Around the Bay race on the horizon, albeit several months away, most of my runs were training focused: speed work drills to make me faster, time and distance to build endurance, hill repeats for strength and stamina. Today's run was all about clearing my head of the clutter so that I could focus on the task at hand. I owed that much to Louisa Frankow.

I owed that much to Anneliese.

FORTIFIED BY THE RUN, a quick lunch of a grilled cheese sandwich and tomato soup, and an even quicker shower, I poured myself a cup of cinnamon rooibos tea and got ready to tackle the rest of the Archives of Ontario available options.

Now that I was relaxed and ready, the task ahead of me wasn't as formidable as I'd first thought. Of the four remaining categories, only Court Records seemed applicable. Correctional Records were limited to those sentenced to a prison term of less than two years and most young offenders. Probation and Parole Records clearly didn't apply, and Judges' Benchbooks and Judgments was meant for cases more than seventy-five years old, with the added requirement of knowing the judge's name.

Okay, then, Court Records it was. A directive to search the Archives Descriptive Database using the phrase "criminal files" and the name of the county or district of interest prompted me to click on yet another link. I entered "criminal files, Toronto, 1956" in the keyword search. Of the one hundred and fifteen entries, not a single one had all three common denominators. It appeared that 1956 had been a very bad year when it came to archiving records. More bad luck.

My last hope under the Court Records archives were the assorted Books associated with criminal trials. These included Minute Books, a brief chronological outline of cases heard before a criminal court, Docket Books for trials held on a particular day, and Procedure Books, which acted as a master day planner. There were also Judgment Books, title self-explanatory, and Order Books, a numerically arranged and bound record of all orders issued by the court.

A search of the database using the recommended keyword, "book" yielded five entries, all for land grants in the nineteenth century. I pounded my fist on the table in frustration. We could archive the warrants for land grants in 1819, but the records from a murder case in 1956 had been destroyed.

Or had they? Maybe I just wasn't looking in the right place. There was a Contact Page at the end, with email and telephone numbers.

> Although unable to do your criminal records research for you, our reference archivists are waiting to assist you. You may telephone or write to them by mail or email or—best of all—visit the Archives of Ontario.

I wasn't up to a visit unless I knew the trip would be worthwhile. I picked up the phone and dialed.

After listening to an automated greeting in English and French, and selecting English communication going forward, I was offered the option to speak to a reference archivist. A woman answered, her tone bright and cheerful. Encouraged, I told her that I was looking into a murder that occurred in Toronto in 1956, and hoped that Archives of Ontario could help.

"Have you tried our online database?" she asked.

"Yes, but I'm not sure I've done everything right. I couldn't find any records."

"Unfortunately, it's possible that the records were destroyed. Not everything made the transfer."

I didn't ask the transfer from where. It didn't matter where the documents came from if they no longer existed. "But it is possible that I missed something, isn't it?"

"Let me walk you through it to be sure you haven't. Go back to the page with the Archives Descriptive Database."

"Done."

"In the Keyword Search, enter 'Toronto, York County, Criminal, 1956,' and then press Search. I'll do it at the same time."

I was pretty sure I'd done that already, but I did it again. And once again, the records I was looking for weren't there.

"Hmmm," the woman said. "Nothing in this batch. Let's try a different approach. Go back to the database, clear the keyword field, and select the Advanced Search option."

I went back and followed her instructions. "Done."

"You'll see three green tabs on the left. Select the central tab *Search Groups of Archival Records*. Enter 'Criminal Records, York, and Supreme Criminal' in the keywords."

I came up with a list of eight results. Only one included 1956, and I'd seen it before. Why hadn't Horst Frankow lived long enough to appeal his case? At least then there might have been a record.

"I'm sorry, there aren't any other places to search," the cheerful voice on the other end of the phone said. "We don't have those records."

I was just about to hang up when another thought crossed my mind. "Would you have details of an occupational accident?"

"We might if there was an autopsy. When was the accident?"

"Last year."

"That would be too soon for archives. You might try the Office of the Chief Coroner. I'm not really sure what the process would be, or if they share those reports."

I'd already read the coroner's report. The details of my father's broken body had been difficult enough to read the first time. I'd also read and reread the reports from the Workplace Safety & Insurance Board and the Ministry of Labor. My father's fall from the thirtieth floor of a condo under construction had been blamed on his safety harness failing, either because it had been faulty or buckled incorrectly. There was nothing in either report that would help me prove he'd been murdered, let alone implicate my grandfather.

I hung up feeling deflated and more than a little defeated, the glow from my earlier run a distant memory. I needed something or someone to cheer me up.

I could have called Chantelle and had her commiserate with me over a glass of wine while we discussed the case, but I just wasn't up to rehashing everything I hadn't learned. I could have invited Arabella over for dinner and a long overdue visit, but since she referred Louisa to Past & Present, she'd likely want an update. I could have gone shopping for a new outfit, but I've never been a believer in retail therapy. I could have done a lot of things, some of them even involving copious amounts of chocolate or butter pecan ice cream.

I called Royce.

16

———

R oyce answered on the first ring. "Hey," I said.

"Hey back," he said, his voice warm. "I've been thinking about you."

Warm voice or not, thinking wasn't the same as calling. For a moment I felt embarrassed. I didn't want Royce to think I was chasing him. Then again, we'd become friends, hadn't we? Friends didn't need an excuse to call each other. Besides, this was the twenty-first century. It was perfectly acceptable for women to call men.

"I've been thinking about you, as well. I find myself in need of company that has nothing to do with Past & Present Investigations, or the case we're investigating. It seems everyone I know is involved in some way. Except you, of course."

Royce chuckled softly. "Well, don't I feel special. And here I was, planning to call and invite you to a play."

"A play? As in the theater?"

"One and the same. Even contractors can enjoy the theater."

He said it in a teasing tone, but thanks to his stockbroker father's dismissal of Royce Contracting, I knew that he could be sensitive when it came to stereotypical views of his profession. I decided to let the comment pass. Whatever response I had was bound to be the wrong one.

"I haven't been to the theater in ages. I'd love to go."

"Before you get too excited, it's not exactly *Kinky Boots* at the Royal Alexandra."

"I love the Royal Alex, but I take it this is local theatre?"

"Not local, as in Marketville, but yes, we're talking regional theater. Porsche has decided to take up acting. She's in a repertory group in Muskoka. They're putting on *Pygmalion*. She's playing the part of Eliza Doolittle."

Porsche was Royce's younger sister. Her woven pillows, and more recently, tapestries, sold for nosebleed money at upscale boutiques in Muskoka's affluent cottage country and Toronto's Yorkville shopping district. "I had no idea Porsche could sing, let alone act."

"None of us did, but then again, Porsche never fails to surprise. She's reserved five tickets for the opening matinee, which happens to be at the end of this month."

Five tickets. "Does that mean—"

"I'm afraid it does. My aunt and both my parents will be there. You know how they feel about Porsche, she's always been their favorite. Porsche just assumed I'd want to bring a date, and for some reason, she thought that date would be you. To be honest, I hesitated about inviting you. I know there will be tension after… well, after this past year."

Royce was right. There was no love lost on either side. Searching for the truth about my mother had seen to that. But I liked Porsche, and if I wanted to have a relationship with Royce, I'd have to make peace with his family. The question was, did I want to have a relationship with Royce, or did I want to keep him as a platonic friend, which wouldn't necessitate getting tangled up with his family. My heart said relationship. My head said don't get hurt again. I always seemed to screw things up, or get screwed trying not to. My father had called it the Barnstable family curse. I called it loser radar. But Royce wasn't a loser. Maybe this time would be different.

"What do you say?" Royce asked, interrupting my thoughts.

"Are you up for it? We'll be in public, so my dysfunctional family will be at their most gracious. And it really would mean a lot to Porsche."

"Let me think about it, okay?"

"Okay."

I heard the note of disappointment in his voice, and attempted to put things back on track. "Hey, I called you, remember? I wanted to see if you'd be interested in dinner. I know it's Monday night, but I have a homemade lasagna in the freezer begging to be reheated, and all the fixings for a salad as long as you're good with balsamic dressing."

"I'm good with balsamic. As for your lasagna, why didn't you open with that? I'll bring the wine. What time do you want me to come over?"

"Any time. I'll be here."

"Then I'll see you at six. And Callie?"

"Yes?"

"I know my family has hurt you in the past, and there's nothing I can do to change that. But Porsche had it right when she assumed I'd want to invite you to her play. I very much want to be a part of your present, whatever form that takes, friendship or something more, although full disclosure here, I am hoping for the something more. I hope you are, too."

Royce hung up before I could answer, which was just as well. I didn't have an answer to give him.

I HAD three hours before Royce came for dinner, which left me plenty of time to get things ready and spruce up a little. Okay, who was I trying to kid? I planned to spruce up more than a little. Still, even at my most narcissistic, a half hour of primping would do, and the lasagna wouldn't go in the oven until after Royce arrived. Making the salad when he was here would give me something to do while we sipped wine and avoided the subject of "us," whatever that meant.

I had time to check our Facebook page and my post on train schedules from Quebec City to Toronto in 1952. There were several Likes and five Comments. The first three were generic, and while I appreciated the feedback, they weren't particularly helpful:

I traveled by train from Toronto to Moncton, New Brunswick in 1955 and had to change trains in Montreal.

Sorry no information, I wasn't born yet, but what a marvelous way to get some research. This is how Facebook should be used.

My dad was a CN conductor on the Toronto to Montreal line. Have no idea how long the trip was but he always stayed over and worked the return trip.

The last two comments provided a bit more information:

Presumably the Canberra docked at Quebec City in the morning for Customs and Immigration. A mid-day Canadian Pacific train would take about 3.5 hours to reach Windsor Station in Montreal.

The traveler would need an hour or two to transfer to the CN Central Station a few blocks away. (This was in the days before CN-CP pool train operations.) Then the fast CN train would take about six hours (3:30 to 9:30 p.m.) to reach Union Station in Toronto.

That would have been part of the Quebec Windsor corridor, and certainly a trip to Toronto would have stopped at Montreal. It might have been a transfer at, or even between, one of the two rail stations in Montreal, Windsor (CPR) or Central (CNR).

There was a link to a Wikipedia page on Windsor Station. I clicked on the link and scanned the entry. It offered a history on the station, now a historical site that housed offices, a hotel, and restaurants. It was interesting, but not particularly relevant to the case at hand.

The fifth and final comment recommended a website called *Old*

Time Trains. I checked out the site and knew I'd hit pay dirt. There were links to dozens of articles, stories, photographs, and archives. I found the Contact Us page and drafted an email.

> Hello. I am searching for information on a German immigrant who lived in Nottingham, England, after WWII, and later immigrated to Canada via the T.S.S. Canberra, arriving July 7, 1952, in Quebec City, and settling in Toronto. What train would she have taken from Quebec City to Toronto—I am assuming a stopover/transfer in Montreal—and how long would the journey have taken? Would it have been on the same day the ship came in? Are passenger lists available? Thank you in advance for any information you might be able to provide.
>
> Sincerely,
>
> Calamity Barnstable, Past & Present Investigations

I reread the email, and satisfied with what I'd written, hit Send. I got ready for Royce's visit: a half hour of fussing and fidgeting with my hair and make-up, and another twenty minutes of trying on and taking off clothes. I ended up in black jeans and a moss-toned sweater that brought out the green in my black-rimmed hazel eyes. I surveyed myself in the full-length mirror, satisfied with my selection. Even so, I might have changed another dozen times if the doorbell hadn't chimed.

Say what you would about Royce, he was always punctual. I like that in a person.

Let's face it. I liked him. And apparently he liked me. It's amazing how a reasonably confident thirty-seven-year-old adult can turn into a sixteen-year-old teenager filled with angst at the sound of a doorbell. I wiped my palms against my jeans and went to answer the door.

⌓

ROYCE HAD BROUGHT a bouquet of mixed flowers—a supermarket special, but pretty nonetheless—a baguette, and two bottles of

Australian wine: one white, one red. He followed me into the kitchen, where I pulled out a vase and two wine glasses. While not nearly as elaborate, the vase brought to mind the one in Olivia's room. I forced the thought out of my head. There would be no thinking of the case tonight.

"I see you've covered all the bases," I said, putting the flowers in the vase and placing them on the ledge of the pass-through. That way, they'd be visible from both the kitchen and office area. "Thank you."

"You're welcome. Can I pour you a glass of Chardonnay?"

"You can."

Royce did so, then poured himself a glass of red. I set the oven to pre-heat and led the way to the comfy chairs under the pass-through. I was already seated when I realized I'd left my computer on. Having an office in my living space did have its drawbacks.

"I should turn that off. I've done enough work for today. I don't want to be tempted to start googling stuff after you leave." I blushed. "Not that I expect you to leave right after dinner or anything."

"I knew what you meant," Royce said with a grin. "You've landed a case already? Impressive."

Since he'd asked, I had no alternative but to update him on Louisa Frankow's request to learn more about her grandmother, but I kept it brief, and the names anonymous. Besides wanting to spend an evening without shoptalk, there was client confidentiality to consider. I also didn't want to talk about my visit to Olivia. Such conversation might lead to talking about Royce's family, a subject I planned to avoid for as long as possible. The oven buzzer went off just as I was telling him about the Facebook posts.

"If we want to eat before midnight, I need to put the lasagna in the oven and get the salad made."

"I'll help you slice and dice."

It was a tight fit, but we were able to work side by side in companionable silence. There are plenty of ways to fancy up a salad, but I veer toward simple ingredients. Romaine lettuce, red and yellow bell peppers, mushrooms, celery. Homemade garlic butter croutons, if I have crusty bread, want to add crunch, and am not worried about the calories. The garlic could have been a concern, but it was already in the lasagna, and besides, we were both eating it.

"Croutons?" I asked. "I can use some of the bread you brought. It's better if it's a day old, but it can still work. There'll still be bread left over for the balsamic oil and vinegar dip I'm making."

"Homemade croutons?"

"Are there any other kind?"

"I've never had homemade croutons. Can I help?"

I took a large sauté pan from the cupboard, added butter, and placed the pan on the stove. "Mince two cloves of garlic while I get the bread ready. When the garlic is ready, melt the butter over medium heat. Add the garlic to the butter with a teaspoon of sea salt as soon as the butter has melted."

I cut the bread into one-inch cubes while Royce took care of the rest.

"Once the butter, garlic, and salt are combined, add the cubes and coat them evenly on all sides," I said. "I'll get the parchment paper onto a baking pan. The croutons take about twenty minutes to bake, but I'll put them in now so they cool off before we eat. I just have to remember to turn them over a couple of times."

"I'll remind you."

"You're a good man."

"I'm going to remind you of that," Royce said, and leaned over to kiss me softly on the forehead, his hands gently cradling my chin.

I wouldn't have to turn off my computer after all. I had a feeling work was going to be the farthest thing from my mind as the evening progressed. I hoped the Barnstable family curse had died with my father.

17

———————

W e'd just finished dinner, and judging by the amount of food Royce was able to consume, he'd enjoyed every morsel.

"Where did you learn to cook?" he asked, pushing his plate to the side.

"My dad was actually a pretty good cook. He didn't have an extensive menu, but he made a mean Hungarian goulash, his perogies were as good as any Ukrainian baba's, and his crepes were to die for. I've never been able to master those. I can't seem to get the batter thin enough. But the one thing he taught me was not to be afraid to try, whether it came to cooking, or baking, or life."

"You must miss him."

"I do, more than I thought possible. It's funny, you know. When your parents are in your life, you don't really think there's a time that they won't be there. Well, maybe you do when they're really old, but my dad was in his mid-fifties, as fit and healthy as someone half his age." I heard my voice crack. "I'm sorry. It's just hard to believe he's gone."

Royce took my hand and held it gently. "I know he died in an accident on the construction site, but I don't know what happened. Did you want to talk about it?"

Every instinct told me to say no, not yet. Dodge the issue for another day, another time. Instead, I found myself oversharing. "I don't believe his death was an accident. According to the Workplace Safety and Insurance Board, and his employer, Southern Ontario Construction, a faulty safety harness was to blame. Either the harness was faulty or he didn't secure it properly, as if he was an imbecile who couldn't fasten a buckle. He fell from the thirtieth floor of a condo under construction and landed on the concrete sidewalk below. He died within moments, if not on impact."

"But if it wasn't an accident, then what was it?"

"I think he might have been murdered." I left out my suspicions that my grandfather was behind it. I needed him to keep an open mind, and Royce was already staring at me with unabashed curiosity.

"Murder? Why would someone want to murder your father?"

Because my dad had left me a letter in a safety deposit box, and the safety harness wasn't the only accident to happen to him at work. Because accepting it really was an unfortunate occupational accident meant I'd have to stop obsessing about his death and move on with that aspect of my life. Because I hated my grandfather and everything he stood for and as long as I could find a way to blame him, I could keep that hatred fueled.

Royce had let go of my hand. I tried to read his expression and realized the talk of death and murder had ruined any chance for a romantic evening. The Barnstable family curse was alive and well. We just couldn't help but bring it on ourselves.

"I'm sorry. I've said too much. You probably think I'm crazy."

Royce shook his head, his brown eyes soft and serious. "I don't think you're crazy, but I do think you're conflicted about your father's accident. Tell me why."

It would be good to have an objective opinion. "There was a letter…"

"Okay."

"Wait here."

I scrambled up the steps, pulled the folder labeled "Dad" from under the bed, took a deep breath, and trundled back down the stairs.

"My dad left a letter in a safety deposit box," I said, sliding the folder over to Royce. "Maybe I'm reading too much into it. The Workplace Safety and Insurance Board and the Ministry of Labor did a thorough investigation."

Royce removed the documents from the folder and began reading, his brow furrowed in concentration. "Can you make a photocopy of the letter and bring me a highlighter?"

I didn't ask why, just went to the printer and made the copy, found a yellow highlighter, handed him both, and watched as he began to highlight specific sections of the letter.

"I'm isolating the paragraphs that are relevant to your concerns," Royce said. "Then we can review each one with an unbiased eye."

I didn't know how unbiased my eyes would be, but the idea had merit. "I'm game if you are, but I think it's best if you start at the beginning."

Royce began reading. I felt my throat constrict hearing the now familiar words spoken out loud.

Dear Calamity, Yes, I know you hate being called Calamity, but I figure if I'm dead, you'll give me a pass. If you're reading this, then I suppose I am. I'm also hoping that you'll forgive me for the Marketville codicil in the will.

He stopped and looked up at me. "Shall I go on?"
I nodded, not trusting my voice.

Of course, I knew there was a chance you'd just wait out the year and let Misty Rivers take over the investigation, and maybe that's what I should have insisted on, especially if I wanted to protect you from hurt or harm. The thing is, I've been trying to protect you from knowing the truth for so many years. I was wrong. You had a right to know, maybe not when you were six, but certainly when you were old enough to understand. Instead, I allowed the years to go by, never talking about your mother. That was as unfair to her memory as it was to you.

Royce paused, his eyes scanning my face. I nodded again, closing my eyes as he read.

Here's what I know: Your mother loved you. She also loved me, although I admit we had our share of ups and downs. What marriage doesn't? Especially with two people who were nothing more than children themselves when they brought you into the world. I do not believe, however, and never have, that your mother left us voluntarily. Something, or someone, forced her to go. For many years, I thought she'd come back. It's the reason I kept the house at 16 Snapdragon Circle. How else would she find us, if not for that house? This was a time well before social media and internet accessibility.

The years ticked by, and after a while even I started to give up hope. Leith Hampton, dear friend that he is for all his pompous ways and multiple marriages, begged me to give up the search years before, after a private investigator, someone I paid a great deal of money to, found out nothing. For a long time, I heeded that advice. After all, the investigator had come highly recommended by a man I trusted implicitly.

Things changed when Misty Rivers rented the house. She told me the house was not haunted, but possessed by your mother's spirit. I know it sounds farfetched, but another renter had insinuated much the same thing.

Misty was convinced your mother had been murdered, and she wanted to help me seek out the truth. I'll admit I was skeptical at first. I'm not a believer in spirits or psychics, but I've never been able to reconcile your mother's disappearance. I decided to put my trust in her.

Royce hesitated. "We're coming to the first section I highlighted. Are you ready?"

"Yes," I said, my voice barely audible.

We had barely scratched the surface when I was almost killed on my lunch break. The job was a new condo development with more than a few complications, and construction was well behind schedule. In an effort to save time, each day one of the workers would take everyone's order and phone it in to a local restaurant and then pick up the food. That day happened to be my day.

He stopped reading. "It could have been any other worker. That day just happened to be your father's day."

"But all the workers knew it was his day," I said, feeling defensive. "They knew he was the one placing and picking up the order."

"Are you saying that you suspect one of the other workers?"

Time for the moment of truth. "No…actually, I think my grandfather might have been responsible for…" My voice trailed off as I saw the doubt creep into Royce's eyes.

"Your grandfather?" Royce stared at me, the doubt turning into something I couldn't read and didn't want to define. "How would your grandfather know it was your father's day to pick up lunch?"

I didn't have an answer for that. After a few moments of silence, Royce turned his attention back to the letter.

I was crossing Yonge Street to get to the sub shop when one of our construction company's vans ran the red light. If it hadn't been for another pedestrian, an elderly man who managed to pull me back with his cane at the last possible second, I would never have had the opportunity to write this letter.

Royce looked at me kindly. "Yonge Street is one of the busiest streets in downtown Toronto. Traffic gridlock is legendary. Vehicles are always trying to avoid waiting at a red light. Running a yellow is expected; the light turning red midway through the intersection is part of the game."

"But it was a company van, which meant someone from Southern Ontario Construction had been driving it."

"Would your grandfather have been driving a company van?"

I was forced to admit it was unlikely. A Cadillac was much more in keeping with his style. "It's possible that my dad spotted the yellow going to red and started crossing before his light turned green. He'd had a tendency to do that."

"The same as almost every other pedestrian in Toronto scurrying to their next destination," Royce said with a smile.

"What about the elderly man and his cane? He hadn't started crossing the road yet. Maybe he sensed danger."

"And maybe he was just being cautious by waiting for the walk signal."

I knew Royce was right. "Just keep reading, okay?"

Royce obliged.

About a week later, another incident occurred, this time as I was leaving the job site. I'd already taken off my hard hat and was just outside the building when a rivet gun fell from thirty floors up, missing my head by less than an inch. If that rivet gun had connected, death would have been instantaneous.

"There's more to the letter," Royce said, "but that's the last highlighted section. The thing is, that rivet gun could have easily struck any other pedestrian. How easy would it be to target a person thirty floors below with any accuracy?"

I had to admit, not so easy, and likely impossible. I rooted around my purse until found my cocoa butter lip balm and smoothed it on my lips, the familiar taste and feel calming my jittery nerves. Could I have been wrong all these months? Could the accidents have just been accidents? Had my hatred of my grandfather clouded my objectivity?

For the first time since my father died, I forced myself to admit that it was entirely possible.

Not just possible. Probable. I slipped the highlighted photocopy back into the file folder, along with the original letter and the rest of my father's death documents: his will, the Workplace Safety and Insurance Board and Ministry of Labor reports, and the coroner's autopsy, all the while avoiding eye contact with Royce.

"I'm sorry," Royce said, taking my hand again. "I should probably go, let you process this."

I pulled my hand away and kept my gaze averted, determined not to cry. "Yeah. You probably should."

I turned off the lights, lit a candle, and sat in the semidarkness after Royce left, trying to make peace with my decision to let this go. I was still sitting there, long after the candle burned out, when the sun came up the next morning.

18

My brain was fogged from going without sleep. I contemplated going for a short run but knew it would be hopeless. Perhaps later on, when the wine wore off. I don't drink a lot of coffee, but I fixed myself a strong cup before turning on my computer to check email. I was pleased to find a response from *Old Time Trains*.

> Thank you for your inquiry. There were a number of passenger trains between Quebec City, Quebec, and Toronto, Ontario, although origin points were always at Canadian Pacific Railway's (CPR) Windsor Station in Montreal. By origin point, I mean that Montreal was a major terminal where trains started and ended. Passengers had to change trains at origin points, as there were no through schedules, even though the timing may have been such that the effect was a through trip. In certain circumstances one or more cars may actually have been taken off one train and added to the other one, thus the passenger need not get off. But, this was highly dependent upon distance traveled and time of day, volume of passengers etc.
>
> The train taken by your German immigrant would have

depended upon the arrival time of the ship, the time required to clear immigration etc., as well as the possibility that she might like a stopover in Quebec City. The more important trains operated by CPR left Quebec City at 1:15 p.m. and 5:00 p.m. seven days per week, arriving in Montreal at 5:00 p.m. and 9:10 p.m. respectively. The trains exiting Quebec City were named Frontenac, most likely named after Chateau Frontenac in Quebec City, and Viger for the Place Viger Hotel in Montreal. The night sleeper train to Toronto was No. 21 Chicago Express. Trains departing Montreal included at 10:15 p.m. (No. 21 night sleeper train), arriving in Toronto at 7:00 a.m. seven days per week.

I do not have passenger lists, but suggest you try the Pier 21 (Canadian Museum of Immigration) history people in Halifax as they have such materials and could possibly provide a contact for Quebec City arrivals.

I hope this information is helpful. All the best to you in your search.

It was a more detailed response than I had hoped for, let alone expected. My first step was to email *Old Time Trains* back with a sincere thank you. My next step was to forward the email to Chantelle.

Chantelle, this was received in response to my Facebook post for information on the train from Quebec City. You mentioned a contact at the Canadian Museum of Immigration. Hopefully they can help us with passenger lists for the trains mentioned. Callie.

That done, I searched for a photo of the No. 21 Chicago Express and found one, along with a detailed history of the train, on *Old Time Trains*. I downloaded the picture to share on the Facebook page, included a link to the photo, and then captioned it:

All Aboard! I've just received a detailed response to my train question from @OldTimeTrains. They have confirmed there would have been a stopover at CPR's Windsor Station in

Montreal, and also provided the names of the trains and when they would have left Quebec City and Montreal. Shown: No. 21 Chicago Express. Thanks to all who chimed in. Your help is appreciated.

Feeling buoyed by the success of my train post, I decided to try another. I scanned Anneliese's three postcards from the T.S.S. *Canberra*, posted them in a group on Facebook with the caption:

Looking for any ephemera from the T.S.S. Canberra, Greek Line, specifically the journey that would have left Southampton, England, around June 25, arriving in Quebec City on July 7, 1952. Other dates, early 1950s, would also be of interest. Menus from the ship, passenger lists, etc. Thanks in advance for any comments and shares.

That posted, and finally starting to feel human again, I made myself some scrambled eggs and toast, along with a cup of cinnamon rooibos tea. I'd just finished it when the phone rang.

Royce.

I answered, determined to keep my voice upbeat. "Hey, what's up?"

"I wanted to thank you again for dinner last night."

"You're welcome. We'll have to do it again some time." I paused, not sure how to bring up the letter, or even if I should. I was still debating when Royce filled the awkward silence.

"Something's been bothering me. About your father's accident. I may have an avenue for you to explore."

"I don't think I have the intestinal fortitude to go down that rabbit hole again."

Silence on the other end. Then, "Why didn't you sue? You lost your father to an occupational accident. If nothing else, a lawsuit would bring out all the facts, hidden and otherwise."

I'm of the opinion that our society has become far too litigious, especially over minor incidents, not that I would classify my father's death as minor. "I'll consider it."

"Whatever you decide. The other reason I called was to find out if you'd be interested in a purely social do-over, this time at my place, with me in charge of dinner. I'm not quite as accomplished as you are, but I have a couple of chicken recipes in my repertoire."

"I like chicken, especially if someone else is doing the cooking. When were you thinking?"

"How about Saturday night?"

"It's a date."

I hung up and found myself humming a few bars of "To Make You Feel My Love." I thought about the Barnstable family curse and laughed. More like "Bad Timing" by Blue Rodeo. Hell, almost anything by Blue Rodeo, especially if Jim Cuddy was the one singing it. That man had a voice made for sad songs.

Maybe this time would be different. I started humming again.

⊕

I WAS STILL HUMMING when an email reply came in from Chantelle.

Well done on the train information, Callie. Based on the response, we can make an educated assumption that Anneliese arrived in Toronto on July 8 or 9 at the latest. It's not a huge piece of the puzzle, but I'd suggest that we include it in our report to Louisa, along with some photos of the trains and train stations. It will help to illustrate Anneliese's journey, and show Louisa that P&P is thorough.

It was a good idea. I made a note and then continued reading.

I've checked with my contact at the Canadian Museum of Immigration at Pier 21, and she has thoroughly checked their collection for the T.S.S. Canberra, Greek Line. I've included her comments in italics, along with my thoughts on each.

"Unfortunately we only have two stories for persons who traveled on the

Canberra. One is about a family who traveled in 1930 and the other is someone who traveled in 1951 but it's not really a story, just a blurb."

Neither of these would be worth following up. It's unfortunate that there are no stories from Anneliese's journey, but not unexpected.

"We do not have any souvenir passenger lists for the Canberra."

This is disappointing news. I notice that you've posted on our Facebook page for ephemera relating to the Canberra. Hopefully this generates the same sort of results as your train post. However, I also had another thought. Before she opened the Glass Dolphin, Arabella had purchased several ocean liner posters and assorted memorabilia from a collector in Niagara Falls. We know that she doesn't have anything in the shop from the Canberra, but if she still has the collector's contact information, and it's still valid, he may have a lead, another collector, or resource to check. It's possible she's already gone down that road and come up empty, but I'll leave it to you to check.

I made another note, this time to call Arabella.

"The immigration records for all post-1935 arrivals are protected under the Privacy Act of Canada and can only be accessed via Access to Information and Privacy, better known as ATIP, by the individuals who immigrated or if the person has been deceased for over twenty years."

We already have Anneliese's immigration records. We also know that Anton Osgoode was on board as a buyer for Eaton's. With the possible exception of Horst Frankow, I don't believe anyone else's immigration status would be relevant. It is, however, an interesting point to consider for future investigations.

Should we decide to submit a written application for Horst, we would be required, at the bare minimum, to supply proof of death, date of birth, and year of entry. We know Horst died in prison, but we don't have a death certificate, and we definitely don't have his date of birth or year of entry into Canada. I don't believe the payback of finding out exactly when and how he immigrated to Canada substantiates the investigative hours required.

"I see that the Canberra left Southampton on June 28, 1952. The crossing took eight days on average."

I've updated the Facebook post to include the date the Canberra left Southampton. We know based on the stamp on Anneliese's immigration paper that she arrived in Quebec City on July 7.

"The UK departure manifest for this crossing may be available via www.ancestry.ca. I would recommend that you obtain a worldwide account with them to access and save the departure list or to go to your local public library as many libraries have accounts that are free for the public to use. You will search the UK, Outward Passenger Lists, 1890-1960 Database."

This is a great tip. Since I already have a worldwide account with Ancestry.ca, I'll follow it up and let you know what comes of it.

 Over and out,
 Chantelle.

⊙

I'D JUST FINISHED READING the email when my phone rang. I looked at the call display. PRIVATE CALLER. I sighed. It was probably someone trying to sell me duct-cleaning services.

"Hello."

"Callie, it's your grandfather."

I was surprised to hear Corbin Osgoode's gravelly voice, and it wasn't a good surprise. I skipped the pleasantries. "What can I do for you?"

"I understand you've been visiting my mother at the nursing home."

"I have. Olivia is a lovely woman."

"I want you to stop."

"I was under the impression she enjoyed my visits."

"Then you were mistaken. Besides, I don't want her living in the past. It isn't healthy."

"Talking about the past is hardly the same as living in the past."

"I'm not willing to discuss it any further. I've already told the administrators at the Cedar County Retirement Residence that you are not to be admitted again. I'm calling you as a courtesy, so you aren't faced with the embarrassment of going there and being turned away."

I wanted to scream or swear at him, but I wasn't about to give him the satisfaction. "Thanks for being so considerate." I hung up before he could get the last word.

⊕

ONCE MY BLOOD pressure had returned to normal, and my desire to punch the wall or throw things had cooled, I picked up my notebook and recorded the facts as I knew them.

- Anton Osgoode had met Anneliese Prei on the *Canberra*. The two of them had a shipboard romance.
- Anneliese was pregnant when she married Horst Frankow. Based on the timeline, the baby could have been either Anton's or Horst's, although Anton was the most likely candidate.
- Anneliese paid Olivia a visit, three-year-old Sophie in tow. According to Olivia, Sophie looked like Anton.
- Olivia confronted Anton, a decision she continues to regret, although she did not elaborate on the reason.
- Shortly after Anneliese and Sophie paid Olivia a visit, Anneliese was struck on the back of the head and died of her injuries.
- The murder weapon was never found. Horst was charged with the murder, and imprisoned for

manslaughter at Kingston Penitentiary, where he was stabbed to death in the shower three weeks later.

Those were the facts. Olivia glancing at the crystal vase as if it were the murder weapon could have been my imagination. In fact, I might even have come to that conclusion if I'd had more time to think it over.

But not now. Not after Corbin Osgoode called to tell me I was being denied access to Olivia. He was hiding something, I was sure of it. Something Olivia knew and hadn't yet told me.

Just what he was hiding remained to be seen. I couldn't wait to find out. And find out, I would. It was just a matter of time.

19

Corbin's call had piqued my curiosity, and not just in regards to my great-grandmother. It was time to find a workplace injury lawyer to look into my father's death. Maybe it was too late, and maybe there was no case, but Royce was right. A lawsuit might lead to more information, or at least, serve to satisfy me that I'd done everything I could.

One of my quirks is a love of talk radio. It's not that I don't like music, but when it comes to working, nothing beats talk radio. I had my favorite shows on Newstalk 1010 Toronto and Talk 640 Toronto, and switched back and forth, depending on the host and topic. It's fascinating to hear the same story spun a dozen different ways, the varying points of views from panelists and callers, especially when it came to politics.

On the weekends, much of talk radio is paid programming, everything from investment advice and gardening to real estate and employment law. The employment lawyer was articulate, and he presented thought-provoking cases. What could he tell me about my father's case?

I looked up his contact information, but felt a bit silly. What would I say? I tapped my pen against the table, summoning up my courage. Then I thought about Corbin, picked up my phone, and dialed.

I updated the receptionist with an abbreviated version of my request, mentioning the radio show. She agreed to put me through to one of the junior partners.

"Kat Fowler. How can I help you?" The voice on the other end sounded young.

"My father died thirteen months ago in an occupational accident. I wondered if there was any chance of suing his employer. Is it too late?"

"You typically have two years to file a claim. Tell me about the accident."

"He was working on a high-rise condo thirty floors up. His safety harness was either defective or not fastened properly. He fell to his death."

"Did your father make a habit out of not wearing or buckling his safety harness?"

"Southern Ontario Construction, his employer, says yes. Apparently there were other employees on the job site who were willing to corroborate the employer's statement."

"It's an interesting scenario, but I'm afraid you won't like my answer."

"Why is that?"

"Your father's company would have been insured under the Workplace Safety and Insurance Board. Unfortunately, you cannot sue the employer because employers cannot be sued for negligence that causes bodily harm to their employees. They pay WSIB premiums to get that protection. However, it is extremely likely that the Ministry of Labor would have investigated the incident and would have laid charges against the company if it found that it was negligent. These would be charges under the Occupational Health and Safety Act."

"The Ministry of Labor ruled the death as an accident. They did not find negligence on the part of Southern Ontario Construction."

"In that case, your only avenue is to sue the manufacturer of the harness, if it can be established that the harness was somehow defective, and if the manufacturer was not covered under the WSIB. For example, if they are an American or foreign company. The value of such a suit can be substantial because not only can you sue on behalf of yourself for 'loss of care, guidance, and companionship,' but also for any loss of income you might sustain in future because of his death."

I'd already done my fair share of research on that safety harness, looking for cases similar to my dad's, and I was surprised the harness had not been made offshore.

"Made in Ontario," I said, knowing as I said it that all hope of a lawsuit had been lost.

"I'm sorry," Kat Fowler said. "In my opinion, it's not a case you can bring forward to the courts, let alone win. You're free to get a second opinion, of course."

I thanked her for her time and hung up. There would be no seeking a second opinion, no relentless pursuit of a truth I'd never uncover, no more reading and rereading my father's last letter to me, analyzing every word until I thought I'd go mad.

It was time to move on.

I changed into my running gear and hit the trails.

⊛

I RETURNED FROM A NINETY-MINUTE RUN, popped some leftover lasagna in the toaster oven, and grabbed a quick shower before checking my mobile for messages.

There was one text from Arabella, no details, just, *Call me when you get in.* Good timing. I could ask about her ocean liner memorabilia collector. I phoned her back.

"The Glass Dolphin, Arabella Carpenter speaking."

"Hey Arabella, it's Callie and great minds think alike. I was planning to call you today. What's up?"

"I've got a lead on some ephemera that might help with your investigation."

"That's great. What did you find?"

"Nothing specific, but I did contact the man who sold me the railway and ocean liner posters. He didn't have anything related to the T.S.S. *Canberra*, but he's friendly with other folks interested in ephemera. He made a few calls, and there's a guy in Toronto who had a relative come over on the *Canberra* in the early 1950s. According to my guy, the collection isn't huge, but it could be of interest, especially if the timeline matches up."

Even if it didn't, it was one more thing we could share with Louisa to demonstrate our efforts. "It sounds promising."

"Yes and no. The man in question has no interest in selling anything in his collection. He distrusts antiques dealers, something about being ripped off a few years back. He won't deal with me on any level. He is, however, willing to talk to you."

"I'd be more than happy to call him."

"I'll give you his number, but fair warning. He wants to meet you in person and see your office before making any decisions. I don't know if he's super cautious or a complete nutbar."

"I appreciate your concern, but if he has something from the *Canberra*, we've got to see it. I'll make sure Chantelle is here when he comes, if that makes you feel any better."

"It does. His name is Geoffrey Burrell, that's g-e-o-f-f not j-e-f-f." Arabella rattled off his phone number and email address and wished me luck.

I called Chantelle to see when she was available, and promised to call her back as soon as I'd connected with Geoffrey Burrell.

I was in luck. Geoffrey answered within two rings. I introduced myself as a partner in Past & Present Investigations.

"I've been expecting your call." Geoffrey's voice had the reedy timbre of an elderly man. "I understand that you're interested in the T.S.S. *Canberra*."

"Yes. Anything you have might be of significance, but we're specifically interested in the journey from Southampton in June 1952. The ship arrived in Quebec City on July 7."

"Forgive my curiosity, but why that particular journey?"

"Our client is trying to find out more about her great-grandmother, who was a passenger on that ship. I'm afraid I can't give you the client's name or the name of the grandmother. There is a confidentiality agreement in place."

"I respect that. Had you told me who the client was, I would have ended this call with a firm, but polite, 'Not interested.'"

"Then you'll help us?"

There was a prolonged silence. I waited. Something told me Geoffrey was not a man to be rushed. I was right.

"Okay, I'll come to your office to show you what I have. If there is anything that could help your client, you can take photocopies to share with them, on one condition. You must promise not to post the images on the internet. Not your website, and certainly not on your Facebook page. I don't want my collection out there in cyberspace."

"You have my word."

"In that case, I can come over tomorrow morning, if you're available."

I checked my notes. "How's ten a.m.? My partner, Chantelle Marchand, will be here as well."

"Ten a.m. is perfect. By the way, I particularly enjoyed Misty's blog today. It was as if she was reaching out, asking me to help. I'm a sucker for a love story." He hung up before I could respond, which was just as well. Once again, I had absolutely no idea what Misty had posted.

20

———

There was a second entry on the *Misty's Messages* page. The card shown was the Two of Cups: a woman in a long white gown on a flowing blue robe, a man wearing a yellow and black tunic and calf-high boots. Both wore a crown of flowers and held a gold cup. The man was reaching out toward the woman, not quite touching. Above them was a winged lion's head. The lion was perched on top of a staff, two snakes coiled around it. I read Misty's message.

The Two of Cups (Element: Water)

Most readers will view the Two of Cups as a lovers' card, and there is certainly an element of love, attraction, and sexuality, but I prefer to interpret this card from the minor arcana under the overarching theme of partnership. Notice the caduceus (the insignia used by the medical profession) and the head of a winged lion, the wings acting like a protective canopy over the man and woman. This symbolizes peace, harmony, and balance.

Misty's Message: The type of partnership depends on whether your connection involves the past, present, or future, but your role, however slight, will be a powerful one that includes mutual trust and respect. Will it reunite two lovers? Perhaps. Or perhaps it will shed light on the lives of past lovers, no longer with us.

Misty had taken the Two of Cups and turned it into a request for information through a mutual partnership. I should have been grateful, something in the way she formulated the post had resonated with Geoffrey Burrell. But it did make me wonder why she put in the part about the lives of past lovers. She wouldn't know about Anneliese and Anton. Could Misty actually have psychic powers? I shook my head. Chantelle must have updated her.

⊕

"GUILTY AS CHARGED," Chantelle said. We were sipping tea and munching on store-bought chocolate chip cookies while we waited for Geoffrey Burrell. If he were the punctual type, he'd be arriving within the next ten minutes.

"Why?"

"Why not? Her last post was effective. She may not be a partner, but she is part of our team. I didn't give her any names, just the basic storyline. I hope you're not upset with me."

"To be honest, I'm relieved. I can deal with Misty interpreting tarot in her own inimitable fashion, especially if it brings us leads or clients, but I'm not ready to label her as a bona fide psychic."

Chantelle laughed. "You're not ready to label anyone a bona fide psychic."

She was right. Nonetheless, *Misty's Messages* did seem to resonate. "I probably shouldn't be so dismissive. Her approach appears to be striking a chord. Maybe we should get her working on some other messages. I don't know what other messages, mind you."

"I'm sure she would have all sorts of ideas, especially if we gave her the slightest bit of direction. And she has done a great job on the website so far."

I admitted I hadn't gotten beyond the most recent post.

"Seriously? You have to check it out. Misty has child pages set up for the major and minor arcana, along with a photo of every single card in the tarot deck. I checked the stats, and both pages are already getting a ton of hits."

I promised to check it out as the doorbell rang. "That will be Geoffrey Burrell."

I've always believed that most people match their voice, i.e. big and boisterous generally meant a person of generous spirit and proportions, whereas soft-spoken and breathy belonged to someone young, sexy, and slender, or maybe a Marilyn Monroe type, a buxom blonde well aware of her charms. If that was the rule, then Geoffrey Burrell was the exception, for he was as thick and portly as his voice was thin and reedy. His height, or lack thereof, didn't help his cause any. I'm five foot six in stocking feet. He was a good two inches shorter than me.

I took Geoffrey's coat and hung it on the hall tree, a fabulous piece I'd found at a local furniture store specializing in Mennonite goods. It had been made from a submerged log that had been salvaged and stained, with railroad spikes as the hooks, and a base carved out of pine. Not only did it look good, it made up for the fact that the front hall closet fit exactly six coats, crammed together.

Geoffrey pulled his mustard yellow sweater over his considerable belly and slipped off his shoes, his black leather briefcase in hand the entire time as if I might take it and run. I adjusted my height estimation of him down by two more inches. The man might have been closing in on eighty and as bald and wrinkled as the day he was brought into the world, but he wore lifts. I stifled a grin. "You don't need to remove your shoes."

"You have such lovely hardwood in here, I'd hate to scuff it up. Besides, I'm most comfortable just wearing socks."

Probably tired of wearing heels, I thought, suppressing a giggle. I invited him in and introduced him to Chantelle.

The pleasantries exchanged, and the offer of tea, coffee, or cookies politely refused, Geoffrey got down to business, opened the briefcase, and pulled out a thin green binder filled with plastic sleeves. I was ridiculously excited at the prospect of finding out what was inside.

"THESE ARE ARCHIVAL POLYESTER SLEEVES," Geoffrey said, his voice taking on a scholarly tone. "They provide a glass-clear, acid-free, non-yellowing or clouding, protective sleeve material which will allow us to handle and view the ephemera without obstruction. Additionally, the sleeves don't crumple and the stiffness offers a good level of support and resistance from damage. Naturally, should you decide to make a photocopy, we can carefully remove the document from its archival sleeve."

I avoided Chantelle's gaze, knowing that we might both burst out laughing if we made eye contact. Geoffrey Burrell had just told me more than I'd ever wanted or needed to know about archival polyester sleeves.

"It's fascinating, the way technology can protect our past," I said, ignoring Chantelle's kick under the table.

"Isn't it?" Geoffrey opened the binder to the first sleeve. "I'm afraid I don't have a lot of material related to the *Canberra*, but you did say anything might be of interest, and I can certainly elaborate on the possible significance of each item as it relates to your case."

Geoffrey gently removed a cream-colored booklet titled "List of Passengers: T.S.S. *Canberra* Greek Line" in blue script. A Greek god, holding a three-pronged spear, was imprinted on the background in soft green. I thought back to my Greek mythology classes in high school. This must be Poseidon, Greek god of the sea. I caught Chantelle's eye and knew she was thinking the same thing I was. Could this be the passenger list from Anneliese's journey?

"I'm afraid it's not from June 1952," he said, bursting my bubble. "The *Canberra* operated for the Greek Line from 1948 through 1954." Geoffrey turned to the Title Page, which was dated Monday, June 4, 1951, for the journey from Montreal to Cherbourg, Southampton, and Bremerhaven.

I felt a twinge of disappointment, but if my face showed anything, Geoffrey was oblivious. "This particular passenger list is not from June 1952, but this is what an intact passenger list would have looked like." He turned a page that listed the ship's officers, lingering for a moment before turning to the next, which listed first class passengers, broken down into three lists: Cherbourg, Southampton, and Bremerhaven. Each list had fewer than a dozen individuals, of which many were members of the same family. In the case of Cherbourg, for example, there were three surnames and ten passengers.

Subsequent pages listed the tourist class passengers, which included seventy-plus names per category. Anton Osgoode was not on the list, not that I expected him to be. Some of the names had penciled checkmarks next to them. "What do the pencil marks mean?"

"Very observant of you, and a good question," Geoffrey said, his tone approving. "Travelers would carefully review and analyze the passenger list. Were any important people on board? Aristocrats, business tycoons, senior clergy, celebrities, and parliamentarians were all of interest. One would look for other passengers from the traveler's home community, if it were shown. This particular list doesn't include the passenger's towns, but many lists did. In this case, my assumption is these tick marks were an aid to remember the names of the other parties seated at their dinner table."

Chantelle was studying the passenger list, her brows furrowed in concentration. "Would a first class passenger have an opportunity to dine or meet someone in tourist class?"

I knew she was thinking of the postcard Anneliese had kept from the first class music salon. Since Anton Osgoode had been buyer for Eaton's, a prestigious job at the time if Olivia was to be believed, he may have been in first class. Anneliese Prei, traveling on a German passport and emigrating from England, would have assuredly been in tourist class.

"Do not let Rose and Jack and the *Titanic* be your guide," Geoffrey said, with a chuckle. "The first class passengers would never mingle with the tourist class. It was simply not done. Should a tourist class passenger have somehow managed to find their way onto the first class deck, which is unlikely if not impossible, they would have been hastily removed and returned to their proper place."

Which meant that the postcard of the music salon was nothing more than a souvenir. It also meant Anton had traveled tourist class. I wondered if that bothered him, or perhaps there was a better chance of finding a guilt-free fling in tourist class. I realized I was being unfair to a man I'd never met, especially since Anneliese wasn't blameless. After all, according to her passport, she was immigrating to Canada because she had a fiancé.

Geoffrey was staring at me expectantly, and I realized that I'd probably missed something while I was spinning stories in my head. "I'm sorry, I was just mulling over everything you've told us so far."

The response appeared to mollify him, because he turned to a section on general information for passengers. There were warnings on opening portholes (definitely not recommended), details on laundry services, lost and found articles, mail and telegrams, baggage, storage of valuables, and religious services. It surprised me to see that deck chairs were rented out at a cost of a dollar and a half per day, pillows and rugs an additional seventy-five cents each.

Anneliese's immigration travel allowance equaled about forty dollars, her journey lasted nine days. Luxuries like deck chairs would have used up almost half of her allotment. I wasn't sure what the rug meant, and asked Geoffrey about it.

"Technically it's a thick woolen blanket, not a rug that you'd put on the floor," Geoffrey said. "The rest of this page is self-explanatory, but I still find it interesting, especially the rental charges."

"I do, too," I said. "It really gives me a sense of the journey."

"I can almost imagine being there," Chantelle said.

Geoffrey beamed. "Exactly. Now you understand why I've been fascinated by this for years. Are you ready to see more?"

Chantelle and I nodded in unison.

The next sleeve offered a glimpse at a daily program of events and activities on the R.M.S. *Sylvania* in July 1957. Program had been spelled *Programme*, as if to fancy things up, despite a notation in italics at the bottom of the page that clearly indicated this program was for the tourist class.

"The designation of R.M.S. stands for Royal Mail Ship or

Steamer, denoting a seagoing vessel that carry mail under contract to the British Royal Mail," Geoffrey said. "As you can see, this is from the *Sylvania's* maiden voyage."

It was evident from the reverence in his tone that Geoffrey was proud of this program, though I was hard pressed to figure out how it related to the Canberra. I was thinking of a way to politely ask when Geoffrey continued.

"While this particular program isn't from the *Canberra*, it's a good example of what you'd expect to find. There would be one program for first class, and one for tourist class. I also selected it because it includes instructions to passengers getting ready to disembark, along with a notation of a time change at midnight."

"They seem to have a lot on the go," I said, taking in the number of things listed. A Quiz Competition; Afternoon Tea Music with *George Forbes and the "Sylvania" Quintet* in the Lounge; Cocktail Hour in the Smoke Room; BBC Radio Broadcast (reception conditions permitting); and a movie night, in this case *Brothers in Law* starring Richard Attenborough, Ian Carmichael, and Terry Thomas. There was a Fancy Dress Parade, followed by a dance featuring *George Forbes and the "Sylvania" Dance Orchestra.*

"These would have been delivered to each cabin on a daily basis," Geoffrey said. "Each of the day's events would have also been posted the afternoon or evening beforehand. There would be exceptions, such as a Costume Ball, where people needed time to conceive and prepare their costumes, or the Farewell Dinner, the timing of that self-evident."

"Fascinating," I said, and meant it. What would it have been like for someone coming to Canada for a new life, someone who'd experienced food rations and the horrors of war firsthand?

I was ready to see what else Geoffrey had. What he'd shown us so far was interesting, but I was getting antsy. I wanted to see something that was part of Anneliese's journey. I avoided eye contact with Chantelle. The last thing we needed was Geoffrey to think we didn't care about his collection.

"I can't wait to see the rest of what you've brought," I said, hoping to hurry him along in the nicest possible way.

The prompt was well received. Geoffrey took us through a handful of lunch and dinner menus from different voyages and different ships, although none were from the Greek Line, let alone the *Canberra*. Nevertheless, he seemed excited about them, so it seemed fitting to ask a question or two.

I couldn't think of a single question. Fortunately, Chantelle came to the rescue.

"Would the menus have been delivered to the staterooms in the same way as the daily event schedules?"

"I don't believe so. I personally have never found a menu specifically addressed to a stateroom," Geoffrey said. "As in a restaurant, the menu for the meal would have been at the table. The environment the ship wanted to create was one of being in a fine hotel with an excellent restaurant. As you can see by the menus, the food would have been quite exotic by most standards."

I had to admit the food did sound exotic. A dinner menu from the *Queen Mary*, dated July 31, 1947, included two soups: Clear Turtle and something called Potage Nelusko. The fish options were equally enticing: Turbot poche, Sauce Riche, and Red Mullet, Meunière. There was also Roast Sirloin of Beef with Horseradish Cream, and Mousseline of Ham, Florentine. Vegetables, potatoes, and desserts covered the gamut from the ordinary, like fresh broccoli or boiled potatoes, to the unexpected, like Praline Parfait or Charlotte Russe, a dessert made with whipped cream, fruit, gelatin, and ladyfingers.

"What about the seating?" I asked. "You mentioned before that passengers would often make tick marks next to the names of their tablemates. But would you always sit with the same group of people?" Meaning, would Anneliese and Anton always have been seated at the same table.

"A passenger would always be seated at their assigned table," Geoffrey said, "although it is not inconceivable that there could have been changes of place within a table's group. People might have occasionally wanted to change tables and that would have been at the discretion of the maître d'. At the end of the voyage, the waiters for your table would be hoping for, and likely expecting, a gratuity."

The groundwork laid for his big reveal, Geoffrey was finally ready to share the last sleeve in the binder.

It was a passenger list, but unlike the previous example, which had been in pristine condition, this one was a bit worse for the wear. The Title Page was there, confirming this was from the *Canberra's* voyage in June 1952 from Bremerhaven, Southampton, and Cherbourg to Quebec City, but the passenger list had been removed. Disappointing, in that it would have been nice to see the names of Anneliese Prei and Anton Osgoode in print, but still something to show Louisa.

"My assumption is that the passenger list had been extricated to give to someone else as a memento, but that's just a guess," Geoffrey said. "It could have been removed for any number of reasons."

"I'm sure our client will be pleased to see this, even without the passengers' names," Chantelle said, and I nodded in agreement.

"You're both too polite to ask why I would have purchased something in such terrible condition," Geoffrey said with a smile.

"It doesn't seem to match the rest of the ephemera in your collection," I said, "but I'm glad you did."

"More politeness, for which I thank you, but I've been saving the best for last. I bought this for the autograph page. I believe I told you that I'm a sucker for a love story."

"You did indeed," I said.

"Maybe I'm reading more into this than there is, but I couldn't resist it. Of course, I realize the names attached to the signatures will mean nothing to you, or your client, but I am sure he or she will love it regardless." Geoffrey flipped to the page and sat back, waiting for our reaction. I suppressed a gasp, not wanting to give anything away. A quick glance at Chantelle found her staring at the page, transfixed.

I couldn't blame her. For there, on the cream-colored card stock, the title Autographs on the top, was the penciled heading of TABLE EIGHT in uppercase. There were thirteen signatures on the page, some written with a flourish, others in a Germanic spiky, cramped script. I knew from the postcard of the *Canberra's* tourist class dining room that the tables seated fourteen. It stood to reason that the owner of the page hadn't signed it, but I found myself longing to know who that person was, because beside each signature there was a small, but intricate, penciled drawing.

"I have never seen anything like it before or since," Geoffrey said. "The artist was quite talented, don't you think? What a wonderful way to remember people years later."

I nodded, fascinated by the images before me. A table tennis racket, a book, the ace of clubs, a racing form, a swim cap, a slice of pie, a teacup, a piano, a radio, a deck chair, and a wine glass.

Only two signatures had a similar drawing next to the signature. It was a double heart, the initials A.P. inside one, and A.O. inside the other.

Anneliese Prei and Anton Osgoode.

21

———

After extracting a written promise that we wouldn't share them on the internet, Geoffrey permitted me to take color photocopies of the documents of interest, including the all-important autograph page.

By unspoken agreement, neither Chantelle nor I mentioned that we recognized any of the names.

"Wow," Chantelle said over and over as soon as he'd left. She was doing laps around the table at a frantic pace.

"Wow, indeed." I dabbed on some cocoa butter lip balm, then dabbed on some more, hoping Chantelle would sit down. She was making me dizzy.

She kept on pacing. "What are the odds that Geoffrey would have that particular autograph page? Not to mention the odds of us being introduced to him?"

I'd been pondering the same questions. I've never believed in the spirit world, nary a word from my father from the great beyond about his death as a case in point. I've also heard stories about murder victims haunting the houses where they were slain until the killer was found. Who hasn't? But I didn't believe them. I pride myself on being a logical person. Spirits, ghosts, and tarot cards defied logic. There was always a plausible explanation, and Misty's latest post and Geoffrey Burrell's autograph page were no exception.

"I think it's a lucky coincidence."

Chantelle rolled her eyes. "Seriously? A lucky coincidence?"

"Coincidence or not, what should we do next?"

"I was thinking of asking Misty to do a reading for us."

I liked Misty well enough, and *Misty's Messages* had netted us a client and a great source, despite my earlier reservations. But there was a limit to what I was willing to share with her.

"I don't want her to know about the autograph page."

"She doesn't have to know about it. We can just ask for a general reading."

I wasn't convinced. "What's she going to say? That the investigation is on the right track? That we should be aware of strangers bearing gifts? I don't see it as a viable option."

Chantelle was not about to be swayed. "Okay, maybe Misty isn't the best choice, but it's still something I want to try. Didn't you tell me that you saw a psychic when you were investigating your mother's disappearance?"

I was forced to admit that I had. "But it wasn't for a reading. I needed someone to interpret the tarot cards I found at Snapdragon Circle."

"And did she? Interpret them?"

"Yes."

"Now we're getting somewhere," Chantelle said, a little bit smug. "What was her name and where do we find her?"

"Her name was Randi and she works out of Sun, Moon and Stars."

"The shop behind Nature's Way Whole and Organic Foods? I knew that they sold crystals and tie-dyed scarves, but I had no idea they had psychics."

"I don't know about the other…psychics…but Randi offers readings using tarot, tea leaves, and personal objects."

Chantelle's gray eyes glistened. "You need to make another appointment with her. I've been doing research on psychics and personal objects. There's a thing called psychometry, also known as token-object reading. It's a form of extrasensory perception characterized by the ability to make associations from an object of unknown history by making physical contact with the object."

"Sounds bogus to me."

"The basic concept is that an individual possessing psychometric abilities holds an object, and from that they are able to tell something about the history of the object, the person who owned it, and the experiences that person had while in the possession of it. The psychometrist may be able to sense what the person was like, what they did, and even how they died."

"Is that so?"

Chantelle either missed my attempt at sarcasm or chose to ignore it. "Sometimes the psychometrist can sense the emotions of the person at a particular time because emotions are most strongly recorded in an object. If Randi had a personal object from Anneliese, it might help. Even one from Sophie couldn't hurt, especially if it's something she inherited from her mother."

"Suppose I was willing to give it a try, we don't have a personal object from either of them. I don't think old photographs qualify as an object."

"Maybe we don't have anything right this minute," Chantelle said, "but there's still Sophie's jewelry box. Will you make an appointment with Randi if there's anything in there that can be traced back to Anneliese?"

"Why don't you make the appointment? It's your idea."

"Because I believe in these sorts of things, which also means I could be easily persuaded. You, on the other hand, are a born skeptic. If it's nothing more than smoke and mirrors, you'll see right through it."

She had a point. "Fine, I'll make the appointment, but only if there's something in the jewelry box worth taking to Randi."

"I'm positive there will be," Chantelle said.

I was pretty sure there would be, too. The thought didn't bring me comfort. Psychometry indeed. Next thing you knew, I'd be planning my day according to my horoscope.

I WAS DEBATING what to include in my report for Louisa when my phone rang. No caller ID.

"Past & Present Investigations, Calamity speaking."

"Hi Callie, it's Louisa. I'm finally back home after the road trip from hell. Don't get me started on the flight from Halifax to Toronto. Anyway, enough about that, you said in your message you'd made some progress."

"We have. There's a lot more to do, but we've made headway, and we have some good leads."

"That's great."

"About the report…there are some loose ends that I'd rather leave out until we can tidy them up. Taken out of context, they might be more confusing than helpful."

"I've been thinking about that. I know initially I requested regular reports, but I've never been good at digesting things in bits and bytes. If you don't mind, I'd prefer to wait until you finished the investigation."

I breathed a silent sigh of relief. It would have felt wrong to withhold information about Anton Osgoode, especially given the autograph page, but I needed to find out what role he played, if any, in Anneliese's murder. Or at least try to find out.

"If you're sure."

"I'm sure. I trust that you're working hard on the case. Now, if we're still having this conversation six months from now, that would be another story."

"Six months? If we're having this conversation three months from now, you should fire us."

"Okay then. Do you still want me to bring you Sophie's chocolate box and jewelry? I'm afraid I haven't had the time to sort through either." Louisa blushed. "Who am I trying to kid? I just couldn't face it so soon after her death. Put me in a business situation, no matter how difficult, and I can be ruthless, but I practice avoidance when it comes to personal matters."

"That's a normal reaction. One day, you'll find comfort in these things. In the meantime, there may be something in there to assist our investigation."

"In that case, I'm going to be in Marketville tomorrow morning to visit one of our franchisees. I'll get everything ready tonight and drop them off on my way there. About ten o'clock, depending on traffic."

"See you then."

Tomorrow morning seemed a long way off. Patience might be a virtue, but it had never been one of mine. I tapped my fingers on the table, trying to figure out what to do next. I couldn't concentrate; the autograph page had rocked me more than I cared to admit. The double hearts meant that Anneliese and Anton hadn't kept their shipboard romance a secret, at least when it came to the autograph artist. The odds were the rest of the people at table eight would have known or suspected as well.

Would any of the tablemates have kept in touch with either Anton or Anneliese? It wouldn't have been as easy then as today, but it was possible.

What if one of them was a blackmailer that went too far? Three years seemed a long time to make it a likely scenario for Anneliese's murder, but a thorough search meant including the names in my newspaper search.

I put the autograph page in front of me and began deciphering the other eleven signatures, some easier than others, adding them to the list of nine names I'd already written down in my notebook.

Twenty names. It seemed overwhelming, but I'd been faced with overwhelming odds when I was searching for the truth about my mother. I could do it again.

At least this time, it wasn't personal.

Except that maybe it was.

Damn those Osgoodes, they were nothing but trouble.

I forced myself to push all thoughts of Anton Osgoode out of my mind and hopped onto the Past & Present Facebook page.

Nothing on my request for ephemera from the T.S.S. *Canberra*. I felt all the more grateful for meeting with Geoffrey Burrell.

I knew posting regularly on Facebook would build our followers, something that was important to the business, but I wasn't sure what to post about. I sipped on a mug of cinnamon rooibos tea, thinking about the possibilities. After a few minutes, I had it. Pearls. Anneliese Prei Frankow had worn a pearl necklace on her wedding day, along with matching pearl drop earrings. There was no chance of finding her pearl necklace, I knew that, but with luck it would garner enough interest to make an interactive post.

I searched online until I found a three-strand pearl necklace similar to the one Anneliese wore on her wedding day and began writing the post.

Pearls: lucky or not?

Ancient Greek culture believed that pearls would promote marital bliss and guard against tears on the wedding day. Modern day superstition purports that pearls are never to be incorporated into an engagement or wedding ring lest they bring "tears to the marriage." Brides are particularly cautioned against wearing pearls on their wedding day lest they begin their new lives with sorrow.

What do you believe, and why?

For a brief moment, I felt like I'd taken a step toward making that other world connection with Anneliese, then I gave myself a mental slap upside the head. I was really getting silly about all of this.

It didn't stop me from hitting the Publish button.

22

—————

Louisa arrived promptly at ten carrying a clear plastic storage tote. I was struck once again at her likeness to Anneliese. As before, she was dressed conservatively, this time wearing a navy blue blazer with matching pants, an off-white camisole, and pearl drop earrings that were eerily similar to the ones Anneliese had worn on her wedding day. Could they be the same earrings?

She handed me the box, which was surprisingly light. "My mom's jewelry and the chocolate box. It's slim pickings, but I hope you're right in that they might be helpful. At any rate, there's no rush to get them back. I have no plans for any of it in the foreseeable future."

"Can I share any of this online, provided we believe that it could help with the search? I'm not saying we will, in fact, the likelihood is remote, but I would like to have the option available. I've drafted up an agreement for you to sign, if you consent." I handed her the document. "Basically it says we can post photographs on Facebook, Twitter, and our website, but we won't post photographs of people. Your name, and the names of all parties, will remain anonymous."

Thankfully, Louisa didn't seem to find anything odd with the request. She read the document, signed it without comment, and got ready to leave. "I'm afraid I'm on the clock and can't stay, but I appreciate your attention to detail. Email me if you have any questions. That's probably the best way to reach me. I have a lot of travel scheduled over the next few weeks, but I tend to check my emails at least once a day, if not more."

"Will do." I hesitated for a moment, but I knew if I didn't ask now, I never would. "I've been admiring your earrings. They have a uniquely old-fashioned quality to them."

Louisa lifted her hand to her ear, smiling as her fingers made contact. "That's because they're really old. They belonged to my mother, used to be clip-on, but she had them converted for pierced ears a few years back. I've been wearing them quite a lot. My mother always said pearls had to be worn to stay alive."

"I've never heard that expression. Is there a matching necklace by any chance?"

"No. Just the earrings."

I felt an unreasonable crush of disappointment. "You're going to think this is an odd request, but is it possible to borrow those earrings for a short time? I promise to give them back to you as soon as I can."

"You want my earrings? How could that benefit the investigation?" Louisa studied me, her brown eyes curious. "Never mind, don't answer that, I don't need to know. I trust you. If you say you need the earrings, you need the earrings." She removed them quickly, handed them over, and slipped out the door. She was gone before I could say thank you.

The first thing I did was pull out the photo of Anneliese on her wedding day. Using a magnifying glass, I zeroed in on the earrings and compared them to the ones Louisa had given me. There was no way to be absolutely certain, but they looked like a match.

I'd have to go through the rest of the jewelry, but I believed we now had our object for Randi. I checked the time. Ten thirty. If I were lucky, Chantelle would still be home.

She had a half hour before she had to head to the gym. I gave her a quick update.

"You've got to go through the jewelry without me." I could hear the regret in her voice. "I've got my own Pilates and spin classes today. I have a two-hour break, and then I'm filling in for one of the other instructors who called in sick. Weights, not my strong suit, no pun intended, but they couldn't find anyone else at the last minute." She chuckled drily. "What does that say about me, I wonder?"

I steered her back on track. "Okay, I'll look at the contents of the jewelry box without you. What about the photos?"

"Can you leave the pix until tomorrow morning? I've got early classes, and I'll let the fitness manager know that I can't take any extra shifts. She'll get sulky if someone calls in sick again, but she'll get over it. I can be there by eleven." Chantelle's voice took on a pleading tone. "It's just that we work well together when it comes to photographs."

"I'll do my best to resist the temptation." Teasing her, but not really. It would take willpower not to slip in a sneak peek. It was like knowing there was butter pecan ice cream in the freezer or potato chips in the cupboard. You might not even crave those things, usually, but suddenly all you could think about was chips and ice cream.

Ice cream, potato chips, and pearls. I was going to dream about them tonight, guaranteed. In the meantime, I had a jewelry box to open. I removed the jeweler's loupe from my Detective Callie drawer, thankful that Arabella Carpenter had recommended it, and got to work.

⊕

THE JEWELRY BOX was a creamy shade of white vinyl with an embossed gold-leaf design that had worn off in several places, and a veneer of ingrained grime that could only have come from decades of use.

It was the sort of jewelry box that had been around since the 1940s and could still be found at your local department store for a few dollars; not what I'd been expecting. I had envisioned polished black lacquer with an intricate cloisonné inlay or something in burnished mahogany with brass trim. I hoped the interior was more promising than the exterior.

I opened the box and a tinny tune started to play. I hummed along with it, searching the recesses of my mind while I tried to identify the song. It took a few bars, but I finally recognized it: "Some Enchanted Evening" from the musical *South Pacific*. I stared at the turquoise velveteen interior. There was a green velvet ring box, and a rectangular leatherette case. The rest of the pieces, a half dozen in all, had been carefully stored inside colorful organza bags. I placed the contents onto the table, trying to decide where to start.

The organza bags won, not so much because I thought they'd be of the most interest, but because I liked to save the best for last, and the ring box held the most promise.

It didn't take long to realize that the organza bags were a bust. There was a silver necklace with a crystal pendant, pretty enough but clearly contemporary; a string of lapis lazuli which might have some value if the stones were genuine—unlikely based on the inexpensive clasp; four sterling silver bangles tarnished black from lack of polishing or use; and a bracelet with alternating silver-tone spacers, amber crystals, and glass beads in butterscotch swirl and chocolate brown. A tag inside the bag identified the bracelet as a CIRCLE OF HOPE bracelet for Golden Rescue, the association that fostered and adopted out golden retrievers in need.

The last two bags held a pair of crystal earrings to match the pendant, and a circle of jade on a leather string. Not a chance either would have been part of Anneliese's wardrobe.

I tackled the leatherette box next. Inside were eight brooches in various shapes and sizes. Three had been stamped AVON and another two SARAH COVENTRY. Based on the designs, I dismissed them as being too recent to be of interest, though I recalled a time when Sarah Coventry home jewelry parties were all the rage.

That left a stickpin with a red metal rose circa 1970s; a gold-tone wreath with garnet and aurora borealis stones, reminding me of a vintage brooch I'd seen at the Glass Dolphin antiques shop; and a round brooch, about an inch in diameter, layered with aquamarine and sapphire stones, gold-tone fleur-de-lis, and clear rhinestones surrounding a large central rhinestone.

I picked up my jeweler's loupe and studied the round brooch. The gold had discolored with dirt and age, and the stones had lost some of their luster, but it would have been lovely once, if not particularly valuable. I'm no expert on vintage jewelry, but this looked like something from the 1950s. The fleur-de-lis, a decidedly French symbol, interested me as well. I wondered if Anneliese had purchased this brooch in Quebec City as a souvenir of her trip.

I took out the photographs of Anneliese again, looking for evidence of the brooch, and found none. Nevertheless, I kept it aside.

That left the green velvet ring box. I opened it up and felt my breath catch in my throat. Because inside the box was a narrow yellow-gold wedding band with delicate filigree detailing. I went back to the photos of Anneliese playing with Sophie and, using the jeweler's loupe once again, brought her hands into closer focus.

There was no question about it. This filigreed wedding band had belonged to Anneliese. How three-year-old Sophie had come into possession of it was anyone's guess, but she had, along with the pearl drop earrings, and most likely, the fleur-de-lis brooch.

It was time to make an appointment with Randi.

23

———

By the time Chantelle arrived the next morning, I was ready to climb the walls. I'd barely managed not to look at the photos without her; only the thought of Chantelle's disappointment stopped me. I placed the wedding band and photos of Anneliese wearing it, the earrings, brooch, and jeweler's loupe on the table in front of her, and set about making tea. Outside of informing her that Louisa had been wearing the earrings, and the ring and brooch had been in the jewelry box, I stayed silent. It was important that Chantelle form her own conclusions.

She took her time, carefully studying each item in turn, and then going back again. "Did you make the appointment with Randi?"

I nodded. "I see her tomorrow morning." The breathy-voiced shopkeeper at Sun, Moon & Stars from last year had answered the phone. I'd been surprised, and a more than a little bit impressed, when she remembered me. Then I realized they'd have caller ID and felt embarrassed.

"Good. You should take all three of these. The ring, we know for sure that it belonged to Anneliese. The photographs prove it. Ditto for the earrings."

"What about the brooch?"

"It definitely has a vintage vibe, and the fleur-de-lis makes me think Anneliese might have purchased it as a souvenir in Quebec City."

"My thoughts exactly. Did you want to see the rest of the jewelry?"

"Do you mind?"

I pushed the box in front of her in answer and sipped my tea while she opened each organza bag, then the leatherette box. It took her less than ten minutes to come to the same conclusion that I had. There was nothing else in the jewelry box that would have belonged to Anneliese.

"When you see Randi, do you think you should take something that belonged to Sophie?"

"I'm allowed to bring up to three items to the session. I could take a few other things with me, in the event Randi relaxes the rule, but if she doesn't I think these are the most important."

"No argument here. Now, let's open that chocolate box."

I did as instructed, removing a manila envelope neatly labeled "Sophie 1961 to 1969." Inside was a small stack of photographs, which I placed in front of us. It saddened me to think that the years 1956 to 1961 had gone unrecorded, that no one had cared enough to take this little girl's picture from age three to seven, or if they had, to protect them from getting lost. I glanced at Chantelle and knew by the way her eyes glistened with tears that she was thinking much the same thing.

Sophie at age eight could be best described as a sturdy child. There were four photos. She was smiling broadly in three, and eating cotton candy in the fourth. There were rides in the background, a Ferris wheel and a roller coaster in one, and merry-go-round and a covered caterpillar in another. She wore stretchy pants and a patterned sweater that had a vaguely European look, and not in the Paris runway fashion sense. Her shoulder length hair was as dark and wavy as Horst's had been fair and straight. I looked for some sign that Horst Frankow was her biological father and found none.

She did, however, bear a striking resemblance to Anton

Osgoode, right down to the dimple in the middle of her chin. I bit my lip, craving my cocoa butter lip balm but resisting the urge. The lip balm was my tell and I didn't need Chantelle asking a bunch of questions right now, especially as my own memories continued to flood in.

"I recognize the caterpillar ride," I said. "It used to be at the Ex. My dad would bring me there every year. These pictures must have been taken there. In fact, I'm sure that's the Food Building in the background of this one."

The Ex, as Torontonians affectionately referred to it, was the Canadian National Exhibition. It ran from mid-August to Labor Day, and had been going strong since the nineteenth century, though admittedly it was a bit long in the tooth these days. But back in 1961, it would have been in its heyday. Besides the amusement park rides and games, I remembered the CNE Bandshell, where up-and-coming or going-going-soon-to-be-gone-and-forgotten musical acts performed. There was also the International Pavilion, which had seemed so exotic with its bonsai trees from Japan, lavender sachets purportedly from France, and the colorful Russian nesting dolls that had charmed and fascinated me. But by far my favorite was the Food Building with its tiny powdered sugar donuts and samples of everything from pancakes to pasta.

"My first time at the CNE was a few years ago when I moved to Marketville with Lance the Loser," Chantelle said. "I remember the hustler at the entrance gates, that guy who sold invisible dogs in a plastic harness on a leash, and the way he called out: 'Doggie, doggie, who wants a doggie?' But I don't recall seeing a caterpillar ride."

"It was in the kid's section of the amusement park, probably deemed unsafe sometime in the last couple of decades. The ride was a string of cars that wound around an undulating track. As it gained momentum, this canopy would come over each of the cars so it resembled a caterpillar. The darkness inside scared me the first time I went on it, but it got old pretty fast."

"If Sophie was at the CNE, in all likelihood her foster parents at the time lived in the Toronto area," Chantelle said. "I also think these were taken by a new pair of foster parents. Otherwise, why wouldn't they have taken photos before this?"

"Someone could have taken her for the day. A friend of the family, maybe."

"I suppose it's possible. Whatever the scenario, we're no further ahead since we don't have any idea who took the pictures."

Maybe we weren't any further ahead, but for the first time since we'd started this investigation I felt a connection to Sophie. Nostalgia can do that to you.

⊕

THE TWO PHOTOGRAPHS of Sophie were labeled "Christmas 1961" on the back. There was the obligatory one on Santa's knee, Sophie looking embarrassed. My guess was that by age eight she had stopped believing—if she'd even kept believing after Anneliese's death. I felt a rush of empathy for this black-eyed girl. How many homes had she lived in by the time this picture was taken?

The other photo had been taken of Sophie standing in front of a Christmas tree, a wide smile on her face. The tree had been decorated with an assortment of mismatched glass ornaments, homemade paper streamers, and tinsel. I smiled, remembering my own elementary school efforts as I carefully cut red and green construction paper into strips, taping each one into circles and linking them together. A silver star, made from aluminum foil by the looks of it, topped the tree.

"It reminds me of the tree my dad and I would decorate when I was growing up, right down to the aluminum foil star and the mismatched ornaments," I said.

Chantelle laughed. "Six kids at Christmas, you should have seen our tree. There were popcorn strings and ornaments made out of cotton wool and scraps of felt and whatever else we made in school. My folks didn't have a ton of money, but we each got one present from mom and dad, and one from Santa, plus our stockings. The gift from our parents was always something sensible like pajamas or slippers. Santa brought the toys and dolls, and the stockings usually held socks, underwear, gum, and our favorite candy. There was always one present for the whole family to share. Those thousand-piece jigsaw puzzles were our favorite. My dad would set them up on a card table in the games room in our basement and we'd all take our turn putting them together."

"You had a games room?"

"Yeah. Ping pong table, pool table, jigsaw puzzle table, one of those hockey games with the metal hockey players, dollhouses, you name it. There were storage crates for each type of toy, and there was hell to pay if we didn't clean up when we were finished playing. It was organized chaos in that room, especially when we were all down there playing with our friends. I sometimes wonder how my parents stood the noise."

Growing up as an only child with a single father, I couldn't begin to imagine the noise, or the crowded games room. I wondered what it would have been like, but I didn't feel a sense of envy. I had treasured our quiet Christmases, one of the few days when my father wasn't working on a job site, and I always got a good stash of books to keep me busy and out of trouble for when he was. Dolls and other toys had never interested me much.

"I wish there was someone else in the picture," Chantelle said, interrupting my thoughts. "Something to give us a clue."

I nodded, but my attention was already on the next picture, a five-by-seven photograph of Sophie in white leather go-go boots and a lime green mini dress with an ivory lace Peter Pan collar. She'd grown several inches taller, and her dark, wavy hair, parted in the center, now reached halfway down her back. I flipped it over to see if anything had been written on the back. There wasn't. "How old are we when we finish grade eight?"

"Thirteen?"

"That's what I thought. I think this is her graduation photo from the eighth grade. Which means we have another five-year gap."

"The boots are cute, but what a ghastly dress," Chantelle said. "The nineteen sixties at its most hideous."

I'm not sure if anyone looks good in lime green, and the color did nothing for Sophie's sallow complexion. She was right about the boots, though. They were cute.

"If it is from her graduation, it's the only one. My guess is the school arranged to take pictures of every student. Unfortunately, there's nothing to tell us who the photographer was, let alone where the school was."

"The school would have been nice, but as for the photographer, I don't think it would matter. The odds of them still being in business would be remote and they would have taken thousands of student photographs over the years. What else have we got? And don't tell me another five-year gap."

"Your wish is my command," I said, flipping to a photo of a large group of teenagers in front of the Horseshoe Falls in Niagara Falls, the *Maid of the Mist* cruising the Niagara River in the background. The kids were smiling in the way you did when you were instructed to say "Cheese." It took me a few moments to pick out Sophie.

"Has to be her grade eight school trip," I said. "Niagara Falls was the typical end-of-year road trip at my school. We started with the Skylon Observation Tower, all of us feeling smug that the Horseshoe Falls on the Canadian side was prettier than the American Falls. Then onto Ripley's Believe It or Not!, Louis Tussaud's Waxworks, and the floral clock. I never did get to ride on the *Maid of the Mist*."

"Why not?"

I shrugged. "Logistics? It was owned by an American company, which meant it left from the US side of the Falls. Imagine getting thirty kids and three teachers across the Rainbow Bridge just to do a short boat tour."

"Still, a school trip to Niagara Falls sounds good to me. We never did anything like that at my school in Ottawa."

"Really?"

"Not that I remember. The first time I visited Niagara Falls I was on my honeymoon with Lance the Loser." Chantelle's voice cracked a little. Although Chantelle would never admit it, I knew she still harbored feelings for him. Or maybe it was because she'd lost and was used to winning. Either way, she was still hurting.

I pushed the photograph toward her and handed her a magnifying glass. "Do you recognize anyone? Besides Sophie?" I didn't tell her I'd already tried and failed.

She frowned in concentration, moving the magnifying glass from face to face. After a few minutes she looked up and shook her head. "No luck, but I could scan it and try to enlarge it on screen."

"Go for it. I'm not holding out a lot of hope, but it can't hurt."

Chantelle got to work on scanning the photo, emailing a copy of it to both of us for later viewing. In the meantime, I laid five strips of small black and white photos on the table, four poses to a strip.

"These were taken inside one of those shopping mall photo booths," I said. "Sophie looks more mature than she did in her grad picture. What do you think? Grade nine summer? That would make her fourteen."

Chantelle slid back into her chair, the scanning complete. "Hmmm." Chantelle studied the photos. "I wonder who the guy hamming it up next to her is? Looks like he's in his late teens, too old to be a boyfriend and too young to be a guardian. Maybe a friend of her foster family?"

The boy was mugging it up for the camera, sticking his tongue out and crossing his eyes while Sophie attempted to mimic him, her smile of happiness infectious. I felt my throat constrict in recognition. It had been fifty years since these were taken, but there wasn't a doubt in my mind. The young man in the pictures was Corbin Osgoode.

My grandfather.

24

———

So Corbin knew Sophie Frankow when she was a girl, and possibly later as an adult. It went a long way toward explaining his insistence that I stop communicating with Olivia. His mother knew about Sophie's existence as a three-year-old child. Olivia may have kept track of her, or found her later in life. Certainly the Osgoodes would have had financial resources to do either. The last thing Corbin wanted was for me to learn about his illegitimate half-sister.

I wondered if Chantelle had made the connection, then realized there was no reason she would. She'd never met my grandfather. The only photograph of Corbin she'd seen had been alongside a thirty-year-old article in the *Toronto Star*.

Once again, I knew I should tell Chantelle what I'd learned from Olivia. And once again, I didn't. All I knew was that I was going to have copies made of the filmstrips. Whether I confronted Corbin with it, or managed to see Olivia one more time and show it to her, remained to be seen.

"There's only one photo left from this batch."

Sophie was blowing out candles on a white-and-pink frosted birthday cake, her wavy hair now reaching her waist. I counted the candles: sixteen. "She was born on March twenty-third. They probably let her stay in the system until after she graduated from the tenth grade in June."

"At least someone threw her a party," Chantelle said, "though I can't imagine being turned out to fend for yourself at sixteen with nothing more than a grade ten education."

There wasn't anything to say to that, so I slid all the photographs back in the manila envelope. "Ready to tackle the rest of the chocolate box?"

"Bring it on."

It contained a mixture of loose photographs, greeting cards, and a thin letter-sized envelope. I sorted the pictures and cards into two piles, setting aside the envelope. "Photos or greeting cards first?"

"Let's stick with photos."

It became quickly apparent that all the photos were of Louisa. Each one had been dated on the back, along with the occasion, Sophie's handwriting small and cramped.

Money may have been scarce, but as with most first-time mothers, every early event had been recorded for posterity. "Louisa's First Christmas, 1982," "Louisa's First Easter, 1983," "Louisa's First Canada Day," and finally, "Louisa's First Birthday." There were a handful of Louisa crawling and walking with the aid of a coffee table, and then without. They were duly labeled "Louisa Learning to Crawl" and "Louisa Learns to Walk." Louisa's resemblance to Anneliese was evident from the beginning.

The photos thinned out after the first birthday, though the annual Christmas and birthday photos continued. With the exception of a couple of girls, the kids in the photos changed as Louisa grew up and made new friends, but the homemade birthday cake remained the same: chocolate with pink icing, a number candle in the center. The photos stopped after her graduation in grade eight, leaving a significant gap until the last photo, her grade twelve graduation and prom in 2000.

"It could be Anneliese in that prom photo," Chantelle said. "That peacock blue really suits her coloring. She looks beautiful."

She did indeed. The dress was sleeveless with a fitted, sequined bodice and a floor-length taffeta skirt. Her blonde hair had been swept into an updo, with loose tendrils softly framing her face. She was wearing the pearl drop earrings.

"I wonder how many special occasions Anneliese's earrings have seen. If they could only talk."

"Maybe the greeting cards will do some talking," Chantelle said.

It was wishful thinking. As with the photographs, all the birthday cards were to Louisa. There was one for every year from age one to eighteen, all signed, "With all my love, Mom."

"She must have moved out after grade twelve to attend university or college."

"We can ask Louisa, but I can't see where it matters to our investigation."

Chantelle had a point, but it was her defeated tone that had me worried. Was she losing faith? Her usually perfect posture had given way to slumped shoulders. I knew from investigating my mother's disappearance that for every positive lead there were a dozen that went nowhere. But she was new to this.

"You're probably right. Anyway, we're down to this single white envelope." I twirled my fingers and hands like a magician, chanting abracadabra. Chantelle rolled her eyes, but at least I had her laughing. I opened the envelope and took out a newspaper clipping, laying it down on the table.

For a moment we sat transfixed, the silence between us palpable as we read, then reread, what was before us.

It was a clipping from an obituary in the *Toronto Star* dated April 19, 1987.

Anton Arthur OSGOODE: 1922-1987

Passed away in Toronto with his family by his side on April 18, 1987, at age 66, following a brief battle with lung cancer. Anton will be deeply missed by his beloved wife, Olivia (née Rosemount), his son, Corbin, and his daughter-in-law, Yvette.

Anton was especially proud of his lengthy career at Eaton's Department Store, where he started as a sales clerk, and worked his way up to Head Buyer, Glass and China. He was a loyal employee and was valued until his retirement in 1986. Anton's buying trips frequently took him to England, Ireland, and beyond. He loved to talk about his shipboard adventures before air travel became the standard.

The rest of the obituary included details of when and where the service would be held in Toronto. There was a photo of Anton, clearly taken before he'd been sick. I was struck by how much Corbin resembled him, especially around the nose and eyes.

But that's not what had captured our attention. It was what Sophie had written at the top of the obituary.

"Uncle Toni."

25

As soon as I read the words "Uncle Toni" I knew that I would have to find a way to visit Olivia again, Corbin be damned.

"It would appear that Anton Osgoode remained involved in Sophie's life," Chantelle said.

I nodded. "The question is, how involved?"

"Involved enough to refer to him as Uncle and keep his obituary. Maybe you can find out from your great-grandmother the next time you pay her a visit."

"Yeah, about that. I've been removed from the approved visitor's list by my grandfather." I filled Chantelle in on Corbin's phone call. "I thought he did it because he was hiding something. Now I'm doubly sure of it."

"Doubly sure? What haven't you told me?"

"It's just an expression." I pulled out my cocoa butter lip balm.

"We're partners. We have to be honest with one another if this business is going to be successful."

I knew she was right, and I was willing to tell her about Corbin being the boy in the photo booth strip, but I still wasn't ready to share the possibility that Anton Osgoode had killed Anneliese. Then it hit me.

"Horst Frankow died in prison."

"Uh, yeah, we knew that," Chantelle said. "Nice stall tactic, but it won't fly."

"I'm not trying to stall. Follow along with me. You're a foster kid, and the only thing you have from your past is a small suitcase with some photos and documents that belonged to your mother. Sophie would have gone through them over and over again, looking for clues. She would have assumed, based on the marriage certificate, that her father was Horst Frankow. I can't believe that no one told her about Horst when she was growing up. Surely the foster care adults would have known."

"We're talking about another time. Things were different then, not so liberated. Given the circumstances, it could have been a confidential placement. At the very least, the foster parents would have been sworn to secrecy. That being said, I have to agree with you. It stands to reason that at some point Sophie would have tried to find him. Maybe not until she was out of the system, maybe not even until she was adult, but she must have tried."

"And when she tried, she learned that he was the bad man who murdered her mother."

"That's my read on it."

"Do you think Louisa knows?"

"No, or she would have said something, don't you think? My guess is Sophie took that secret to her grave. But we're going to have to tell Louisa when we file our final report."

"You don't think she'd want to know about this before then?"

"Louisa prefers a single, final report, versus ongoing updates. Besides, we might find information to the contrary."

"Aha. Information to the contrary. Are we coming to the doubly sure part yet?"

"Let's just say that there's something that I need to follow up. I promise to tell you what I've learned as soon as I have, whatever the outcome, but it's something I have to do on my own. I hope you'll be okay with that."

Chantelle leaned back, her gray eyes appraising me. I'm not

sure what she was looking for, but I must have passed the test. "I can wait."

I wanted to hug her. "Thank you."

"Is that it? Because something tells me there's more."

I'm always amazed by how easily Chantelle can read me. Most of the time, I'm grateful, especially when it works in my favor. Right about now, I wish I could be a little less transparent.

"It's about the boy in the photo booth filmstrip. I recognized him."

"You did? Who is he? How do you know him? He'd have to be in his late fifties by now."

"Sixty-two, actually, and last time we spoke, he warned me off this investigation."

"Are you saying what I think you're saying? That the boy in the photo is your grandfather?"

I nodded. "The one and only Corbin Osgoode."

"Then you have to confront him and make him tell you what he knows."

"You don't know my grandfather. Confrontation won't work. He'll just shut me out." *The way he shut my mother out when she told him she was pregnant at seventeen.* "I need to come up with a different strategy."

"What sort of different strategy?"

"Honestly? I don't know. I still believe Olivia holds the key. There has to be some way to see her again."

"I could try. Corbin has forbidden you to see Olivia, but that came from him, not her."

"She did seem to enjoy my visits." I thought about it for a moment. "It could work. I told her you were the one who sparked my interest in genealogy, and that I was working on my family tree. So it wouldn't seem completely out of place if you went there on my behalf. The only question is, should you take the photo strip with Sophie and Corbin with you?"

"I can bring it to show her as a last resort, but I think it would seem less invasive if I can just get her talking. How to get her talking will be the challenge."

"What about your genealogy research on Horst and Anneliese? You could tell her that I became fascinated with their family tree once I realized that Sophie was a relative, and that you agreed to help me."

"That's a good angle, but I've hit a brick wall on both. Entering their names in the database didn't generate a single lead."

"Is that typical?"

"No, but then again, this search is atypical. Usually there's more information. A record of parents and siblings, for example, and where and when they were born. The names of the siblings, siblings' spouses, and so on, with each name adding another rung in the ladder. The only information we have on Horst is his first and last name. There wasn't even a middle name on the marriage certificate. We don't know when he immigrated to Canada, or from where. I can check UK departure manifests, but there are a lot of them, and I have no idea where to start. We can assume he met Anneliese in Nottingham, but that's a big assumption and doesn't get us far. I'm not even sure it's important."

"Speaking of the UK departure manifest, did you find Anneliese's name on the T.S.S. *Canberra?*

"Bad news there. There are plenty of departure manifests on record, but not that particular one." Chantelle gave a rueful smile. "It could be worse. At least we have the autograph page. The manifest would have listed every single passenger, but honestly, what could we have done with the information?"

What indeed? I didn't know, but it would have been nice to find out. I noted the glum look on Chantelle's face and attempted to cheer her up. "At least we know the basics from Anneliese's passport: her date of birth, that she was born in Stettin, Germany. And of course, we know the date of her death. That should help you find out more."

Chantelle sighed. "Except Stettin is now Szczecin, Poland. In 1945 the Nazis issued an evacuation order, and most of the city's German population fled, likely with not much more than the clothes on their backs, their records destroyed or, possibly, buried deep inside a church basement somewhere in Europe. If Anneliese had any relatives, dead or alive, they aren't listed in the Ancestry database. What can I say? Genealogy is a wonderful thing, but it's not magic."

The results were disappointing, but not entirely unexpected. It stood to reason that if Anneliese or Horst had any living relatives, someone would have come forward for Sophie, or there would have been some evidence of it in Anneliese's train case, a photograph or a letter, something.

"It's okay. You can still use that as your cover story when you visit Olivia. Be honest and tell her you couldn't find anything, but play up my disappointment. Tell her I'm trying to find out all I can about Sophie. Which is true."

"I'll go tomorrow. Let's just hope she's willing to see me."

"If she doesn't, we'll have to go with Plan B."

"And that would be?"

"Confronting Corbin without confrontation? And before you ask me how I plan to do that, let me answer. I have no idea."

"Maybe Randi will have the answer," Chantelle said, laughing.

I laughed along with her. "Or Misty. I'll call her up and ask for a tarot card reading, maybe we'll hold a séance in the living room."

Chantelle was still chuckling when she left.

26
***

I fussed over the objects I planned to take to Randi. Anneliese, Sophie, and Louisa had all worn the pearl earrings. Would that complicate things? I had the fleur-de-lis brooch and her wedding ring. Maybe that would be enough.

After an absurd amount of deliberation, I stuck with my original decision to take all three. I'd gone from a complete skeptic to a hopeful cynic who should do some reading up on psychometry. A Google search came up with multiple links. After a quick scan, I found one that explained the concept more thoroughly than Chantelle.

> Psychometry is based on the theory that the human mind radiates an aura in all directions, which impresses everything within its orbit. Since all objects are porous, the minute holes in the object's surface collect fragments of the mental aura of the person who possessed the object. If an object has been passed on down the family, it will contain information about its previous owners.

That sounded promising, but I wasn't quite ready to take off my cynic's cloak. I searched for scientific evidence, psychometry and was rewarded for my efforts.

There is no scientific evidence that psychometry exists. Skeptics explain alleged successes of psychometry by cold reading and confirmation bias.

Cold reading is a technique used by mentalists, psychics, fortunetellers, mediums, and illusionists. A practiced cold reader can quickly obtain a great deal of information by analyzing the person's body language, age, clothing, hairstyle, race or ethnicity, manner of speech, etc., all without any prior knowledge.

Randi was one step ahead of me there. She had plenty of prior knowledge of me, and trying to change my hair, speech, or clothing wasn't going to make a difference. At least this time it wasn't about me, or a family member.

Cold readings typically employ high-probability guesses, quickly picking up on signals as to whether their guesses are in the right direction or not, then emphasizing and reinforcing chance connections and quickly moving on from missed guesses.

Before starting the actual reading, the reader will try to elicit cooperation from the subject. They may say something along the lines of, "I may see images that are a bit unclear which might mean more to you than to me. If you help, it may uncover more than if you do not."

I laughed out loud. Did people really fall for that? I kept reading.

Once assured of the subject's cooperation, the reader will make a number of probing statements or questions and assess their replies, both verbal and nonverbal. Subtle cues, such as changes in facial expression or body language, can determine whether a particular line of questioning is effective. Promising avenues of inquiry are pursued, and unproductive ones quickly abandoned.

The reader will continue to refine and restate facts shared by the subject, reinforcing the reader's alleged psychic ability.

I would have to be on my guard when it came to a cold reading, although I'd never been great at maintaining a poker face. I googled, "How do psychics use confirmation bias?" and found what I was looking for.

Confirmation bias is one reason why a psychic may only average one accurate hit for every dozen guesses, yet will be described as "totally accurate" by the client after the reading. People place a lot more importance on confirmatory evidence than on contradictory evidence.

Using cold reading techniques, the psychic will make several ambiguous statements. The subject will selectively, though unconsciously, remember those statements made by the psychic that apply to their lives versus those that don't. For example, a psychic will give a very general description about a relative and their relationship with the subject, saying something like, "Why do I sense this distance?" The subject's response might be that their father lived on the other side of the country, or it might be that their father was detached, the kind of man who didn't like to show love for the family. Either way, the psychic has new information to use later, along with other "revelations."

Forewarned was forearmed. Maybe there was something to psychometry, and maybe there wasn't. I would see Randi tomorrow as promised, but with a healthy dose of common sense and skepticism.

⚲

I KNEW I should start on the newspaper research, but memories of the hours spent at the Cedar County Reference Library looking for clues in my mother's disappearance had been tedious work. I'd spent hours staring into a microfiche reader, and I'd had Shirley there to help me.

At least this search would be online in the comfort of my home office, but I suspected it would be every bit as tedious. A big part of me also worried that I would find out things about Anneliese or Anton better left in the past. I knew I was procrastinating, but I decided to check our Facebook page before I tackled the archives.

There were three new page Likes, several post Likes, and a couple of Shares. The pearl necklace in particular seemed to have struck a chord. One comment suggested that the three strands represented the past, present, and future. *Almost certainly a wedding gift from groom to bride, no tears intended.* It didn't advance our investigation, but I loved the concept, and small details such as this, included in my report to Louisa, would demonstrate an attention to detail.

The first thing I did was open the photo of Sophie and her classmates in Niagara Falls that Chantelle had scanned. Enlarged, the faces were grainy but distinguishable. I studied each face carefully, looking for anything or anyone that might stand out. Nothing did.

Disappointed, I shifted my attention back to our website.

Misty had posted another message, this time with a photo of the Seven of Cups. The card depicted the silhouette figure of a man, his back to the reader. He appeared to be mesmerized by the seven golden cups floating on a cumulus cloud in front of him. Each cup contained a different object. In the top row there was a beautiful blue head unattached to a body, a veiled figure reaching outwards, creating a mysterious mushroom-shaped ghost-like persona, and a snake coiling its way out of the cup. In the bottom row there was a blue castle, overflowing jewel-like treasures, a laurel wreath with a skull drawn in the cup beneath it, and a blue dragon.

Seven of Cups (Element: Water)

The suit of cups represents emotions. There are many theories on what the contents of each cup represents. Some believe they represent temptation. Others believe these objects are nothing more than illusions. My belief is that they represent the many choices an individual can make, although each path will offer some challenge and possible risk. For example, the castle is without windows, the head is without a body, while the cup beneath the laurel wreath has a skull drawn into it. At what cost was the win for the victor?

MISTY'S MESSAGE: There is a difference between contemplation and procrastination. Have you been deliberating on a course of action or have you been avoiding it? There are many different paths you can choose, each with its own set of consequences. The important thing is to take action so that you may learn from it and move forward.

Damn, it was as if Misty was speaking directly to me and my foot dragging on the archives search. The skeptic in me knew the answer: if the message hadn't concerned me I would pass it by. And if her message resonated with me, it would also resonate with others. I shared each of her posts on our Facebook page, scheduling them two days apart in the hopes of creating some buzz. That done, I tweeted the latest one out on Twitter with a photo and a #tarot, and set up a Pinterest *Misty's Messages* board under the Past & Present Investigations account, creating a pin for each post.

I emailed Misty, cc to Chantelle, letting them know what I'd done, and asked Misty to update Pinterest, Facebook, and Twitter whenever she wrote a new message, and encouraged her to create an Instagram account. I tried to convince myself that I wasn't procrastinating, that I was setting things in motion so that I wouldn't get sidetracked the next time Misty posted a message, but I knew she was right. It was time to take action and move forward.

IT STARTED OUT WELL. I entered "Historical Newspapers" in the search string for the Toronto Public Library and found links for the *Toronto Star* and the *Globe and Mail.*

I clicked on the tutorial on the *Toronto Star* archives page. It gave a detailed example on Hurricane Hazel in 1954. Encouraged by the ease of the search process, I hit the Access Online button, only to find out that I needed a library card to access the archives. It would be free if I lived, worked, or owned property in Toronto, but otherwise the most economical option was a thirty dollar charge for a three month period. I was ready to whip out my credit card when I read the fine print. I had to apply for the card in person with proper identification. True, I could apply at any branch, but the closest branch was still an hour's drive away. I started an online chat with a library representative, hoping that the rules could be bent, if not broken. The suggestion was met with a firm no. I could imagine the stony-eyed stare on the other end and signed off with a polite thank you, cursing under my breath.

Did I know someone with a library card? Chantelle? Royce? Misty? I made a note to myself to ask.

I tried going directly to the *Globe and Mail* and *Toronto Star* websites next. I struck out with the *Globe*—all roads led me back to the Toronto Public Library—but I found an archives list for the *Star*. I entered in "Anneliese" in the Search box, along with a date range of March 23 to June 1, 1956, knowing that I could always broaden or narrow the search. There were several pages available. I clicked on the first one, hoping for a PDF but getting a list of payment options from one week to three months. I considered it, but the format wasn't nearly as user friendly as the library's page.

Frustrated, I looked for other alternatives, and stumbled upon a site that created the records for libraries, colleges, and other institutions. The Historical Newspapers section was lengthy, with several US, Canadian, and international publications. I clicked on the link to the *Star* and was taken to a page describing the paper, and the archives available. There was even an offer of a free trial if I contacted the Sales department. I called, only to be told that all the sales representatives were busy, but that the next available representative would be with me shortly.

I hung up after a twenty-minute wait on hold and decided to call it a day. Tomorrow was my visit with Randi, which left a drive to Toronto on Saturday. At least the traffic would be lighter. I just had to get home in time to get ready for my dinner with Royce. It meant an early start to get in my Saturday run, but unless I wanted to go back to the Cedar County Reference Library and delve through pages and pages of microfilm, I didn't see any other option.

Procrastination One, Archives Zero.

27

———————

Sun, Moon & Stars was tucked at the back of Nature's Way Whole & Organic Foods, an expansive store that capitalized on all things organic, including a dizzying array of baked goods—many made with grains I'd never even heard of—as well as a plentitude of gluten-free products. There was also a massive section devoted entirely to the vegan lifestyle. If you couldn't find something to eat at Nature's Way, you were too picky to live.

On the opposite end of the sprawling spectrum you had Sun, Moon & Stars, a minute retail space packed with a treasure trove of trinkets, textiles, natural stone jewelry, healing crystals, books on the occult, and flowing cotton garments with tie-dyed patterns, shiny beads, and silk embroidery. A hand-painted ceramic incense holder in the shape of a lotus flower held a stick of sandalwood incense.

The shopkeeper fluttered toward me, a flurry of multi-colored silk scarves swirling around her. She smiled in greeting, waving a slender hand adorned with silver rings on every finger. "Callie, so good to see you again. Did the smudging do the trick?"

On my previous visit, Randi had encouraged me to smudge the Snapdragon house with white sage to cleanse it of negative energy. I'd felt ridiculous chanting "I am removing all negative energy and replacing it with positive energy," while waving the smoldering sage stick in the air as I wandered from room to room. But at the time I would have tried just about anything, and I suppose things were no different now. I was here to see Randi with three objects in my handbag, hoping for answers I didn't expect to find, and wondering if I should be smudging the Edward Street house.

"I believe it did. I can't imagine how you remembered after all this time."

She laughed, a breathy sound that matched her voice, and fluttered her scarves. "We don't get many skeptics in here. The merely curious and the true believers, certainly, but outright skeptics are a rarity. I'll let Randi know you're here."

I was thumbing through a book on tarot when Randi drifted into the room, her long, dark hair falling in loose waves down to her waist. There are few people in this world who radiate kindness, beauty, and charisma. Randi, with her cinnamon-colored skin and eyes the color of lapis lazuli, was the personification of all three. She could have bottled and sold her essence like some sort of magic potion. I felt the first layer of my skepticism dissolve and cursed myself for it.

When I'd been here last, Randi's space had been painted floor-to-ceiling in an inky midnight blue. The walls had since been repainted in a deep shade of lavender, the ceiling a complementary shade of milky mauve. A myriad of tiny pot lights twinkled like stars overhead, casting a soft glow over the room. A gigantic candle in a tall wrought iron stand burned softly in one corner, the scent a soothing lilac vanilla. The only furnishings were a black lacquer rectangular desk and two chairs upholstered in a dark navy needlepoint fabric. There was a sun embroidered on the back of one, and the four phases of the moon on the back of the other. Randi sat cross-legged on the chair with the sun, her feet tucked underneath her, and gestured to the other. Several colorful bangles jangled on her right arm.

"Welcome back, Callie," Randi said. "Did you find everything you were looking for on your search for your mother?" Her voice had a soft, musical lilt to it, with the faintest trace of a British accent.

"Let's just say some secrets might have been better left buried under whatever rock they'd been hiding under, but thank you for asking."

"No one's past is without blemish, although some are more acne scarred than others. It is inevitable when we delve into the past that we discover things we would have rather not known. That is the price we pay to learn the truth. In the end, the truth, in all of its incarnations, is all we really have."

Was I here expecting some version of the truth, or because Chantelle had coerced me into coming? What about Randi? Was she going to tell the truth, or create a fictional scenario based on cold readings and confirmation bias? I was mulling over the possibilities when Randi spoke again.

"Am I to assume you are here for another journey into the past?"

When I made the appointment, I had forgotten that I'd advertised the Grand Opening of Past & Present Investigations in the *Marketville Post*, including my name and email information as the main contact. How much did Randi know? Had she been to the website? Our Facebook page? Maybe yes, maybe no, but it was better to be upfront and tell her. If it was all out in the open, she couldn't use it as one of her revelation techniques.

"I've started a business with a friend, Past & Present Investigations." I updated her on the basic premise, leaving out the details of the Frankow case. Those had to remain confidential, and not just out of respect for the client. If I was to trust anything Randi told me, I had to know she was doing so without a lot of backstory.

Randi clapped her hands, her bracelets tinkling like wind chimes. "Congratulations. It's wonderful how you have taken something painful and transformed it into a new path in life. That shows great strength of character."

A new path in life. Had Randi read Misty's latest message about the Seven of Cups? Or was I reading too much into what might only be a simple choice of words?

"I'm not sure how strong my character is, but I will say it's been tested on more than one occasion. I'm here today with three objects. Each one is part of a current investigation. I'm afraid I can't share the details with you."

"Nor would I want you to. Such information would cloud my vision, rendering it unreliable." Randi smiled, revealing a row of perfectly straight pearl-white teeth. "I'm sure you've been online researching psychometry, which is the official term for object reading. Unfortunately there are plenty of charlatans out there, and it is those individuals who give the legitimate practitioner a bad reputation. I assure you that I don't rely on cold reading or confirmation bias. Some objects speak to me, and some do not, regardless of their history. Armed with that knowledge, are you prepared to go ahead with an open mind?"

I nodded, feeling somewhat reassured if not altogether convinced.

"Very well. Let's see what you have brought for me today."

I decided to start with the brooch. If I was correct in my assumption that Anneliese had purchased it in Quebec City, it was the oldest of the three items. I took it out of the organza bag and handed it over to Randi.

She rested the brooch on a tiny black velvet pillow and bent over to study it from all angles, using a pencil-length LED flashlight and a jeweler's loupe. After several minutes, she straightened.

"The fleur-de-lis suggests a French connection, but I would say this was purchased in Quebec, not France. The styling is not European, and the quality, while a step above what one might have found in Woolworth's Department Store, is far from haute couture. The stones are rhinestones, not precious gems, but then I suspect you knew that already, especially since the gold finish has tarnished. Silver tarnishes, but gold does not. As for a timeline, I would place this brooch as being made in the early-to-mid 1950s. There are no maker's marks, but that in itself isn't unusual for the time period."

So far Randi wasn't telling me anything I hadn't figured out on my own. I tried to hide my disappointment. I must have failed, because Randi addressed it head on.

"Have faith, my skeptical friend. The first thing I do with an object is to analyze it in a clinical manner. Only once I have done that can I connect to it spiritually. It is this combination that allows me to speculate on the meaning of each object, and its relationship to the owner."

She picked up the brooch, closed her eyes, and placed her clenched right fist on the left side of her chest, over her heart. I wasn't sure whether to laugh or cry and instead did neither, silently watching Randi's theatrical performance. Because I was sure it was a performance, staged for my benefit so that I wouldn't feel ripped off when I paid her at the end of my visit.

Randi opened her eyes and rested the brooch back on the black velvet case. "This brooch was almost certainly a gift from a lover to a woman met on a ship. It may seem fanciful to you, but I believe the aquamarine stones represent the ocean, the sapphire blue the night sky, and the clear rhinestones the stars. From my clinical observation, I would suggest it was purchased in Quebec City or Montreal."

Not a souvenir but a gift from a lover. I hadn't thought of that. Had Anton Osgoode given the brooch to Anneliese as a memento of their affair? It was a possible explanation, and one the romantic side of me preferred. The cynic in me remained uncertain. If Randi had visited our Facebook page, she would have seen my post looking for ephemera related to the T.S.S. *Canberra*. I'd even done her the favor of listing the departure date from Southampton and the arrival date in Quebec City, adding that the woman was a German immigrant. My posts asking for information on rail travel would have filled in more blanks. Add the brooch into the mix and a good storyteller could create an entire world.

At least I hadn't posted anything about Anton Osgoode. "Can you tell me anything about the lovers?"

"Let me look at each item of jewelry first. Perhaps then I can draw some additional conclusions. I make no such promises. As I said before, not all objects speak to me, no matter their history."

It was an honest answer, albeit one that conveniently skirted the question. I handed over the pearl drop earrings and watched in silence as Randi went through her ritual, first studying the earrings from all angles, and then holding them against her heart. I wasn't sure if I was amused or entranced by her performance.

"These earrings almost certainly started life as clip-ons," Randi began. "I believe the transformation to pierced was done long after the original owner passed them along, possibly to a daughter." Her brow creased into a frown. "Maybe a granddaughter. It's confusing. I'm getting mixed messages. They were almost certainly intended as a wedding gift. Is there a matching necklace?"

Once again, I thought about our Facebook page and the photo I'd posted of the pearl necklace. Despite trying to keep an open mind, I was becoming increasingly suspicious. "There was a matching pearl necklace. Three strands. The owner wore them at her wedding."

"Did you bring the necklace with you?"

"I don't have it. I have only seen her wearing it in a photograph."

"Did you bring the photograph with you?"

"I was told to bring no more than three objects."

"A rules follower. I never would have guessed it," Randi said with a smile. "Actually, a photo would have been acceptable, possibly desirable, but you can always return with it, should either one of us deem it necessary. You said there were three strands of pearls?"

"Yes. I thought the three strands might be symbolic of the past, present, and future." No need to mention I'd gotten the idea from a Facebook follower. Then again, if she'd been to our Facebook page, she would have known that.

"That's very astute of you. I was going to suggest the same thing." The frown returned. "I believe these earrings have been worn during times of great joy and greater despair, possibly even danger."

If Randi thought I'd start sharing what I knew, she had another thing coming. There would be no cold readings coming off this woman. I handed her the wedding band. "Perhaps this will help you."

I was expecting a repeat of the black velvet pillow routine. Instead I watched, openmouthed, as Randi dropped the ring, grabbed the back of her head, and then doubled over, clutching her stomach in pain.

"Are you okay?"

Randi stared at me, tears welling in her deep blue eyes. "The woman who wore this ring was murdered in cold blood. I believe she was hit on the back of her head with a heavy object."

She picked up the ring and closed her eyes for a moment, her breathing ragged. "She knew her killer. It was someone she loved… no, maybe not loved, but definitely someone she trusted." She opened her eyes, her stare accusatory. "You knew, didn't you?"

"Yes, I knew. I'm sorry. I didn't realize it would be painful for you. I'm trying to find out the truth about her killer. There is some doubt in my mind that the person incarcerated for it was responsible."

"Remember what I told you earlier. In the end, the truth is all we have. Please bring me anything you have that belonged to this woman, anything at all. I will do this without any cost to you or your client. The woman who owned this ring deserves justice."

I wasn't willing to share anything with Anneliese's name on it, such as her passport, immigration paper, or Sophie's birth certificate, but I could bring Anneliese's train case, and perhaps the postcards and photographs that were inside it.

Even as I planned my next visit with Randi for Tuesday of the following week, I knew it wouldn't be enough. I had to find a way to get that crystal vase from Olivia's room.

But how?

✻

I CALLED Chantelle from the parking lot outside of Sun, Moon & Stars, anxious to find out how she made out.

"Did you get to see Olivia?"

"Yes and no."

"Either you saw her or you didn't."

"Let me start at the beginning and tell it my way, okay?"

I knew Chantelle well enough to know that she wouldn't be hurried, at least when it came to telling a story. "Okay."

"I went to reception, where the platinum blonde at the front desk made me feel as if I was there to spring an inmate versus visit a resident."

"Yeah, she's got that act down pat."

"That she does. Anyway, I told her I was a friend of the Osgoode family, which technically isn't a lie. I am a friend of yours, and you are part of the family. I'd brought a bunch of yellow daisies with me, and some homemade shortbread. I offered her a couple of cookies to have on her coffee break. She politely refused, but the gesture seemed to placate her because she acquiesced and called Olivia's room. Olivia agreed to see me."

"Fantastic."

"Not so fast. I said 'seemed to placate her.' I got to Olivia's room and had no sooner given her my cover story, when who charged into the room but Corbin Osgoode. He asked how I knew his mother. I had to admit that I didn't know her, but that I was there as a friend of the family." Chantelle sighed heavily. "He's quite a piece of work, your grandfather. I felt about as welcome as a cockroach at a housewarming party. As for Olivia, she might be his mother, but he's definitely the boss of her. He turned me out on my ear, figuratively speaking of course, but another minute in that room, I have no doubt he would have gotten physical, or at least threatened it."

For a moment I was too disappointed to speak. Then I got angry. "Who is Corbin Osgoode to threaten my friends or tell Olivia who she can or cannot see? Especially since she had agreed to your visit."

"There's more," Chantelle said. "Before Corbin stormed in, Olivia told me that she was disappointed you hadn't come back to take her out for lunch. Which means—"

"Olivia didn't know that Corbin had forbidden me to see her."

"Exactly. You were right, Callie. That man is hiding something, something Olivia knows. In amongst his rage, I sensed fear."

Rage and fear. I'd experienced both in my dealings with Corbin Osgoode before, as had my father. Well, this time the roles were reversed. One way or another I was going to expose that secret, no matter what it took.

This wasn't just about Anneliese Prei Frankow any longer. My grandfather had just made it personal.

28

———

Sometimes procrastination pays off. Either that, or you get lucky. I was checking my Maps app to determine which branch of the Toronto Public Library would be my quickest option for getting a library card when the phone rang. I checked the call display, hoping it wasn't Royce calling to cancel our dinner tonight. It was ridiculous how much I was looking forward to the evening.

It was Shirley Harrington.

"Shirley, I wasn't expecting to hear from you until late April. Is everything okay?"

"Perfectly fine now that I'm back in Marketville," she said, chuckling. "It seems I'm not snowbird material. Six weeks in Florida is about my limit. It might be different if I was married and staying down there with my husband, or if I was sharing the condo I rented with a friend, but as a single, I got bored. Of course, I've been home two days and I'm still bored silly. I'm seriously regretting my decision to retire."

"Your words are music to my ears." I proceeded to fill her in on the concept behind Past & Present Investigations.

"That's fantastic. First, I'm thrilled that you have decided to make your home in Marketville permanent, and I'm doubly thrilled that you've sold Snapdragon Circle and found a property on Edward Street. It's such a great street with all its pubs and independent shops and restaurants. I can't imagine you would have ever felt entirely comfortable at the old house, given everything you discovered while living there."

"You're right on all counts, and Edward Street is definitely a better fit for operating a home-based business. I'd considered buying another subdivision house, but the realtor cautioned me. There are subdivision and town bylaws to consider, and we're hoping this location encourages occasional walk-in traffic."

"We?"

"Sorry, I'm skipping ahead. Chantelle Marchand is my partner. She'll be doing genealogical research, among other things. I'm the general dogsbody. Advertising, managing the website and social media, meeting with clients, writing reports, you name it, I'll be doing it." *Even going to see a psychometrist.*

"I'm so glad for both of you," Shirley said, and I could hear the smile in her voice.

"There's more. We've asked Misty Rivers to help us. She's added a section about tarot on the website. She posts a *Misty's Messages* blog using a tarot card."

"Tarot," Shirley said, and this time I could almost hear her laughing.

"It was Chantelle's idea. I'll admit I wasn't thrilled at first, but *Misty's Messages* brought us our first client, as well as some valuable information on the assignment. Arabella's also on board on an as-needed basis in the event there are antiques to appraise, or anything antiques related, really. It was actually Arabella that referred the client to us, and *Misty's Messages* on the website sealed the deal."

"I'm intrigued. Send me the link, I'll take a browse around."

"I will. But as I was saying earlier, your regret over retiring is music to my ears. There's a reason for that. Chantelle and I would like you to join our team."

"You would? Really?"

"We can't pay you much to start with, but—"

"No buts. You'd be doing me a favor. I wasn't kidding when I told you that I'm bored out of my mind. I would love to be part of your team. I just don't know how I could contribute."

"Don't sell yourself short." I told her about wanting to review *Toronto Star* and *Globe and Mail* archives from the 1950s. "It seems that the Toronto Public Library now has everything archived online, but you need a library card to access it, and you have to apply in person for the card."

"You want me to help you with the archives research?"

"I know it sounds dull, especially since you left the Cedar County Reference Library for a new life, but yes, in answer to your question, that's exactly what we'd want you to do. You could pick your title. How does Chief Research Analyst sound?"

"It sounds perfect," Shirley said. "I'll go to the library today and get a card. There's a branch at Warden and Steeles that's close to a friend's house. I'll give her a call, see if we can meet up for dinner."

"Thank you. You have no idea how much that simplifies my life. I'll have to update you on the case before we get started. I'd rather do that in person. It would be best if you saw what we've got so far so you can focus your search. When is your earliest availability?"

"How does tomorrow morning sound? I'm anxious to get started."

"I don't mind working on a Sunday if you don't."

"I've just had six weeks of mind-numbing R and R. Working on a Sunday will be a welcome diversion. Besides, I'm treating this like an adventure. What's a good time to meet?"

I didn't know how my date with Royce would go. Would I end up staying over? Did I want to stay over? I wasn't sure. Either way, my training schedule called for a six-mile run and run club met at eight thirty.

"Why don't you come by around eleven? It shouldn't take more than a couple of hours to go through everything, and then I'll make lunch."

"Eleven works for me, and lunch would be great."

"How does tourtiere and salad sound?" I asked, knowing how much Shirley loved my version of the French Canadian meat pie.

"Like I'm not in Florida any more. And I couldn't be happier."

I WENT to the grocery store to pick up the fixings for a tossed salad and the ingredients for tomorrow's lunch. If I made the tourtiere today, it would only require reheating tomorrow. Not to mention that the activity would keep my mind off of my dinner with Royce. I was as excited as a teenager going to her first prom.

My next stop was the liquor store to pick up a nice bottle of white wine. Royce had told me not to bring anything, but my father raised me right. You didn't go to someone's house for dinner without taking something for the host, and I would feel silly bringing him flowers. Taking food would imply I didn't trust his cooking.

The errands done, I returned home, turned on the radio, and got to work. First, bake a potato, peel, and mash. Next, combine the lean ground pork with chopped onions, potato, spices, and water. Simmer until thick, about an hour. While that was going, I made the pastry and rolled it out, humming along to the songs on the radio as I did it. It was comforting to make comfort food.

And yet, I was still worried. I was looking forward to the evening, really looking forward to it if I was completely honest. But what if we tried dating and it didn't work out? I didn't want to sacrifice our friendship.

My worry also went a lot deeper than Royce. I was worried about the case. It was a great relief that Shirley would be helping me search the archives, but what if we found out things I didn't want to know? Or that Louisa wouldn't want to know? True, I had forewarned her, and we both knew the risks of delving into the past, but knowing the risks or being faced with the cold, harsh truth were two different things. Then there was the business with my grandfather. Corbin Osgoode was hiding something, and I needed to find out what it was. I also had to find a way to speak to Olivia again, and to get the crystal vase from her room to bring to Randi. Despite hours of thinking about it, I had yet to come up with a plausible plan.

I sighed. I had forty-five minutes to spare now that the pie was assembled and put in the oven. Worrying about worrying would do nothing more than ruin my evening. I hopped onto the website and almost laughed out loud when I saw Misty's latest message. Chantelle must have told her about my date with Royce.

The card shown was the Ten of Cups. The ten golden cups formed a rainbow arc in a blue sky. Beneath it was a man, his arm wrapped around the waist of a woman. Two children were playing off to the side. A small white house with a red roof stood in the distance, beyond a flowing stream and green fields. Except the card was upside down. I frowned. So far, in all of *Misty's Messages* the cards had been right side up. I proceeded to read it, my curiosity piqued.

THE TEN OF CUPS (ELEMENT: WATER)

The Cups are often viewed as the happiest of the four suits, and this card certainly exudes happiness and contentment, the love of family and home. The most obvious interpretation is a romantic one of love and marriage or a long-term relationship. Less obvious, but I believe equally relevant, the card also represents clarity on personal beliefs and core values, and the creation of a life that is aligned to those values, both personally and professionally.

While some readers interpret the reversed Ten of Cups as an indicator of dissatisfaction, I believe it remains a card full of promise and joy, even though there are challenges ahead.

MISTY'S MESSAGE: Sometimes the lines between the past and present blur our future. Facing challenges head-on will ultimately result in learning the truth. Do not allow anyone to thwart your quest for truth, no matter how deeply the secrets are buried in the past.

Realize, however, that not all answers lie in the past. When it comes to romantic relationships, stop questioning everything about it and set aside past heartbreaks. Until you do so, true happiness cannot follow. Trust your heart, and realize everything worth having takes time to build.

I had expected the message to be all about falling in love, and Misty had certainly gotten her point across with her comment about setting aside past heartbreaks. But she had also managed to twist the narrative so that it was still relevant to the business. *Do not allow anyone to thwart your quest for the truth, no matter how far the secret is buried in the past.*

I wanted to email Misty and tell her not to worry. I was ready to trust my heart. No more loser radar for this woman. As for my quest to find the truth out about the past, Corbin Osgoode had met his match. The next time I saw the Ten of Cups, it was going to be upright and standing. Just like me.

29

I tried on a half dozen outfits from dressy to denim. I wanted to look nice, but this was dinner at Royce's house, not some swanky restaurant, and he tended to dress in blue jeans and a golf shirt, no matter what the occasion. In the end, I selected a pair of black skinny jeans and an emerald twill sweater that brought the green out in my hazel eyes. I did my best to tame my hair with a flat iron and a couple of barrettes. Silver hoop earrings. Minimal make-up, mascara, and lip-gloss. My hair might be a nightmare to manage, but at least I had good skin. I surveyed myself in the mirror, satisfied with the result.

The drive to my old neighborhood took ten minutes. I smiled at the familiar street names: Day Lily Drive, Lady's Slipper Lane, Coneflower Crescent. I turned left off Trillium Way onto Snapdragon Circle and almost pulled into the driveway at number 16 out of habit, stopping myself just in time.

I saw the blinds flicker at 14 and knew that my previous next-door neighbor, Ella Cole, was up to her old tricks, watching the coming and goings of everyone on the cul de sac and willing to report on it to anyone who would listen. I grabbed the bottle of wine, hopped out of the car, and rang Royce's doorbell before Ella could come out and start a conversation. I liked her well enough, but I wasn't in the mood to explain what I was doing visiting Royce. I grinned. She'd figure it out soon enough if my car was still here in the morning.

Royce answered the door promptly, pecking me on the cheek and admonishing me for bringing anything. His bungalow was open concept, with the hallway leading directly into the kitchen, dining, and living area. His design and workmanship were evident throughout, from the black granite countertops to the gleaming hardwood floors and taupe-toned walls. The table had been set with white linen napkins, black-and-white plates, silver cutlery, and a centerpiece of miniature red roses and baby's breath.

"You've outdone yourself," I said. "Everything looks beautiful."

Royce smiled. "I wanted to be sure you'd come back. Have a seat and I'll get you a glass of wine."

He poured Chardonnay into two long-stemmed wine glasses while I sank into a comfy black leather sofa surrounded by textured, tapestry-like pillows in shades of bronze, gold, and cream. I recognized Porsche's handiwork. I realized in that moment that I'd completely forgotten about Royce's invitation to go to Muskoka and watch his sister play Eliza Doolittle in *Pygmalion*.

"How are the play preparations going?" I asked, accepting the glass of wine.

"According to Porsche, she's having the time of her life, though I suspect she has aspirations for greater things. Will you be coming as my date? Opening day is two weeks today, a matinee. We could stay at my parent's place, or I could make reservations at one of the local resorts. Or we could come back to Marketville if you'd rather not stay over. It's a lot of driving in one day, but it's manageable. It would mean a lot to Porsche—to both of us—if you could be there."

I thought about sitting with his parents and aunt. I wasn't sure I was ready for that yet, if ever. Then again, if I didn't get over that aversion, my relationship with Royce didn't stand a chance. But that didn't mean I had to stay at their cottage.

"Let's see how things go between now and then. A local resort might be nice."

"Does that mean you'll come with me?"

"I think it does."

DINNER WAS PERFECTION. Herbed boneless breast of chicken stuffed with spinach and ricotta, roasted miniature potatoes, and a medley of broccoli, cauliflower, and julienne carrots. Dessert was crème caramel, sinfully delicious, followed by decaf coffee with Irish Cream in the living room. Tomorrow morning's run wouldn't make up for the calories, but I savored every last bite. Much more of this, and I might not even get to run club in the morning.

"Simply delicious," I said, curling my legs under me and making myself very comfortable. "How did you know that crème caramel was my favorite?"

"I didn't," Royce said. "It's mine. Just one more thing we have in common."

It was as close to a romantic overture as we'd had all evening, which is to say there hadn't been one. Instead of being disappointed, I found myself feeling oddly reassured. I've jumped into relationships feet first before, only to find myself standing inside a ring of fire. I've also learned the hard way that loving someone doesn't always mean liking someone. I liked Royce, in fact, I liked him a lot. Even better, I knew the feeling was mutual. There was a strong physical attraction, no question about it, but above all else, we were friends.

I found myself telling him about Anneliese Prei, the photographs and postcards in the train case, her marriage, baby, and eventual murder. I left out names to keep things reasonably confidential, referring to her as "the grandmother," Louisa as "my client," and Sophie as "my client's mother," not that Royce was going to talk to anyone about it. I also left out the part about going to see Randi. Somehow I didn't think Royce would buy into the whole object-reading business. I still wasn't sure how I felt about it.

"This woman, she's become much more than the grandmother of a client to you, hasn't she?" Royce asked, after I'd finished. "She's gotten under your skin."

I admitted that she had. "The frustrating thing is that I know someone who might have more information, but I've been forbidden from seeing her."

"Forbidden? Sounds very cloak-and-dagger. Who is this someone?"

"An elderly woman. She lives at the Cedar County Retirement Residence, the one on the corner of Mavis and Lester. Her son has told the front desk I'm not to visit. The sad thing is, the two times I did visit with her she seemed to enjoy it. And I'm quite sure she wasn't aware of his directive."

"What floor is she on?"

"The third. Why?"

"I might be able to help you with that."

"Really? How?"

"Royce Contracting has been hired to renovate a storage room on the third floor. Right now, it's filled with stuff no one wanted to throw out, but never uses. Management wants to convert the space for use as a movie theater. You could help me sort the wheat from the chaff, what goes to charity, what can be recycled or repurposed, and what's junk to go to the dump."

"The movie theater sounds like a great plan, but I'm not sure how going through rubbish is going to help me."

"I've invited the residents to a meeting at ten a.m. on Tuesday in the board room. Management felt getting everyone involved would increase interest in the project. I'm supposed to get the list of names tomorrow. Who is your resident and what's her room number?"

"Room eighteen. Her name is Olivia Osgoode."

"Olivia Osgoode. Your great-grandmother, I take it?"

I nodded.

"And the son who won't let you visit with her?"

"My grandfather, Corbin Osgoode."

Royce leaned back in his seat, eyebrows arched, cheeks sucked in. "The plot definitely thickens."

I'D LIKE to tell you that the remainder of the evening went from cold case to hot romance, but the truth was that Royce and I spent more time talking about Anneliese Prei, including her affair with Anton Osgoode, than we did about our own potential relationship. Royce was fascinated that Louisa had hired me, not knowing we were related. We stopped drinking alcohol by eight, moving on to sparkling water and, eventually, peppermint tea with a touch of honey. It was the tea that told me tonight wasn't going to be the night. What can I say? Talking about an old murder isn't exactly an aphrodisiac. Neither is peppermint tea no matter how much honey you stir into it.

I left a few minutes past midnight and noticed the lights were all off at Ella Cole's house, as well as at Chantelle's across the street. Both women would be disappointed to find my car gone.

Who was I kidding? I was disappointed that my car would be gone.

I WOKE up at six a.m., despite not getting to bed until after one. Alone in the darkness of my bedroom, I mulled over the evening with Royce. There had definitely been mixed signals. The lovely dinner, combined with his invitation to stay overnight at a Muskoka resort when we went to watch Porsche's play, versus a virtually romance-free evening. The sole exception was an almost platonic goodnight kiss at the door, with the promise to call me Monday, as soon as he'd connected with the Cedar County Retirement Home's management team. I'd punched the pillow a few times and tossed and turned a few more, thinking about Misty's message: *Trust your heart, and realize everything worth having takes time to build*, before finally falling into an unsettled sleep.

Shirley arrived promptly at eleven, suntanned and freckled from her six weeks in Florida, her brown eyes sparkling with anticipation as she proudly flashed her Toronto Public Library card. She may have been in her mid-sixties, but her figure was that of someone much younger. I knew she liked to golf and that she played tennis regularly. I suspected she also worked out at the gym.

"Do you still drink your coffee decaffeinated with double sugar?"

Shirley beamed. "Great memory."

"We did spend a lot of time together last year."

"That we did."

I got the coffee going and poured, made myself a cup of Earl Grey tea, and then walked Shirley through the evidence from start to finish, pausing only to put the tourtiere in the oven. I even told her about meeting with Olivia Osgoode, though I left out my suspicions about the crystal vase and Anton's part in the murder.

I also neglected to show her Anton's obituary marked "Uncle Toni." I knew she'd come across the obituary in her search, that much was a given. But the Uncle Toni part, I wasn't quite ready to share that bit of information. I needed Shirley's research and opinions to be unbiased. At least, that's what I told myself.

Shirley wrote copious notes as we went along, occasionally underlining something, and, difficult as it was, I refrained from offering any conjecture. It was one o'clock before we finished.

"Perfect timing," I said, getting up and stretching. "Let me toss the salad and get the tourtiere out of the oven. We can discuss the case after lunch. I'd like to start searching through the online newspaper archives first thing tomorrow morning, provided that works for you."

"I'll be here at nine. As for my thoughts, I'd like to read my notes and think things through. I have a couple of theories, but I need to sort through everything first, alone in my own space. I hope you're not disappointed by that."

Disappointed? I wanted to stand up and cheer. "Not only am I not disappointed, I'm relieved. I didn't relish the thought of poring over newspaper archives. Then again, I've been unfolding this saga for days, and you've seen everything over the course of a couple of hours. It must be overwhelming."

"Overwhelming? Perhaps a little, but it's also the most fun I've had since the last time we worked together. I thought I might make a list of the names we need to search, as well. I'm sure you have one already, but it won't hurt to compare lists."

"Agreed. Now let's have lunch so you can get out of here and start theorizing and making those lists."

SHIRLEY HAD JUST LEFT when my phone rang. I checked the caller display. Royce.

"Hi, what's up?"

"I wanted to apologize," he said.

"Apologize? Whatever for?"

"For not letting you know how I feel about you. For letting the case of Anneliese Prei get in the way of what was supposed to be a romantic evening."

"Oh. That. It's okay. I'm as much to blame as you are, maybe more."

"It's not okay. I'm interested in you, Callie, and not just as a friend or a confidante. I'd like us to try for something more."

My mouth went dry as I searched for the right thing to say. "I'd like that, too."

"What are you doing this afternoon?"

"I thought I might go for the run I skipped this morning. Read a book. Watch some TV. Nothing that couldn't be changed."

"In that case, I'll be over in thirty minutes. And Callie?"

"Uh huh?"

"This visit will be strictly pleasure. No talk of Past & Present, ongoing investigations, and especially no talk about old murders. Deal?"

"Deal." I hung up and made a mad dash to my dresser drawer, pulling out a brand new set of sexy black lace lingerie. My intimate apparel efforts hadn't been appreciated last night, but today was a new day and I was feeling optimistic. Thank heavens I'd gone shopping with Chantelle. Otherwise I'd be wearing sensible cotton undies and an oversized race T-shirt. Hardly the look I was going for.

It was time for our strictly-pleasure moment.

30

———

R oyce left at seven o'clock the next morning after a quick breakfast of scrambled eggs and toast, promising to call me with a time to visit the Cedar County Retirement Home. It was the first reference to the case that he'd made, and he followed it up with a long, passionate kiss that almost led us right back to the bedroom.

I showered and changed, thinking about the night before while I got ready for my day with Shirley. Everything had been so easy with him, so comfortable. We'd even made plans for a trip to Niagara-on-the-Lake and Niagara Falls once the Frankow case was filed and finalized. Sightseeing, slot machines, and steamy sex, Royce had said. The deliberately wolfish grin on his face when he suggested it that made me laugh. Could the Barnstable family curse finally be over?

℞

SHIRLEY ARRIVED Monday morning exactly on schedule, forcing me to get my head out of the future and firmly back to the past. We sat across the table from each other, notebooks out, pens in hand.

"The first thing we need to do is compare our list of names to research in the archives," she said.

"Agreed. Call out if there's a name you don't have written down. Otherwise, let's just get through the list. The primary focus has to be Anneliese Prei, Anneliese (Prei) Frankow, Horst Frankow, and Sophie Frankow."

"I had Louisa written down," Shirley said, looking at her notes.

"So did I, initially, but we're looking at a murder that took place in 1956. Louisa wasn't born until 1982. The task ahead is formidable enough without looking for extra work."

"A valid point." Shirley crossed Louisa's name off her list. "Who else do you have?"

"The witnesses to the christening, whom I assume were the godparents, Adam and Helena Bradford. The pastor who performed the ceremony, G. Walther. And the eleven signatures on the autograph page from the T.S.S. *Canberra*." I slid my notebook toward her so she could compare them to what she had.

Shirley checked off name by name, only pausing once. "This signature. Helena Brown. I wondered if she might have immigrated to Canada to marry Adam, becoming Helena Bradford. Helen is a fairly common name, but Helena? Not as common."

I couldn't believe both Chantelle and I had missed such an obvious connection. It proved you could never have too many sets of eyes on the same problem. "You're right. I can get Chantelle on that. If there's a marriage certificate, she might find it on Ancestry.ca. Do you mind if I email her now? The sooner she gets this, the sooner she can get on it."

"Go for it."

I finished off the email and hit Send. "Anything else?"

"I also have Anton Osgoode, the father listed on the birth certificate."

If Shirley had made the Osgoode connection, she was too diplomatic to mention it. "Yes, please look up Anton. Also his wife, Olivia."

"Got it, Anton and Olivia. We're definitely on the same page. At least so far."

I frowned. "What do you mean, at least so far?"

"I would like to do the archives research on my own."

I didn't know whether to be disappointed or relieved. I'd been looking forward to finding something—anything, but honestly, I hadn't been looking forward to the drudgery of the actual work. Perhaps Shirley sensed my procrastination had been deliberate avoidance and was trying to spare me. If that were the case, it would be unfair to burden her with the entire archives research.

"Can I ask why?"

Shirley blushed, her freckles standing out on her tanned face. "I miss it, Callie. The research, the thrill of the hunt, the exhilaration of the find. But frankly, it's easier if I do this my way, in the comfort of my own home, where I can go off on a tangent if I want to, without feeling as though I'm holding up progress or wasting time. I give you my word that I'll keep my billable hours to a minimum, and I promise to update you on a daily basis. Heck, I'll do it hourly if you want. But I really want to do this on my own. Of course, it is your company. I'll play it however you want."

"Actually, you'd be doing me a huge favor. I have some other things to take care of that are quite pressing." *Like Olivia Osgoode and the crystal vase. Like scrolling through thousands of photographs from the* Telegram, *something I felt compelled to do myself.* "I just don't want you to feel as if I'm taking advantage of you."

"Trust me, if I ever feel that way, I'll tell you. For now, I'm looking forward to getting started. The sooner, the better."

I smiled. "Then get out of here and get started."

Was it my imagination or did Shirley positively skip out of the house?

⚲

ROYCE CALLED a few minutes after Shirley left. "Good news. Olivia Osgoode was one of the first residents to sign up."

It was great news, better than I'd hoped for. I thanked Royce and promised him that I'd be there with a half hour to spare. Now all I had to do was find a way for Olivia to give me the crystal vase.

I WENT online to find the York University *Toronto Telegram* Archives. I found them under the York Space Institutional Repository as part of the Clara Thomas Archives and Special Collections. It appeared to be a formidable task: ten thousand, two hundred and ninety-four images. Fortunately, there were a few search options, including one that allowed me to enter a date and the number of images per batch, ranging from five to one hundred. I typed in 1956, selected batches of twenty in ascending order, and hit enter.

The first image was dated January 1, 1956. It was a cute photo of two cats playing with a watering can. The caption was "Cat: Owned by Mrs. Harold Walker." It made me smile, but it also reminded me that this exercise could become a huge time suck if I didn't stay focused.

The first reference to a murder included several photographs starting on March 31, with the headline MURDER AND SUICIDE IN HAMILTON, ONTARIO. Intrigued, I googled for more information, but all links led back to the *Telegram* photograph archives. Just as well. I didn't need another murder to investigate.

There were several photos of Woodbine Racetrack, many with the added tag "Not used." A few of a house fire, again in Hamilton, with the caption "Children set fire to home and then saved parents and family." More searching led me to "Torso found" and "Body of murder victim found in Hamilton cemetery." Both were interesting, but neither was remotely connected to Anneliese Prei. It became quickly apparent that the archives, while seemingly extensive and dating back to 1927, had huge gaps in each year represented. I was about to give up hope when I saw "Young mother murdered in own home." Dated April 9, 1956, there was an artist's drawing of the interior of a house. A woman was shown lying face down on the floor, arms sprawled overhead. A man in a suit was depicted standing over her, holding a large, but unidentifiable, object. It could have been a vase, a pot, any number of things. A young girl was shown hiding under the kitchen table. Uppercase labels within the drawing read "YOUNG MOTHER STRUCK WITH BLUNT OBJECT IN

Her Home." "Man with blunt Object." "Three-year-old daughter hid under the kitchen table."

Sophie hiding under the table was a new detail. She must have waited until the bad man had left before going to the neighbor, but how much could she have seen? Based on the drawing, no more than the man's shoes and his pants below the knees. Definitely not his face.

I also wondered why there was a drawing and not a photograph. Had the police refused photojournalists entry to the scene? Why were there no names associated with the victim and murderer? Were they being withheld to find and notify next of kin? I continued searching, but there was no further reference to the murder or the trial. It was as if it had never happened, as if this solitary drawing was the figment of the artist's imagination. I checked the credits, hoping the artist would be credited. Unfortunately, "Telegram Staff" had been listed under Photographer and Creator.

Frustrated and disappointed, I emailed the link to Shirley and Chantelle with a brief note explaining that there were no other references in the *Telegram*. I could only hope that the *Star* and the *Globe* would offer better results. In the meantime, I had to put my faith in Operation Olivia and the crystal vase.

31

I arrived at the Cedar County Retirement Residence by nine thirty on Tuesday morning, where I received a grudging clearance along with directions to the boardroom from Platinum Blonde. I was tempted to go to the third floor and knock on Olivia's door, but resisted the urge. I didn't need to get kicked out of the building, and I didn't want to cause Royce any grief.

The boardroom was long and narrow, with off-white walls, mahogany wainscoting, and a mahogany table that had been polished until it gleamed. A matching sideboard held a tray of on the rocks glasses, four pitchers of water filled with water and lemon slices, and two plates of assorted cookies. Chairs upholstered in buttercup yellow and burgundy sateen had been placed around the table. A quick count revealed a total of twenty-five chairs, twelve per side, and one at the head. Royce was already there, alternately fidgeting with his laptop and a movie screen. He looked up when he saw me and smiled. "PowerPoint presentation. Hopefully I don't put anyone to sleep."

I gestured to the chairs. "I wasn't expecting this many people."

Royce laughed. "Most of those chairs will be empty. There were only eight names on my list. Do you think I should move some of those chairs and place them along the wall? Or just leave it as is?"

"Eight chairs to a side will be plenty. I'll take care of it while you obsess about your PowerPoint setup."

I rearranged the chairs, poured ten glasses of lemon water and placed them and the plates of cookies on the table. I checked my watch. Nine forty-five. It was almost show time. I tapped the table for good luck in a "knock on wood" gesture.

The first resident arrived a few seconds later, followed closely by the others. Royce greeted them at the door, while I checked their names off his list. Everyone was present and accounted for by nine fifty-five.

Everyone but Olivia. I was almost in panic mode when Royce leaned over and whispered in my ear.

"I took a chance and spoke to Olivia last night. She's expecting you in her room." He straightened up and said, "Thank you, Ms. Barnstable, for helping me to set up and greet everyone. Your assistance was much appreciated."

The seven residents sitting around the table clapped politely, murmuring their goodbyes while I made my exit. I glanced furtively down the hall in both directions, making sure Platinum Blonde was nowhere to be found. Once convinced I was in the clear, I made a beeline to the stairs and ran up to the third floor, taking two steps at a time. The elevator was too risky.

⌖

I KNOCKED on Olivia's door, my palms as moist as my mouth was dry. There was no response for what seemed like several minutes, but was in all likelihood no more than a few seconds. I heard the lock click and waited for the door to open.

"Come on in, Callie," Olivia said. "I've been waiting for you."

I followed Olivia, waited until she settled herself into her chair, and then took a seat on the black leather sofa. She looked older today than she had a week ago, as if someone had stolen the sparkle from her.

"Thank you for persevering," she said. "I had no idea my son forbade you to visit until your friend came to see me. I apologize for causing you any embarrassment or discomfort. Corbin means well, but he can be a bit of a pompous ass. I blame Anton and myself. I coddled him for far too long, and Anton filled his head with all sorts of nonsense about the Osgoode name. Being a buyer for Eaton's was prestigious, but it wasn't as if Corbin was heir to a throne."

"I didn't blame you, Olivia. I knew it wasn't your idea to ban me from visiting. But I'm curious why Corbin felt the need to do so."

Olivia shook her head. "I don't understand it. He knows I get lonely. Besides, you're family."

Family. Corbin Osgoode would never consider me family. He'd made that clear on several occasions. My grandmother, Yvette, had made overtures, but no matter what she said or tried to do, Corbin ruled that household.

But what about Olivia? Did I come clean or keep stringing her along with a sanitized version of the truth? I studied the elderly woman before me and found the answer in her eyes.

"I have a story to tell you, Great-grandmother, if you're willing to listen." It was the first time I'd called her anything but Olivia, but she didn't flinch or tell me to call her Olivia. Instead, she reached out to me with arthritic hands.

"I'm willing to listen. And call me Gran."

Gran. I thought about how Corbin and Yvette would react and suppressed a grin. "Gran...I misled you earlier about the reason for my visit. It wasn't because I was working on my family tree."

"I don't understand. Are you saying you aren't working on your family tree?"

"I am, or at least I've started one, but that's not the real reason for coming to see you."

"And what is?" Eyebrows raised, lips pursed.

"I think you know that I spent last year trying to learn the truth about my mother's disappearance in 1986."

"Yvette filled me in. I'm sorry that things turned out as they did. I'm even sorrier that you spent all those years with your father as your only family. We were wrong."

I shrugged. "It could have been worse. My father was a good man and a loving parent. Anyway, this isn't about that, although I suppose in a way it is. I learned a lot about investigating the past last year. I decided to start my own business using that knowledge. I call it Past & Present Investigations. My friend, Chantelle Marchand, is my business partner."

Olivia clapped. "You have Anton's blood running through your veins. Make lemonade from lemons, he would say, and serve it up in a nice crystal pitcher with matching glasses."

"I don't know about lemons and lemonade. I do know I couldn't bear to go back to working nine-to-five at a call center, and I'm not rich enough or old enough to retire. Past & Present Investigations seemed like the perfect solution. So far, we only have one client, although I'm sure there will be others. It's that client's case that brought me here."

"May I ask who the client is?"

We'd arrived at the moment of truth. Was I breaking client confidentiality by revealing Louisa's name? Almost certainly. But was it breaking confidentiality to share the names of Sophie Frankow and Anneliese Prei Frankow? It was a fine line, but one I had to cross.

"Before I say anything more, I need to know that what I tell you stays between us. I can't have you talking to Corbin or Yvette about this. Or anyone else for that matter."

"You have my word. There's been far too much buried in my past. Now, tell me, who is your client?"

"I can't reveal the name of my client, but I can tell you that the investigation has led us to Anneliese Prei Frankow and her daughter, Sophie."

"So you knew, when you came here that very first day, that Anton was Sophie's father?"

I felt myself blush. "We found a Certificate of Baptism for Sophie. Anneliese was named as the mother. Anton was named as the father. I knew from my family tree research that Anton was my great-grandfather."

I was expecting Olivia to get all huffy with me, possibly even throw me out. Instead, she laughed, a rich, throaty sound that belied her age. "How very enterprising of you. I admire a woman with chutzpah. Have you figured out what Sophie's relation to you is?"

I laughed along with her. "No. Every time I try I get a headache. It seems so complicated."

"Complicated or not, I don't believe it's a coincidence that your client came to you with this case."

"What do you mean? I don't believe my client is aware of my connection to Sophie Frankow, though I will have to include that information in my final report."

"I don't mean it wasn't a coincidence in that way. I meant it was fate." Olivia tilted her head to the right and studied me through narrowed eyes. "I've always believed fate is the universe's way of putting things in order. The reason Anton died young and left me a widow so early."

Coincidence or fate? I didn't know. "I'm not sure what to believe any more. The past few months, this case, have altered my perspective in so many ways. I've never believed in spirits or psychics, but a few days ago, I went to see a psychometrist."

"There was a guy on television back in the seventies, the Amazing Kreskin. He billed himself as a mentalist, claimed he could read minds. I recall he did not want to be considered a psychic."

"This isn't the same thing. A psychometrist is someone who purports to read objects, not minds. The theory is that objects are porous and can store an owner's history and emotions. I took some jewelry that belonged to Anneliese."

"Fascinating. Did you learn anything?"

"Perhaps. I'm still skeptical about the science behind it. There are plenty of naysayers who believe the information is garnered through cold readings and confirmation bias. I was careful not to give anything away, but Past & Present has a website and Facebook page, and Randi—that's the psychometrist's name—did a lot of talking about the actual objects versus their history."

"And yet, something about what Randi said resonated with you, despite your inner cynic."

I nodded. "Randi told me Anneliese was killed by someone she trusted, perhaps even loved, though she wasn't as sure about the love part. I'll admit it took me by surprise. How would holding a piece of jewelry lead her to that conclusion? It also made me wonder what other objects could tell me about the past. Like your lovely crystal vase, for example. I've been admiring the etchings. The birds, the envelope and pen, the cornflower. It tells a story. Perhaps two lovers who could only contact each other by writing letters."

"I've never been much of a romantic," Olivia said. Her posture had gone from relaxed to rigid, her expression from interested to incensed. "Are you implying that this vase was a gift from Anton to Anneliese? If so, how on earth would it have come into my possession?"

If I told Olivia what I really thought—that Anton was the killer, and not Horst, that the vase was the murder weapon—she would almost certainly ask me to leave and never come back. Even worse, she'd likely tell Corbin all about it. The last thing I needed to experience was Corbin's wrath. I formulated my response carefully.

"I think the vase originally belonged to Anneliese, and that it was a gift to her from Anton. It's the sort of thing he'd bring back from a buying trip in England. Perhaps he even gave it to her on the ship. I believe that she returned it to him when she married Horst, and he gave it to you. Even so—"

"Even so, you want to take this vase to your psychometrist."

"I realize it's a lot to ask, but it would still hold some history of Anneliese, provided psychometry can be trusted. I'm not convinced it can be, but I owe it to my client to try every avenue, no matter how unorthodox."

I'm not sure what I was expecting, but the gratitude in her eyes wasn't it. I was sure she knew what her husband had done, and she'd been protecting him, and his memory, all these years. I'd given her a plausible explanation for owning the crystal vase. Her voice quivered as she pointed to it with a trembling hand.

"Take the vase and keep it. I've lived with it for far too long."

32

A saner person might have taken the vase and run, and rest assured, I wasted no time storing it into the canvas bag I'd stashed in my purse on the off-chance I'd get lucky, but I wanted to find out more about Sophie's "Uncle Toni" reference on Anton's obituary. I wasn't sure what Olivia knew, but I had to find out.

"I have a couple of things to show you, Gran."

Olivia attempted a smile. "Do I want to see them?"

"I don't know. They connect Sophie Frankow to Anton…and Corbin. It may explain why Corbin stopped me from seeing you."

"You have a way of piquing my interest and piercing my heart at the same time," Olivia said. "Let's see what you have."

"You once told me that despite his philandering ways, Anton wouldn't have walked away from the responsibility of a child. Not if he knew. By your own admission, he did know about her because you told him about Anneliese's visit." I opened my purse, took out the obituary Sophie had marked "Uncle Toni," and handed it to her.

"Anton wanted to adopt Sophie," Olivia said, her voice so quiet that I had to strain to hear. "I would have none of it. No one knew he was her father. I certainly had no knowledge of his name on her

Certificate of Baptism. Besides, we had Corbin to consider. He was entering his preteen years, for heaven's sake. That's a tough enough time in a boy's life. He didn't need the stigma of an illegitimate half-sister. We argued for weeks, but Anton eventually agreed to drop it."

"So you didn't know that he'd connected with Sophie."

"Oh, I knew eventually, although Anton kept me in the dark for several years. Sophie went into foster care after Horst was arrested. I convinced myself it was for the best. She'd find new parents to adopt her, people who chose her, not people who felt…obligated."

"Except new parents didn't come her way. Sophie stayed in the system until she aged out at the ripe old age of sixteen with a grade ten education. From what I can gather, her time in foster care was less than ideal." I saw Olivia flinch and felt like a bully, but surely she didn't expect me to believe the fairy-tale-ending story she was trying to spin.

"I didn't know any of that—at least not until much later. I'm embarrassed to admit I'd all but forgotten about her, at least until the day Anton, Corbin, and I went to the Yorkdale Shopping Centre. It was the latest shiny new thing in 1964, an enclosed shopping mall, by far the biggest in Canada at the time, and one of the largest in the world."

I'm not a huge fan of shopping malls in general, preferring small, indie, and specialized shops to mass-market chains, but even I've been to Yorkdale, if only to window shop at one of the many upscale merchants. Even so, I'd never given a moment's thought to when it was built. It had just always been there.

It was as if Olivia read my thoughts. "Did you know, when it opened, that Yorkdale was the first Canadian mall to include two major department stores under the same roof, Eaton's, and its biggest rival, Simpsons? Sadly, neither survived the '90s, but at the time Eaton's and Simpsons were considered iconic."

"Let me guess. Eaton's and Simpsons both had well-stocked crystal and glass departments. Anton wanted to check out the competition."

Olivia laughed. "Exactly. Corbin, of course, was bored out of his mind. He was nineteen at the time, and more interested in pickup trucks and trashy girls than teacups and trinkets. Anton was trying to entertain him with tales of his buying trips when I spotted Sophie giggling over china patterns with an acne-ridden teenaged girl. Sophie was only eleven at the time, but I would have recognized her anywhere. Or should I say, I would have recognized Anton's daughter, and Corbin's sister, anywhere."

"It must have been a shock to see her."

"Not as much of a shock as when she ran up to Anton, hugged him, and called him 'Uncle Toni.'"

"What did you do?"

"What could I do? Make a scene in public? Embarrass everyone, including my son? There would be plenty of time for recriminations once we got home. Sophie's friend seemed to think I knew Sophie, and no one corrected her. Later, Anton said she lived in the same foster home as Sophie. He didn't mention her name and it was the last time I saw the girl or Sophie."

"What about Anton?"

"He never admitted it, but I know that he continued to see Sophie, albeit infrequently, until her sixteenth birthday. As long as he was discreet about it, I could turn a blind eye. It was easier for everyone that way."

"What about Corbin?"

"That day in Simpsons there was no sign of recognition on either side. To the best of my knowledge, they never saw each other again."

Except that they had, and I had the photo booth filmstrip to prove it. In that moment, I decided not to show it to Olivia after all. There was no reason to hurt her, no reason to let her know that both her husband and her son had deceived her. Corbin, on the other hand, was fair game. I would wait until the time was right. I got up to leave. "You look exhausted. I should probably go, let you get some rest."

"Before you do, there's something..." Her voice trailed off, uncertain.

I sat back down, curious. What other secrets could my great-grandmother be hiding? "What sort of something?"

Olivia pulled a photo album from behind the throw pillow beside her and handed it to me, her arthritic hands shaking at the effort. "I wasn't sure when to give this to you, but I think the time is right."

My fingers traced the embossed gold lettering on the brown leather cover.

Abigail Osgoode: 1967-1980.

My mother.

33

———

I've only seen a handful of pictures of my mother as an adult, and those only as recently as this past year. Her wedding photo, four family photos, taken the year I was five, a few grainy images in the local newspaper talking up Abigail Osgoode's volunteer efforts. Olivia shook her head when I told her.

"Your father was always too proud and too stubborn by half," she said, sorrow etched into every line of her face. "I had reprints made of every single photo in that album, sent them by courier, made certain Jimmy would have to sign for the package. I can almost forgive him for not showing them to you…almost…but to think he destroyed them. It breaks my heart."

And mine, not that I would ever admit it. "He probably thought he was protecting me." Or maybe he was protecting himself. My fingers retraced the gold embossed lettering. *Abigail Osgoode: 1967-1980* "Would you do me a favor?"

"If I can."

"Would you look at these with me?"

"I was hoping you'd ask."

I DROVE HOME, the album on the seat beside me, my mind spinning in a million different directions. I'd always thought of my grandfather as spoiled, but the photographs of my mother illustrated an idyllic upbringing. It was all so very different from my own suburban, single parent childhood, my early years filled with delivering newspapers and babysitting, the teen years working part-time as a cashier at a cut-rate grocery store. No such minimum wage labor for Abigail Osgoode, her summers spent lounging on the shores of Lake Miakoda, her winter vacations at Alpine ski resorts. Annual school photos showed a pretty, blue-eyed blonde with nice clothes and the confident air of the entitled.

Listening to Olivia share the stories behind the pictures, her voice filled with pride, I could begin to imagine how Corbin and Yvette must have felt when their pampered princess announced her pregnancy at seventeen. How had a girl from Moore Gate Manor wound up with a working class guy like Jimmy Barnstable?

"Abigail was given the choice of abortion or adoption," my great-grandmother had said, her voice tinged with regret. "No one considered that she would choose keeping the baby and marrying Jimmy."

My father had told me as much, the same set of demands coming from his own parents. He never forgave either family. I felt myself shut down emotionally and closed the album with a decisive snap. I was gone before my great-grandmother could see me cry.

ONCE BACK HOME I pushed all thoughts of Abigail Osgoode from my mind and forced myself to consider what else I'd learned from my visit with Olivia. She knew that Anton had connected with Sophie, though she'd been unaware of Corbin's involvement. The revelation held more questions than answers. Had Corbin seen Sophie many times, or just the once? How had Anton convinced his son not to tell his mother, and when did the visits stop? Olivia seemed to think that Sophie's sixteenth birthday marked the end of their association. I wasn't so sure. I was about to call Chantelle to update her when the phone rang. Shirley.

"I've gone through the archives," she said, her excitement palpable. "Let me tell you, it's a lot easier when everything is online. Beats the old microfiche system by a mile. I've made notes, printed copies of everything relevant, and put it in a binder for you. I can come over whenever you're ready."

As much as my visit to Olivia had emotionally exhausted me, I had an appointment with Randi in the morning, and I didn't want to dampen Shirley's enthusiasm by putting her off until Thursday. Besides, I was eager to find out what she'd learned.

"No time like the present. I'll see if Chantelle can make it."

Shirley agreed to come over within the hour. Chantelle, on the other hand, had back-to-back classes at the gym, but a free day on Wednesday.

We scheduled a meeting for Wednesday afternoon, when I would fill her in on everything I'd learned, including whatever Randi had to tell me about the crystal vase, and Chantelle could share her findings from Ancestry.ca.

True to her word, Shirley arrived within the hour, a bounce in her step and a glint in her eyes that hadn't been there previously. The blue plastic binder she carried was thinner than I'd hoped for, but it was quality, not quantity, that counted, right?

We took seats side by side at the table and got right to it.

"I wanted to get used to navigating the online archives, so I started with the names from the autograph page," Shirley said. "I didn't expect them to lead anywhere, and I was right. Not a single mention of any of them in the *Star* or the *Globe*. My next step was to search for Anneliese Frankow." Shirley opened the binder. It was filled with newspaper clippings tucked inside plastic sleeves.

"There were fewer stories than I anticipated, and nothing from when she was alive. I've sorted into batches. This first batch reports the murder. The next four batches include Horst's arrest, preliminary inquiry, trial, and subsequent death in prison. There are no references to him after that, not even an obituary."

Shirley was right in that there weren't a ton of stories, though I hadn't expected Anneliese to make the papers for any reason other than her untimely death. I counted twelve in the first batch, eight from the *Star* and four from the *Globe*, and started with the first one from the *Toronto Star*. The headline read MOM MURDERED AT HOME. There was no photograph. There was also no by-line.

"Not having a by-line back then isn't unusual," Shirley explained, when I commented on it. She pointed out several other stories without. "In fact, by-lines weren't commonplace in newspapers until the 1970s, although staff writers were typically credited. Then, as today, newspapers often relied on freelancers, or in industry jargon, stringers. Stringers usually had an ongoing relationship with one or more news organizations, and they would be paid by the piece rather than receiving a salary. A stringer's work was largely uncredited."

It meant there would be no way of finding out which journalist had covered the story. While disappointing, the reality was sixty years later they would almost certainly be a dead end, both figuratively and factually. I proceeded to read the article.

> Anneliese Frankow, a twenty-four-year-old wife and mother of one, was found murdered in the kitchen of her home. No arrests have been made. At the police department's request, neighbors of Mrs. Frankow have declined comment at this time. However, we have since learned that Mrs. Frankow was born in Germany, immigrated to England, and came to Canada in 1952 to marry Horst Frankow. Mr. Frankow was not available for comment.

Not available for comment. Was he being questioned at the time? Or had he refused to speak with the press? I wasn't sure if publication bans existed back then, or if it was a courtesy daily newspapers extended to police in a time when twenty-four hour news cycles and tabloid journalism didn't exist. Either way, the outcome was the same.

An almost identical story appeared in the same day's issue of the *Globe and Mail*. Once again, there was no photo and no by-line.

Given the story's similarity to the one in the *Star*, I assumed the same stringer had filed it with both papers.

I skimmed through the rest of stories. Despite daily updates, few additional details surfaced. To compensate, the reports rehashed the facts as known. Anneliese had been in her kitchen. Her three-year-old daughter had been playing under the kitchen table when her mother was struck on the back of the head with a blunt object. The daughter, who was never named, ran to a neighbor saying a bad man had hurt her mother. Nothing I hadn't already known.

A photo of Anneliese and Horst on their wedding day, almost identical to the one in the train case, had been used over and over. One neighbor, who asked to remain anonymous, eventually came forward, adding a little bit extra to each day's report in the *Star*, as if savoring her fifteen minutes of invisible fame. At least I assumed the neighbor was female. The murder had taken place during the day, after all, when most husbands were at work, and housewives looked for diversion.

Horst and Anneliese were a quiet couple who liked to keep to themselves.

Anneliese doted on her daughter. Sometimes, I thought Horst was jealous of her.

Horst was very protective of Anneliese, you might even call him possessive, but then who could blame him? Anneliese was a looker.

I would often hear them argue when the windows were open.

Visitors? There was a woman once, but I only saw her backside as she was leaving. Anneliese told me she was the wife of an old friend. Never did get her name.

And then, a rueful confession.

I wasn't home the morning it happened. I always do my day's

grocery shopping at ten, home by eleven. You can set a clock by me.

"Our gossip isn't the one Sophie went running to," I said.

"A regret the woman likely took to her grave," Shirley said, grinning. "But it is unfortunate. Had she been home, she would almost certainly have seen or heard something."

Except she always did her food shopping at ten, home by eleven. What if Anneliese had told Anton that the best time to come over was between ten and eleven?

Or maybe Horst killed Anneliese after all. Who better to know his neighbor's routine? I could imagine Anneliese telling Horst, laughing at the woman's dull predictability. I pushed the thought aside for the moment and showed Shirley the drawing from the *Telegram*. "This suggests the daughter was hiding under the table, not playing."

"Does it matter?" Shirley asked. "Either way, the poor lamb was there to witness her mother's death. She must have had nightmares for the rest of her life."

"According to Louisa, she did."

"Well, thank heavens Horst didn't know she was under that table. Then again, maybe he did, but couldn't bring himself to kill his own daughter."

Or maybe he wasn't the killer. "Let's go to the next batch."

Horst's arrest on May 1 made front-page news in the *Star* and page two of the *Globe*. Both recapped everything they'd written before, both used the same wedding photo of Anneliese and Horst. The *Star's* reporter noted that a preliminary inquiry had been scheduled for June 7. The Crown Attorney was quoted, "The purpose of the preliminary inquiry is to determine if there is sufficient evidence to set the matter down for trial. In practice, the inquiry is used to test the strength of the Crown's case."

The reports receded to the back pages for the next couple of days, eventually disappearing until June 6 and 7, when there was a reminder in the *Star* about the impending inquiry. On June 8, the preliminary trial made front page news once again, along with pencil drawings of Horst, dark circles under his eyes and sunken cheeks in stark contrast to his fair hair, a too-big suit that hung on a skeletal frame. I scanned both reports quickly. The bottom line was that the trial would commence on September 10, and was expected to last a week or less.

"The trial is covered in these pages," Shirley said, flipping to the next section in the binder. "I'll sum them up for you now, and let you read them at your leisure, if that works for you."

"It does."

"The thing that struck me most was that there was no direct evidence that Horst killed Anneliese. There were, however, plenty of witnesses who came forward to testify about Horst's jealousy and temper, mostly neighbors, but also some local shopkeepers. There were reports of bruising on her arms, as if Anneliese had been grabbed in a rough manner. The Crown did a commendable job painting the picture of a husband who was easily enraged."

"What about the murder weapon?" I asked, thinking about the crystal vase.

"Never found, although the police explained that it would likely have been something heavy found in the house, a frying pan or a pot. There would have been sufficient time, they said, to dispose of the item before Anneliese's body was discovered, or to simply scour it clean and put it back in the cupboard. Remember, there was no DNA evidence back then. It was a plausible explanation."

I shook my head. "No murder weapon and no direct evidence. It's hard to believe Horst was convicted of manslaughter, even with the testimony of the neighbors and shopkeepers."

"Look at the pencil drawings. He has the appearance of a condemned man. But the nail in his coffin was Guenther Walther."

G. Walther. "The pastor who baptized Sophie?"

"One and the same. Walther testified that according to Anneliese, Horst Frankow was not Sophie's biological father. A copy of the Certificate of Baptism was put into evidence, but the name of the father was excluded from all newspaper reports as 'not relevant' to the trial. I'm assuming the judge ordered the papers to refrain from including Anton's name, but that's just an assumption.

I have no idea if there was a limit on reporting testimony back then."

I tried to process everything Shirley had told me. Horst would almost certainly have had grounds for appeal—if he had lived long enough to file for one.

"That's everything on Anneliese and Horst," Shirley said, interrupting my thoughts. She turned to the last page in the binder. "There was no mention of Anton Osgoode in any of the reports then, or later. The only thing I found was his obituary in the *Star*. I've included it in the binder. Since there is no mention of Anneliese or Sophie, I didn't delve into it any further."

I appreciated Shirley's attempt to spare me any embarrassment. "Thank you."

Shirley smiled, kindness emanating from her. "If that's all, I'll leave this with you and be on my way."

"You've done such a thorough job, and in record time. Louisa will be very pleased. Send me an invoice for the hours you've put in, and I do mean all of the hours. Our client expects to pay for services rendered."

"Very well, I will, on one condition. Promise that you'll hire me again in the future."

"You have my word."

After Shirley left, I read the clippings from start to finish, and then reread them three more times looking for anything I might have missed, an inconsistency between reports, a random fact that hadn't resonated.

I kept going back to one statement. *Visitors? There was a woman once, but I only saw her backside as she was leaving. Anneliese told me she was the wife of an old friend. Never did get her name.*

Olivia?

34

I was quick to hop out of bed as soon as the alarm buzzed the next morning instead of hitting the Snooze button. I was going to pay Randi a visit, and I was actually looking forward to it.

I'd made the decision to bring nothing more with me than the vase and the suitcase. If Randi truly could read objects, I didn't want that reality cluttered with facts garnered from postcards and photographs.

As before, the breathy-voiced shopkeeper welcomed me as I entered Sun, Moon & Stars. Randi flitted down the stairs moments later and invited me into her room on the second floor. After we took our seats and exchanged basic pleasantries, I opened the train case, removed the crystal vase, leaving it inside its canvas carrying case, and put it on the floor next to my chair. Then I placed the case on the top of the desk.

"I'd like you to start with this," I said, all business. No cold reading from this client.

Randi pulled the train case toward her, her ringed fingers studying every exterior seam before opening it. More careful examination, eyes open and closed, the eventual lifting of it to her heart.

"This suitcase originally belonged to your murdered woman." It was a statement, not a question.

I nodded. It was a natural assumption. Nothing supernatural there.

"So many secrets inside. Photographs. Postcards. Important documents. Some were long hidden beneath the seams at the bottom."

I didn't respond. Chantelle had re-stitched the seams, and she'd done a good job of it, far better than I could have, but it didn't take a psychometrist to see that they'd been tampered with. And why tamper with them unless something was hidden underneath? The cynic in me returned.

"This type of suitcase was known as a cosmetic case back in the 1950s," Randi said. "They were also referred to as train cases, although it almost certainly made a journey over water, as well as by rail. I sense it has traveled to many houses, and not always under the happiest of circumstances." Randi rocked back and forth, the case now in her lap, eyes shut, her face skewed in concentration.

I was starting to feel antsy, and more than a little bit silly. Perhaps she sensed my impatience because Randi opened her eyes and slid the train case toward me in a gesture of frustration. "I'm sorry. There are just too many impressions. Some are very old, others very new. I can't seem to distinguish one from the other. It's all a jumble. Perhaps if I had more time, but no, I don't think so."

I'll admit I was disappointed, though it did reaffirm my earlier skepticism. I took the case and placed it on the floor. "I have one other object. A vase." I slipped it out of the bag and gently placed it on the desk.

Once again, Randi went through her ritual, turning it upside down and over again. "This is a specially designed crystal vase," Randi began. "It is signed and dated 'R.C. Riedel nineteen- fifty-something,' at the bottom, although I'm sure you've discovered that for yourself. I'm not sure if that's a two or a five at the end. It's very faint, it could be either. The craftsmanship and style is undoubtedly Czechoslovakian."

I hadn't discovered anything for myself. In fact, I hadn't taken the vase out of the canvas bag since Olivia had handed it to me. Some investigator. "Of course."

Randi placed the vase against her chest, her breath becoming ragged as perspiration formed on her brow. "I also believe you've found your blunt object. There is anger and pain, but there is also deep love, and something else. Jealousy? Fear?"

Was Randi expecting me to answer? I remained silent. She closed her eyes again, her fingers tracing the patterns in the crystal. After a moment she began to nod as her breathing returned to normal. "I'm seeing an image now."

"What sort of image?"

"There's a mountain filled with roses of every color." Randi's eyes fluttered open, a smile spreading across her lovely face. "What time is it?"

I looked at my watch. "Eleven fifteen."

"Eleven fifteen. Make note of the date and time, Callie. The women who owned this vase are finally at peace."

⚲

IT WASN'T until I arrived home that I realized the significance of Randi's words. Not "the woman who owned this vase," but "the women." I paced until Chantelle arrived an hour later, anxious to share the binder of news clippings Shirley had accumulated, and to discuss my visits with Olivia and Randi.

Chantelle was equally eager to share her news. I let her go first.

"Shirley was right," she said. "The Helena Brown on the T.S.S. *Canberra* autograph page was Sophie's godmother, Helena Bradford. She immigrated to Canada to marry Adam Bradford. As you can imagine, both Brown and Bradford are common last names, but I stuck with it, and managed to find a record of them, and their marriage, on Ancestry.ca."

"That's fantastic."

"Not so fast. They're both deceased, though Helena outlived Adam by about a decade. Regardless, if they knew what became of

Sophie, or where she was fostered, or if they knew anything about Anton or Corbin, they took that knowledge to their graves."

My disappointment must have shown because Chantelle became defensive.

"I know it's not as exciting as it could be, but I thought it would demonstrate how thorough we were. Especially since my guess is you're not about to confront Corbin any time soon."

It was my turn to be defensive. "I'm waiting for the right time."

"I'd say there's no time like the present. We need that loose end tied up before we can present our final report, and we're pretty much there."

She had a point. "Fine. I'll call him now. In the meantime, here's what Shirley came up with from the archives. Start reading and let me know what you think." I blushed. "Do you mind reading them out on the deck? I need privacy if I'm going confront Corbin. I'll join you in a few minutes."

Chantelle trundled outside without argument. I summoned up my courage and dialed. Yvette answered the phone.

"Hello, Yvette, this is Callie." I couldn't bring myself to call her grandmother. "Is Corbin available?"

"Hello, Callie." Her tone was considerably cooler than the last time we spoke. I suspected she'd gotten a tongue lashing from Corbin for giving me Olivia's address.

"I'm sorry, this isn't a good time, unless you're calling to apologize for stealing Olivia's vase."

"I didn't steal her vase, she gave it to me."

"Owned it for sixty years, guarded it as though it were priceless, and then just handed it over when you visited her on Tuesday morning? After you were expressly forbidden from doing so. Did you think we wouldn't find out? Never mind, don't answer that. I will give you top points for timing. It was impeccable."

Impeccable timing? "I have no idea what you're talking about."

I heard her sharp intake of breath, then, "I'll let Corbin know that you called. He's busy making…I wouldn't wait by the phone." She hung up before I could say anything else.

I made a pot of tea to calm my nerves, set up a tray with two mugs and six peanut butter cookies, and went out to find Chantelle.

"Thanks, I was just going to come in and make a cup of tea. It's a bit chilly out here."

"Not as chilly as the reception I just got from Yvette. As was to be expected, His Highness was not to be disturbed. Busy making something or the other. If he doesn't call me by tomorrow, I'll try again."

"That's all you can do."

"Did you read all the newspaper reports?"

Chantelle nodded. "I skimmed them quickly to get the gist. I'll read them over more carefully at home. There isn't anything in there we didn't already know or suspect, outside of the pastor testifying. One thing did stand out, though."

"What was it?"

"Hold on, let me find it." She flipped through the pages. "Here it is, and I quote, '*Visitors? There was a woman once, but I only saw her backside as she was leaving. Anneliese told me she was the wife of an old friend. Never did get her name.*' I wondered if the wife of an old friend might have been Olivia."

"I wondered the same thing. I'll ask her the next time I see her *if* I can manage to get by security. I expect it will be difficult, if not impossible. Yvette just accused me of stealing Olivia's crystal vase."

"So you got the vase? Did Randi see it?"

"She did, the vase and the train case. The train case was a bust. Apparently it had too many impressions. She couldn't distinguish one from the other. The vase, however…"

I went to the cupboard where I'd stored it, took it out, and handed it to Chantelle.

"It's very decorative. And heavy."

"It's Czechoslovakian crystal, and yeah, it is heavy. I almost dropped it the first time I picked it up. It's lovely, though, isn't it? The two lovebirds, the pen, and the envelope."

"It's hard to believe something so pretty could have been used to kill Anneliese." Chantelle turned it over. "It's dated on the bottom,

1950-something. It's hard to make out, but it must be a two, since Anton and Anneliese met in 1952. What did Randi say about it?"

"She believes it's the blunt object that killed Anneliese. She also claimed to have seen an image of a mountain filled with roses." I paused. "It was the oddest thing. She asked me what time it was, and I said eleven fifteen, and then she told me to remember the time and date. She said the women who had owned the vase were finally at peace."

"The women, plural?"

"Yeah. I assume she meant Anneliese and Olivia. I suppose keeping the vase all these years served to remind her of Anton's..." I paused midstream. "I need to read Anton's obituary again."

"His obituary? Whatever for?"

"I need to double check something." I went to my files and pulled it out, skimming it quickly to find Olivia's maiden name. Damn. Maybe there was something to this psychometry business after all.

"Anton Osgoode didn't kill Anneliese. Olivia did."

Chantelle stared at me, openmouthed. "Olivia? But Sophie said there was a bad man, not a bad woman."

"Sophie was three years old and playing under the table. All she would have seen was the person's shoes. Maybe Olivia was wearing pants. Maybe Sophie said bad 'mom,' not bad 'man.'"

"I suppose it's possible."

"Not just possible, probable. It explains Olivia's guilt all these years. The reason the vase was one of the few things she brought with her to the retirement home. It served as a reminder of what she did. Killing Anneliese. Allowing Horst to go to prison for the crime. She felt responsible for his death as well as Anneliese's. I think she went to visit Anneliese the time the neighbor spotted her, saw the vase, and knew it must have come from Anton."

"But the vase, it was dated 1952," Chantelle said.

I shook my head. "You assumed it would have been 1952, but it could just as easily be 1955."

Chantelle turned the vase over again and nodded. "It *could* be a five. Are you thinking that Anton and Anneliese had taken up again, that perhaps Sophie was the catalyst?"

"I do. It explains why Horst was so jealous, not that there was any excuse for the way he treated Anneliese. Or maybe his temper was the thing that sent her back to Anton. That, and what she believed would be best for Sophie. Listing Anton's name on her Certificate of Baptism, why else would Anneliese risk doing that unless she was through with Horst and planning to start a new life with Anton?"

"Okay, let's say I buy into your theory. How did you arrive at it?"

"I'm sorry, I thought you made the connection."

"What connection?"

"Olivia's maiden name, it's on Anton's obituary. Olivia Osgoode, née Rosemount."

"Rosemount," Chantelle said.

"Rosemount," I said. "As in a mountain filled with roses."

35

I spent the better part of Wednesday evening and Thursday morning completing our final report for Louisa, who had agreed to come by Thursday evening after work. I compiled everything the team had learned and filed it in chronological order for context. I felt a sense of pride as I flipped through the pages of documents and photographs.

"There were a lot of questions, but I think we've found most of the answers," I told Louisa on the phone. *Oh, and by the way, we're related.* Hmmm…might have to fine-tune the approach for that one.

⊕

CHANTELLE and I walked Louisa through Anneliese's journey, starting with the passport and her immigration records, and winding our way through the key players, from Horst to Olivia, Anton, and Corbin. It wasn't easy, but I told her about our conclusion that Olivia, not Horst, had killed Anneliese.

"We think she said a 'bad mom' killed her mother, not a 'bad man,'" I said.

"A bad mom," Louisa said. "Are you going to report Olivia?"

Until that moment, the thought had never crossed my mind. I was mulling it over when Chantelle spoke.

"No. She's ninety-one. The likelihood of Olivia getting charged after all these years and surviving a murder trial, are slim to none. Besides, it's only our conjecture that Olivia killed Anneliese. There's no solid evidence."

Louisa nodded. "I think I can accept that."

"It's going to take some time for you to sort things out in your head," Chantelle said. "Take your time, read everything over, and we'll have another meeting in a week or so to answer any questions you might have. You set the pace. I can imagine it's all a bit overwhelming."

"There is one other thing," I said. "Your grandfather, Anton Osgoode."

"Yes, what about him?"

"It would appear he's also my great-grandfather."

Louisa's eyes widened. "We're related?"

I nodded. "I haven't been able to figure out the proper associative term. Half-cousins? Second cousins? Every time I go there, I get a headache. Regardless, I probably should have told you as soon as I found out."

"Nonsense. I instructed you to wait until you had your report finalized, and that's exactly what you did. Besides, it's kind of nice to know that I have family again. That is, if you'd like to be family. Even if we're cousins a billion times removed, I've always wanted a little sister." Louisa's voice was choked with emotion.

I used to dream about having an older sister when I was a kid. "There's nothing I'd like more," I said, smiling, and for a brief moment, it felt as though Anneliese was smiling back at me. I glanced at Chantelle and knew she saw it, too.

"By the way, I meant to tell you how much I loved Misty's post yesterday," Louisa said, breaking the spell. "I knew the minute I read it that you'd completed your investigation. Justice. That's what it feels like to me. Justice for Anneliese. She deserved to have her story told. I can't really explain it, but I feel as if she's finally at peace."

A mountain filled with roses.

"I think she finally is."

I CHECKED THE PAST & Present website as soon as Chantelle and Louisa had left, curious to read Misty's latest post.

As Louisa had indicated, the card illustrated was Justice. The woman depicted sat on a throne, a purple velvet backdrop behind her. She wore a long, flowing red robe with a green cape, and a gold crown with a green stone, probably an emerald, in the center. In her left hand, she held a sword pointing toward the sky. The scales of justice, perfectly balanced, were on her right.

XI JUSTICE (MAJOR ARCANA)

As the eleventh card in the Major Arcana, this comes in the middle, with ten before it and ten after. Notice how the scales are perfectly balanced as they are with the statues of Lady Justice we are familiar with. However, unlike Lady Justice, whose sword is pointed toward the ground, this sword is pointing upwards. Another difference is the eyes. Lady Justice wears a blindfold. Our Justice stares at us, eyes wide open.

MISTY'S MESSAGE: If you have been seeking justice, your journey is nearing an end. Realize, however, that true justice is only achieved if we seek and accept the truth with complete honesty, and balance it with what we have learned.

Complete honesty. With Louisa. With Corbin. With myself. *Thanks for the nudge, Misty.* I would think of the best way to confront Corbin, and like it or not, he would hear me out. There was one more piece of this puzzle, and it belonged to Louisa. She deserved to know everything I could tell her about her mother and grandmother, just like…just like I deserved to know everything I could find out about my mother and great-grandmother.

THE PHONE CALL came early Friday morning, waking me from a dreamless sleep. I checked the call display and was surprised to see Hampton & Associates on the screen.

"Leith? What's up? Did someone die?" I laughed when I said it, but he didn't laugh back.

"Actually, Calamity, someone did die. I've arranged a meeting for tomorrow at ten, along with the other beneficiaries. It's imperative that you attend."

"But tomorrow is Saturday," I said, my head foggy from lack of sleep. "You don't work on Saturdays."

Leith let out one of his theatrical sighs. "I've made an exception in this case."

"It's just that I've been invited to a play in Muskoka." With Royce. Who I hadn't seen in more than a week. Then my brain clicked into focus. "Wait a second. You said the other beneficiaries. Are you saying that I've inherited…I don't understand. Who died?"

"Your great-grandmother, Olivia Osgoode. She passed away on Tuesday morning. I'm sorry to be the one to tell you. I thought you knew."

"Olivia's dead? Why didn't anyone call me?" Why didn't Yvette tell me? At least it explained what Corbin had been making when I called. Funeral arrangements. To which I would not be invited, or welcome.

"I can't answer that, although it may explain why she hired me. Apparently Olivia didn't trust the family's legal counsel. She told me the firm didn't have her best interests at heart. Or rather, your best interests."

My best interests? Gran had left me something in her will? "You said Olivia died on Tuesday morning. Do you know what time?"

A shuffling of papers. "Eleven fifteen."

Eleven fifteen. The time Randi said both women were finally at peace. I was still trying to wrap my head around everything when Leith spoke again.

"Ten o'clock tomorrow at my office on Bay Street. Don't be late. And Calamity?"

"Yes?"

"'Wear your armor. I don't think it's going to be a pleasant experience."

⊕

I CALLED CHANTELLE FIRST. She listened to me cry, didn't ask any questions, and promised to come over on Saturday night with white wine and cheese pizza.

I phoned Royce next and broke the news. As much as he commiserated with me about Olivia, I sensed relief when I told him I'd have to miss Porsche's play. Perhaps the thought of me sitting with his parents and aunt fell under "seemed like a good idea when I asked you, but now that it's almost here, I'm not sure I can deal with it." Then again, maybe I was reading too much into it. Or maybe that's how I felt. Was I secretly relieved? I hung up, feeling unsettled. Neither of us had mentioned a trip to Niagara Falls.

36

———

Corbin's face was flushed purple with anger as he paced around the boardroom of Hampton & Associates.

"This whole thing is preposterous," my grandfather said.

"Sit down, Corbin," Yvette said.

"I'll sit when I'm good and ready." He pointed at me, his hand trembling with rage. "What I want to know is—why is *she* here?"

"If by she, you mean Calamity," Leith said, "she is here as a beneficiary of Olivia Osgoode's will."

"Impossible. I was the sole beneficiary, at least before she sweet-talked her way into my mother's heart with her cookies and carnations." He sniggered. "Calamity. Aptly named. At least her parents did something right."

I wanted to stand up and tear his eyes out. Instead I stayed seated and took out my cocoa butter lip balm, finding small comfort in the ritual of dabbing it on my lips.

"Actually, Olivia changed her will several months ago," Leith said. "That would have been long before Calamity made contact. Therefore, I can assure you there was no coercion. Now if you would please take a seat next to your wife, I'll begin."

Yvette gave me a sideways glance, and to my surprise, a

surreptitious wink. She'd all but accused me of stealing Olivia's vase, and here she was rooting for me, even if it was only from the sidelines. Or had I imagined the wink? As Corbin took his seat, Yvette's face transformed into an expressionless mask.

Leith began reading the will. "I, Olivia Marie Rosemount Osgoode, hereby declare that this is my last will and testament and that I hereby revoke, cancel, and annul all wills and codicils previously made by me either jointly or severally. I declare that I am of sound mind and legal age to make this will and that this last will and testament expresses my wishes without undue influence or duress."

My mind drifted back fourteen months ago when I sat in this same boardroom listening to the reading of my father's will. I forced myself back to the present. It wouldn't do to zone out right now.

"…hereby leave the sum of one hundred thousand dollars to my son, Corbin Anton Osgoode. The remainder of my estate, property, and effects, I bequeath to my great-granddaughter, Calamity Doris Barnstable."

"One hundred thousand dollars?" Corbin sputtered. "But Mother had close to half a million dollars in assets. I should know, I've been handling her financial affairs for the past five years."

"Four hundred and sixty-five thousand to be exact," Leith said. "Give or take a hundred dollars and change on either side."

My eyes flicked from Corbin, to Yvette, to Leith and back again. Surely there was some mistake? "Are you saying that I've inherited three hundred and sixty-five thousand dollars?"

"That's exactly what I'm saying," Leith said. "You would have inherited everything, but I advised Olivia against that. It's difficult, if not impossible, to challenge a will if you've inherited a substantial amount from it. I suspect most courts would consider one hundred thousand dollars substantial."

The reality of the situation seemed to dawn on Corbin. I watched as his posture deflated, but I didn't feel any pity. Surprisingly, I didn't feel victorious, either. There were no winners here. Not now that Olivia was dead. I found myself missing a woman I'd barely gotten to know. No matter her past, she was still my great-grandmother, and I had liked her.

"I don't care what you say," Corbin said. "I can fight this. It's incomprehensible that Mother would have left the bulk of her estate to this…this woman."

Seriously? *This woman?* I'd been waiting for the right time. That time was now.

"Perhaps she found out about you and Sophie," I said, taking pleasure in the way my grandfather flinched at the sound of her name. "It was bad enough that her husband lied to her. But her only son? I suspect Olivia found it unconscionable."

Yvette moved her chair back a few inches, separating herself from her husband. "Who's Sophie?"

Corbin didn't answer. Instead he stared at me, his eyes blazing with hatred. "How do you know about Sophie?"

"I have a strip of photos of the two of you, taken inside one of those shopping mall photo booths. You really shouldn't mug it up for the camera like that. So juvenile."

"Photos…Sophie promised to burn those. It was a mistake meeting her that day, an even bigger mistake having those pictures taken. I'll admit that I was curious about her. Why did she call my father 'Uncle Toni' that day at Yorkdale? But in the end I realized that Sophie was nothing more than a mistake. She could never compete with me, a real Osgoode." He threw his head back and laughed. "Just like you were a mistake, Calamity. No amount of money will ever change that." Corbin took Yvette's hand. "C'mon, we're out of here. My lawyer will be in touch."

Yvette shook off his hand, but she followed her husband out of the room nonetheless. I waited until the door closed before starting to cry.

Leith reached across the boardroom table and handed me a silk handkerchief. "There'll be plenty of time for that later, Calamity. I haven't finished reading the will yet."

"I don't understand."

"I'm afraid there is one condition. A cold case Olivia wants Past & Present to investigate. She added the codicil after finding out about your business." He smiled. "I gather she was impressed by your initiative. Of course, you're free to decline, in which case Corbin will inherit the estate in its entirety."

I rocked back in my chair, thinking about the codicil in my father's will. The one that insisted I find out what happened to my mother thirty years before. My father had believed in me, and that belief had taken me on a quest for the truth. It was that journey which led me to Marketville, to my new career, to Olivia, and eventually, to this moment. Was that justice, or was it fate? Maybe it was a combination of both. All I knew was that I couldn't let my great-grandmother down, and I couldn't let Corbin win.

"Tell me about the case."

THE END

ACKNOWLEDGMENTS

Beyond writing the words, every novel requires hours of research, much of it never making the printed page. A day or two of looking into old train schedules, for example, might lead to nothing more than a single paragraph, possibly two. But those details, however minor, matter. So, too, do the many people and resources that help the author behind the scenes. While space precludes me from listing everyone, I would be remiss if I didn't recognize (in alphabetical order) the following:

Michelle Banfield, for her ongoing friendship and support.

Susan Daly, an award-winning author and Toronto Public Library cardholder, for sending me examples of online newspaper archives and never questioning why.

Kathleen Costa, beta reader extraordinaire. This book is better because of her.

Erin, Archives of Ontario archivist, for helping me navigate Criminal Justice Records from 1956.

Rosemary Graham, for her hawk-eyed proofreading, as well as her willingness to debate the punctuation issue of the T.S.S./T.D. *Canberra* vs. the CMoS-sanctioned TSS/TD. In the end, historical material won the day.

R. L. Kennedy, the man behind the website Old Time Trains, www.trainweb.org/oldtimetrains.

Ti Locke, every author's dream editor.

Hunter Martin, for his endless patience with me while designing the cover.

Larry Owen, for tirelessly answering my "what-if" 1950s legal questions.

Carole McGill Plant for a realtor's perspective on Danforth Village, Toronto.

Lior Samfiru, for his legal opinion on Ontario employment law regarding occupational accidents leading to death.

John Sayers, for sharing his treasure trove of ocean liner memorabilia, and for his invaluable suggestion that Anton Osgoode be employed by Eaton's as a buyer, crystal and fine china.

The Canadian Museum of Immigration at Pier 21 for information and postcards of the T.S.S. *Canberra*.

York University Archives and Special Collections: Clara Thomas Archives and Special Collections.

Last, but not least, my heartfelt thanks to my husband, Mike Sheluk, for his unfailing love, faith, and encouragement, and to my mother, Anneliese Penz, who was with me in spirit while I wrote this story.

A FOOL'S JOURNEY

A Marketville Mystery #3

Judy Penz Sheluk

Four Chapter Preview

1

I stared at Leith Hampton, déjà vu enveloping me. It had been fifteen months since the first time I'd sat in the law office of Hampton & Associates. An unexpected connection had brought me back to learn of another inheritance. And once again, there were strings attached. What can I say? In my life, nothing is ever as simple as it seems on the surface.

This time, I'd inherited $365,000 from my great-grandmother, Olivia Marie Rosemount Osgoode. I'd met her for the first time a few weeks earlier while attempting to sift through the life and times of Anneliese Prei.

I liked Olivia, though I'm not sure I knew her long enough or well enough to claim the emotion I felt for her was love. It was hard to forgive someone who, along with her son, Corbin, and his wife, Yvette—I prefer not to think of them as my grandparents—had disowned my seventeen-year-old mother when she became pregnant with me. My father went to his grave despising anyone who bore the Osgoode name, and a lot of his bitterness had been passed on to me. I wondered what he'd think, now that I was the primary beneficiary of her last will and testament. I suspect his personal code of ethics might have led him to refuse the money. I'm not quite as principled.

"You said there was a condition," I said, and waited for one of Leith's well-practiced courtroom sighs.

He nodded, the theatrical sigh coming on the heels of the nod. "Olivia was fascinated by Past & Present Investigations. Fascinated and proud. She began to worry that a significant sum of money might decrease your need, and ultimately your desire, to find another case."

"So she found one for me?"

Leith nodded again. "I'll admit I wasn't completely on board with the idea, but Olivia was a stubborn woman, and no amount of discussion was going to dissuade her."

Stubborn I could understand. I'd inherited the same trait from my father, apparently burrowed deep into my DNA. I turned my attention back to Leith, who was still talking.

"Of course, you're free to decline, in which case your inheritance will revert to Corbin Osgoode."

I thought about my grandfather's fury at the reading of the will and suppressed a smile. "I wouldn't dream of declining, and not just because of the money. Tell me about the case."

THE CASE, Leith informed me, was the story of Brandon Colbeck, a twenty-year-old college student who left home in March 2000 to "find himself." He was never heard from again.

"The family is, understandably, still looking for answers," Leith said. "Did Brandon come into harm's way? Or did he simply decide to disappear and start a new life? His mother, a woman by the name of Lorna Colbeck-Westlake, admits, albeit reluctantly, that there had been some harsh words spoken by her husband, Michael Westlake, after Brandon dropped out of college. However, both insist that they never wanted Brandon to leave home. Rather, he'd been given some 'tough love' choices in the hope that it would provide motivation. It was a popular strategy, back in the day. It may still be, in some circles."

He slid a thin leather briefcase across the mahogany boardroom table. "The little that Olivia accumulated is in here. I will warn you, there's not much to go on. A couple of newspaper clippings, one that is dated four years ago, another quite recent. Barely enough to bother with, and yet…" Leith spread his arms out, palms upward, and shrugged.

I was getting used to going on not much. What I wasn't used to was having my great-grandmother getting involved, especially from the grave. "I'll admit I don't know a lot about our family, but the name Brandon Colbeck means nothing to me. Are we related?"

"Brandon's great-grandmother is Eleanor Colbeck, a friend of Olivia's at the Cedar County Retirement Residence. A year ago, Eleanor was diagnosed with Mild Cognitive Impairment or MCI. I'm told it's a condition that doesn't get better, only worse, and the decline can be rapid. Eleanor was close to her grandson and six weeks ago, she received a telephone call from a man claiming to be Brandon Colbeck. He said he missed her and wanted to come home, but didn't have the funds available to travel."

"Let me guess, he asked her for money."

"Not in so many words, though he did mention a friend in a similar situation whose father had used a wire service like Western Union. The family reported the call to the police, who determined it was a scam, one of many that targets the elderly. Nonetheless, Eleanor remains convinced that the call came from her grandson, based on the fact that he'd called her Nana Ellie."

Eleanor Colbeck. Now *that* name rang a bell, though I wasn't sure why. "The name sounds familiar."

"Eleanor contributed to several community-based charitable initiatives, long before you moved to Marketville. Cedar County Retirement is far from inexpensive and Eleanor has been living there for the past decade. As her condition worsens, medical expenses increase."

"Where I know her name from probably isn't important," I said, knowing that I'd keep digging until I remembered or discovered the truth. I tapped my fingers against the briefcase. "You say there's not much in here. Am I expected to find out where Brandon went and what happened to him? Or am I to determine the call was a fake? Does the family approve of my getting involved? What's the bottom line?"

Leith leaned back and smiled for the first time. "Olivia may have been old, but when it came to legalities, she was on top of her game. The family is willing to assist you in whatever way possible. I have signed affidavits from Lorna Colbeck-Westlake, her husband, Michael Westlake, Brandon's stepsister, Jeanine Westlake, as well as Eleanor Colbeck, granting Past & Present Investigations carte blanche to do whatever is necessary to find Brandon. They are also willing to sit down with you at any time, though from what I gather, they know little, if anything, beyond what's already been reported."

"What about written permission to post relevant material on the Past & Present website or on social media sites like Facebook and Instagram?"

"Inside the briefcase you'll find a notarized document to cover exactly that concern, signed by each member of the family. As for the bottom line, in order to inherit you must make a reasonable investigative effort over the next three months. After that, you're free to walk away without further obligation."

Three months. I wanted to solve it in two.

2

I left Hampton & Associates with a briefcase firmly tucked under my arm. I hustled my way down Bay Street to Union Station, hoping to catch the noon GO train leaving for Marketville. I had planned to spend a few hours in Toronto, checking out the Royal Ontario Museum and the tony shops of Yorkville before grabbing dinner at one of the many restaurants on the way to the GO. Now all I could think about was getting home. I needed to develop a plan.

I managed to reach Union with three minutes to spare and sprinted up the stairs to Platform Twelve, breathless by the time I reached the top tiered "Quiet Zone" of the train, and grateful for the silence it afforded. I found an empty seat, sat down, and got to work. The trip to Marketville would take just over an hour, and I didn't intend to waste a minute of it.

Leith had warned me that there wasn't much to go on and there wasn't. The manila folder, neatly labeled "BRANDON COLBECK," contained two carefully clipped articles from the *Marketville Post*, and some handwritten notes by Olivia Osgoode. Still, I couldn't help but smile at the thought of my great-grandmother investigating a cold case at the age of ninety-one. Maybe we shared more than stubbornness in our DNA.

I unfolded the first clipping, smoothing out the creases. It was dated Thursday, March 19, 2015.

"BRANDON COLBECK STILL MISSING 15 YEARS AFTER DISAPPEARANCE" the headline stated. A color photograph of a young man in his late teens or early twenties took up a quarter of the page. He appeared to be standing on a dock, ripples of blue water behind him, though the photo had been cropped close to focus on Brandon's smiling face. It was a nice face, free of guile, with full lips, warm brown eyes, and a well-proportioned nose. His hair was blowing in the breeze, wavy copper with glints of gold. He looked happy. I set about reading the story for the first time, knowing it would have piqued my interest had I lived in Marketville at the time it was published. The byline, "Jenny Lynn Simcoe, with files from G.G. Pietrangelo," piqued my curiosity all the more. I'd met Gloria Grace during my investigation into my mother's disappearance. She'd left the *Marketville Post* a dozen years ago to start her own photographic studio. How much did she remember about this cold case? I made a mental note to find out and turned my attention back to the article.

> THE FAMILY of Brandon Colbeck is still hoping to be reunited with him nearly fifteen years after his disappearance. Brandon was twenty on March 9, 2000 when he left a note for his parents that said he was leaving home. "I was completely blindsided," said Lorna Colbeck-Westlake, Brandon's mother. "Brandon borrowed my car that morning to go job hunting. He dropped me off at my office and was upbeat about the prospect of finding work."
>
> When Brandon didn't pick up his mother at the prearranged time, a co-worker drove her home. "I remember being embarrassed and more than a little annoyed," said Lorna. "At the time I just assumed it was Brandon being unreliable."
>
> Annoyance turned to shock when Lorna found a note from Brandon on the kitchen counter. "He wrote he was going to 'find himself,' and told us where he'd left the car. I ran to his bedroom,"

said his mother. "He'd taken his laptop, toiletries, and most of his clothes, but no identification, not even his health card or driver's license. I called Michael in a panic."

Michael Westlake is Lorna's husband and Brandon's stepfather. The couple found Lorna's unlocked vehicle in the parking lot of a neighborhood strip mall. The keys were underneath the driver's floor mat. There was no trace of Brandon.

Although it's been fifteen years, the family has not given up hope. "We believe Brandon wanted a fresh start, which is why he didn't take his ID," said Westlake, reiterating a statement from an earlier interview. "He'd dropped out of college in his second year, moved back home without a plan, and didn't seem motivated to find gainful employment."

"There was tension in the house," admitted Jeanine Westlake, Brandon's stepsister, who was twelve at the time of his disappearance. "My dad was a firm believer in tough love, and that only intensified after my brother quit school. Brandon didn't respond well to that approach."

Brandon Colbeck's profile has now been added to the Ontario Registry of Missing and Unidentified Adults, along with two age-progressed sketches supplied by the Cedar County Police Department's Forensic Identification Unit. His grandmother, Eleanor Colbeck, best known for her widespread community philanthropy, was recently interviewed at her retirement residence in Marketville. She believes the pictures are an accurate representation of what Brandon may now look like at age thirty-five.

"I have never stopped believing that my grandson is alive and well," said Eleanor, her eyes glistening with tears. "I'm waiting for the day when the telephone rings and Brandon says, 'Nana Ellie, I've missed you. I'm ready to come home.'"

Nana Ellie. There it was for any scammer to read. The term of endearment that had convinced Eleanor Colbeck that her grandson was still alive. Add the implication of Eleanor's advanced age and wealth, and I could understand why the police had dismissed the telephone call as a scam.

But there were questions the article didn't answer, and Olivia had written them down. I smiled. They were the same questions I would have asked.

- Who is Brandon's biological father? Where is he now? Did he play any part in Brandon's upbringing?
- How old was Brandon when Mike and Lorna met and got married?
- Who were Brandon's friends?
- How close were Brandon and Jeanine? Did he confide in his sister about his plans to leave?
- Why did Brandon drop out of college?

I wondered if Eleanor Colbeck had the answer to any of those questions, or if they were locked inside her mind, no longer accessible. I reread the article, thought for a moment and then added one final point.

- Find Michael Westlake's earlier interview (and G.G. Pietrangelo)

I moved on to the second clipping. It was dated 2018, nearly three years to the day after the first, the headline announcing, "PHONE CALL SCAMMERS TARGET GRANDPARENTS." Once again the byline was that of Jenny Lynn Simcoe, this time without a nod to G.G. Pietrangelo.

THERE HAVE been numerous reports of unsuspecting seniors receiving phone calls from callers claiming to be a grandchild in need of money. Referred to by police as the 'grandparent scam,' these calls play directly on the emotions of the elderly. For example, a scammer will call an older person and pretend to be their grandchild. In one scenario, the caller will ask if they know who is calling. When the grandparent guesses the name of one of their grandchildren, the scammer pretends to be that grandchild, then tells the grandparent that they are in a financial bind. Typically, they will also ask the grandparent not to tell anyone else about their situation because they are ashamed or embarrassed.

In another scenario, the caller knows the name of the grandchild along with one or two key facts, information culled from social media posts or newspaper articles, and assumes their identity.

While not all scams targeting seniors involve grandchildren, they inevitably include requests for money, usually by Western Union wire transfer. "There are as many variations of the grandparent scam as there are grandparents," said Detective Aaron Beecham, who heads the Cedar County Police Department's recently formed Fraud Investigation unit. "If you have a senior in your life, please take the time to educate them about scams targeting the elderly."

For a list of the latest scams, visit the Cedar County Police Department's website and click on the Fraud tab. To file a report, call 555-835-5763, ext. 35.

Detective Aaron Beecham. That name also sounded vaguely familiar, but I couldn't place it, not that it mattered. It angered me to think there were unscrupulous people whose sole purpose in life was to swindle seniors.

What about the real Brandon Colbeck? Was he long dead and buried in an unknown grave? Or was he still alive, living somewhere under a different name, perhaps with kids of his own? If so, what sort of person left his family in limbo for nearly twenty years, and why?

I was still mulling things over when the train pulled into the Marketville station.

3

____

I called Chantelle as soon as I got home, anxious to get her on the case. "Do you have any plans for dinner?"

She laughed. "I wish. Sadly, Prince Charming has yet to come my way. Not even a frog, which at this point, I might actually consider. Then I think about Lance the Loser and I come back to my senses."

Lance was Chantelle's ex-husband, and I knew that despite her cavalier attitude about him she was still hurting, especially since he'd left her for an adolescent—her words, not mine, though she wasn't far off the mark. "You'll meet the right guy when the time is right," I said.

"I'm not holding my breath. How did your meeting go with Leith Hampton?"

"It was…interesting. Olivia left me some money in her will. More than some, actually. Enough to pay off my mortgage."

"Wow, well done, you. I assume Corbin was less than impressed."

"You could say that. He accused me of undue influence. I gather he was the sole beneficiary until a few months ago. Leith assured him that Olivia had revised her will long before I reentered her life."

"She knew about you, even though you didn't know about her? I expect that infuriated him all the more."

"He was livid," I said, thinking back to the scene in Leith's office, the way my grandfather had spat out the words that would hurt me forever, my grandmother sitting stone-faced and silent beside him. *You were a mistake, Calamity. No amount of money will ever change that.*

"He threatened to contest the will. Leith doesn't believe Corbin stands a chance, since he also inherited a sizable sum, but who knows? I'm not counting on the money until probate is granted, which, as I understand it, can take about a year. Of course, if Corbin does contest the will, the timeline will almost certainly be prolonged. In the meantime, there is a slight catch."

"What sort of catch?"

"In order to inherit, Past & Present has to attempt to solve a cold case."

"Attempt, meaning we don't have to solve it, we just have to try?"

"According to Leith, it's the effort during the next three months that counts, not the end result." I bit my lip. "The thing is, Chantelle, I'm not sure I could accept the money if we didn't find out the truth."

"Then we'll have to find out the truth, won't we?"

"Exactly. Can you come over tonight? I can fill you in on the details over pizza and wine."

"I thought you'd never ask."

✎

CURIOSITY GOT the better of me and I decided to check out the online Ontario Registry of Missing and Unidentified Adults while I waited for Chantelle. The web page was attractive and easy to navigate, with three blocks at the top of the home page: *Search*

Unidentified Adults, Search Missing Adults, and *Publications*. Beneath these were the dated bullet points: *Recent News* and *Updates*.

I'm not sure why I started by clicking on Unidentified Adults, since I was looking for a missing adult, but that's what I did. I was taken to a page where I could enter a number of parameters: Gender, Race, Date of Discovery, Location of Discovery, Province of Discovery, Hair Color, Eye Color, Age (Low) and (High), and Weight (Low) and (High) and Keywords. I left all fields blank and hit Submit, surprised and saddened to find eight pages with twenty-five cases per page, most with the caption "no image available." Two hundred unidentified men and women, their bodies, or in most cases, their remains, discovered as far back as the 1960s, and no one had come forward to claim them. Did they not have families, or in the absence of family, at least someone who cared? Or was there an assumption that the person had left voluntarily and didn't want to be found? Whatever the situation, it was heartbreaking to think that their death didn't matter.

I spent the next three hours reading each entry, looking for signs of Brandon in the case files, all the while fully aware that the police and members of Brandon's family would have scoured the records many times over. I'm not sure if I was actually expecting to find something they missed—*Calamity Barnstable solves the case in a matter of hours,* the headlines screamed—but the only results of my search were a stiff neck, a sore back, and a pervading feeling of doom and gloom.

I got up, stretched, made a cup of cinnamon rooibos tea, and settled back to the task at hand, this time clicking on the Missing Adults page. The news here was even bleaker, with eighteen pages of twenty-five missing adults in the database, one going as far back as 1935. *Four hundred and fifty missing adults*, I thought, doing the mental math. I entered Brandon Colbeck's name in the appropriate Search fields, and was directed to the data about his case.

SUMMARY
Date of Disappearance: March 9, 2000
Location of Disappearance: Marketville, Ontario

AGE AT DISAPPEARANCE: 20 years
HEIGHT (ESTIMATE): 5'9"
WEIGHT (ESTIMATE): 150 lbs.
HAIR: reddish brown, wavy
EYE COLOR: Dark brown
GENDER: Male
RACE: Caucasian
ALIASES: None known

DETAILS

DENTAL INFORMATION: Teeth - described as good
MEDICAL INFORMATION: Unknown
CLOTHING/JEWELRY: Sheepskin-lined jean jacket
OTHER PERSONAL ITEMS: Dell Laptop Computer
NOTABLE IDENTIFIERS: Upper left arm: A black outline of the
bottom quarter of the sun emanating multiple rays, shining on the
face of a wavy-haired boy. At the time of Brandon's disappearance,
this tattoo was recent. It may since have been colorized or enlarged.
ADDITIONAL INFORMATION: After failing during his second year at
Cedar County College in Lakeside, Brandon returned to live with
his parents in Marketville in late January. He had been studying
Computer Science.
Until a few months before his disappearance, Brandon had been a
straight-A student, described as having an inquisitive mind and
quick wit. His behavior started to change in his second year at
Cedar County College, although the family is unsure of the reason.
As his grades dropped, he began to withdraw from family and
friends until there was virtually no contact.

The rest of the entry recapped what had been in the news
articles, noting he had not tried to contact family or friends.

There were two SOURCE LINKS, the first leading to the *Marketville
Post* article dated March 19, 2015. There were no prior newspaper
reports, not that I was surprised. The "earlier interview" mentioned
would almost certainly have been within a few months of Brandon's
disappearance, predating online coverage. I hoped Gloria Grace still

had her files, and that she'd be willing to share what she knew with us.

The second link led to a "Find Brandon Colbeck" Facebook page listing Jeanine Westlake as the administrator. She'd posted the same photo and sketches as those on the Ontario Registry for Missing and Unidentified Adults website, but despite multiple shares and eighty-nine friends, there was nothing in the way of helpful comments, and all activity ground to a halt in early 2016. I made a note: *why 2016?* Too many dead ends?

Under RELATED PHOTOS, there were four thumbnails that could be enlarged to full size by clicking on each individual photo. The top photo was the now familiar *Marketville Post* photograph of Brandon. Beneath it there were two full-page, age-progressed artist sketches, one depicting Brandon with short hair, parted on the right, the other with shoulder-length hair, parted in the center, and a slightly scruffy beard, lips closed, with a hint of smile. He had a narrow face with high cheekbones and a perfectly proportioned nose. He was a good-looking man, even scruffed up. Both sketches were signed and dated March 1, 2015. How much more would he have aged in another four years? Would the reddish-brown hair now be tinged with gray?

The fourth thumbnail was a rough sketch of the tattoo. It looked incomplete, a black outline of something more to come, and yet there was something oddly familiar about it. I stared at it for a several minutes, enlarging in on my screen, zoning in and out, frustrated that nothing came to me. I knew I'd seen this somewhere.

I went back to the images, saving each one to a "Brandon Colbeck" folder on my computer, then printed all three sketches. One thing I've learned from my past investigations is that being organized makes everything easier going forward.

I just wished I could shake the feeling that nothing else about this case was going to be easy.

$$4$$
____

Chantelle arrived a little after five, her tablet in one hand, a bottle of white wine in the other. I handed her the manila folder in exchange for the wine, and updated her on everything Leith had told me.

"The main article raises more questions than it answers," I said. "I jotted down what came to me and would like you to do the same."

Chantelle nodded, sat down at the long mission oak dining room table that doubled as a desk, and began reading.

"With files from G.G. Pietrangelo," she said, looking up.

"Gloria Grace is definitely on my to-contact list."

She nodded again, turning her attention back to the article. I ordered the pizza—extra sauce with hot peppers—poured us each a glass of wine, forced myself not to pace, and dabbed on some cocoa butter lip balm. The lip balm helped a little. The wine helped a little more.

"There's a fair bit to read between the lines, isn't there?" Chantelle said, after she'd finished.

"Does the name Detective Aaron Beecham mean anything to you?"

Chantelle wrinkled her brow in concentration, then shook her head. "No, should it?"

"Probably not." I handed her the two age-progressed sketches of Brandon Colbeck. "These are on the Ontario Registry of Missing and Unidentified Adults mentioned in the newspaper article."

"Interesting," Chantelle said, her fingers tracing the outline of Brandon's jawline. "In the one with the short hair, he looks like any number of clean-cut, thirty-something men. The one with the long hair and slightly scruffy beard lends him an appearance of someone who's been living on the street."

"Really? I didn't interpret it that way, I just thought of a free spirit, maybe someone who worked in a field where being clean-cut isn't an expectation. But, yeah, you could be right."

Chantelle bit her lip. "You know, as detailed as these sketches are, they don't look like the young man in the photograph. At least, not to me."

"I thought that too, at first, but these are black-and-white sketches versus a color photograph and the sketches were done fifteen years *after* he disappeared. People change a lot between twenty and thirty-five. I know I did. Plus, according to the newspaper, Eleanor Colbeck believes these are accurate representations of what Brandon might look like now. Maybe she saw a resemblance between this older version of Brandon and his mother or biological father. Even the stepsister, Jeanine, could bear a likeness from the mother's side. I've learned that age-progression is a combination of science and art, similar to facial reconstruction. Not an exact likeness, but someone who knows the person should see enough of a resemblance to recognize them."

"Valid points," Chantelle conceded. "What else have you got?"

I handed her the rough sketch of the tattoo. "According to the Registry, this tattoo is on his left upper arm. I know it's incomplete, but does it remind you of anything? I keep thinking I've seen this before."

"Hmmm. Not really. But I'm not an expert on tattoos."

"Probably just my imagination then," I said, but I knew it would niggle.

"We could always take this to a tattoo parlor and see what they have to say."

It was a good idea, one I'd add to my growing to-do list. "There's one more thing, a journal that belonged to Olivia. I thumbed through it before you got here. Her handwriting isn't easy to decipher, and it's not much more than a list of questions, versus answers. I'm not sure whether that's because she ran out of time, or because Eleanor's cognitive issues had advanced to the point where her memories were no longer reliable. Overall, it's not much help."

"It's a starting point." Chantelle logged into her tablet and began typing. That's one of the differences between us. I tend to be more of a pen and paper thinker. The other difference is that even with her blonde hair tied in a ponytail and her face devoid of makeup, Chantelle was drop-dead gorgeous, with charcoal gray eyes that seemed to smolder and a killer body developed from years of working as a personal trainer and fitness class instructor. I'm not unattractive—black-rimmed hazel eyes being my best feature, though I could live without my unruly chestnut curls—and as a runner I'm in decent physical shape, but I'll never be in her league. Then again, despite Chantelle's obvious attempts at flirtation, I'd been the one Royce Ashford had asked out.

The thought of Royce momentarily distracted me. We'd left things in limbo, neither one of us quite sure where our relationship was headed, or if we even wanted a relationship. I pushed him out of my mind and gave Chantelle my undivided attention.

"Now that you've seen everything I have, does anything stand out? Beyond the files from G.G. Pietrangelo?"

"My gut feeling is that Michael Westlake and Brandon Colbeck were at loggerheads, and it didn't start with Brandon dropping out of college. The whole 'tough love' business that Jeanine alludes to, for example."

"What else?"

"I'd want to know who Brandon's biological father is, what role he might have played in his son's upbringing, if he played one at all. His name is noticeably absent from the report. I also wonder when Michael Westlake entered Brandon's life."

"Great minds think alike. What are your thoughts about Jeanine? She'd be thirty-one now, if my math is correct, eight years younger than Brandon. I'm an only child, completely out of my element on this one. You, on the other hand, had five siblings. Would you have confided to one of them if you were going to leave? Would any one or all of them have confided in you?"

"I honestly don't know," Chantelle said. "It would depend on how much we wanted to leave, and why. I come from a close family, and I don't think that's just because we were related by blood. My parents tried to treat us all equally, albeit differently based on our individual personality traits. Was that the case in the Colbeck-Westlake household? It's something we need to find out, though whether anyone will tell us the complete truth remains to be seen. I definitely think Jeanine knows more than was reported in the article."

"My thoughts exactly. Lorna may also be hiding something. She claimed to be blindsided by Brandon's disappearance, but we only have her word for that. Maybe she's trying to protect her husband. Or Jeanine? From what or who is the question."

"We need to interview Lorna, Michael, Jeanine, and Eleanor, but we may only get one kick at the can," Chantelle said, "and that's if they agree to see us."

"The family has signed affidavits giving Past & Present carte blanche, and Leith assured me that they are willing to cooperate in any way. The questions we ask will be as important as the answers we hope to get. We'll have to do some prep work before approaching anyone."

"Agreed. I'm also curious about Brandon's friends, before, during, and after college. Hopefully someone in the family will be able to provide that information."

Who were Brandon's friends? "There's a 'Find Brandon Colbeck Facebook' page on the Registry, with Jeanine Westlake as administrator. It's been inactive since 2016, but the group has eighty-nine friends." I shuddered at the thought of tracing all eighty-nine, sure that both Jeanine and the police would have already done that, but knew it might have to be done. "I'm not sure how easy any of this is going to be."

"If it was easy, the police would have solved the case long ago," Chantelle said with a smile. "Let's consider ways the team can help us."

In addition to Chantelle and me, the Past & Present "team" consisted of Shirley Harrington, a retired research librarian, Misty Rivers, a self-proclaimed psychic who posted tarot messages on our website and social media channels—surprisingly well-received despite my initial skepticism—and, on an "as needed" basis whenever antiques and collectibles came into the mix, Arabella Carpenter. Shirley's skillset in digging through newspaper archives would definitely come into play, but I couldn't imagine how Arabella or Misty would be of assistance in this particular case. Arabella wouldn't expect to be consulted, but Misty would, and she'd definitely want to be involved, though how tarot would figure in was anyone's guess.

Chantelle read my mind. "We can skip Arabella for this one, but we should hold a team meeting with Shirley and Misty."

"Agreed. When are you available?"

"My shift at the gym doesn't start until three o'clock Monday afternoon, so Monday morning would work for me."

"I'll try to set something up tomorrow."

Chantelle was already tapping away on her phone. "Just sent them both a text. Now where's that pizza delivery guy?"

The doorbell rang in that moment. "He must have heard you," I said, grinning. "Get the napkins and plates. I'll get the pizza. First we eat, then we brainstorm."

⊕

ABOUT THE AUTHOR

 Judy Penz Sheluk is the author of the Glass Dolphin Mysteries and the Marketville Mysteries. Her short stories appear in several collections.

In addition to writing mysteries, she has spent many years working as a freelance writer and editor; her articles have appeared in dozens of U.S. and Canadian consumer and trade publications.

Judy is a member of Sisters in Crime – International/Guppy Chapter/Toronto, International Thriller Writers, the Short Mystery Fiction Society, South Simcoe Arts Council, and Crime Writers of Canada, where she serves on the Board of Directors.

You can find Judy at judypenzsheluk.com.

facebook.com/JudyPenzSheluk

twitter.com/JudyPenzSheluk

instagram.com/judypenzsheluk

bookbub.com/authors/judypenzsheluk

pinterest.com/judypenzsheluk

goodreads.com/wwwjudypenzshelukcom

amazon.com/author/judypenzsheluk